REGRET

Henry Scott

ACKNOWLEDGMENTS

Published by Pretty Lake Publishing House

For any inquiries regarding this book, please email:
henryscott@henryscottauthor.com

As Always for Tracy

OTHER TITLES BY

HENRY SCOTT

THE REDEMPTION SERIES

REVENGE
REGRET
RETURN
REVEALED
RECKONING
REMEMBER

STAND ALONE NOVELS

THE MANDELA AFFECTION

MONSTYR

Prologue

The decision in this case was obvious, though Judge Patrick Doyle pretended to listen to the arguments. For over twenty years, he'd sat on this bench, and he always hated when cases like this found their way into his courtroom. With a neutral look, the Judge considered the young man sitting behind the defense table. The boy's head hung low while his leg twitched up and down nervously like a jackhammer trying to chip away at the floor.

Scanning the file, Judge Doyle read the boy's life had not been easy, growing up in the South Side of Chicago with a deceased father and an overworked mother. The only bright spot in the child's life was a school principal who'd acted as a surrogate dad. Both supporters, the boy's tiny mother and the large administrator, sat directly behind the defense table wearing their Sunday best. The mother had been repeatedly threatened by the bailiff with removal for her outbursts. In contrast, the dark-skinned man had not uttered a word during the entire trial. His calm presence had provided much-needed support for the fourteen-year old boy accused of rape.

To draw the Judge's attention back to the proceedings, the State's Attorney cleared his throat. Judge Doyle lifted his head and nodded at the skinny man with thinning hair who said, "And, that is why the State believes you should find the defendant delinquent, your Honor."

"Bullshit," the boy's mother whispered loud enough for the entire room to hear.

Judge Doyle banged his gavel down hard enough for the water to slosh out of his drinking glass. He shouted, "This is your final warning. One more word from you, and I will find you in contempt. Am I understood?"

"Yes, your Honor," the mother replied as sarcastically as she could.

The court recorder finished her transcription. She chanced a glance at Judge Doyle and offered him the tiniest of smiles. She made it no secret that she found him attractive. Judge Doyle remained stoic.

When it was apparent there would be no further outbursts, the defense attorney gave his young client a reassuring pat on the arm and stood up. He smoothed the creases of his department store suit and began his closing statement.

"Your Honor, I am appalled that the State has wasted your time today, not to mention my client's. I don't need to remind you that the facts in this case are overwhelmingly in favor of his innocence. The State brought no physical evidence that would tie my client to the crime. Furthermore, I'd like to remind the court that my client has a solid alibi for the time in question. He was at home caring for his little sister, as witnessed by his principal."

The Defense moved to the center of the courtroom. "The only evidence the State has against my client is his confession. A confession that was obtained through the outright abuse of the interrogating officers. He was questioned for over ten hours without a lawyer or legal guardian present. The officers provided him key elements of the case and then claimed he was incriminating himself. They lied, manipulated, and controlled a minor who did not have the mental capacity to understand the severity of the situation."

Judge Doyle reconsidered a key point from the Defense's persuasive argument and made a note on his legal pad. He did feel sorry for the boy. Frowning, he underlined it twice with thick angry lines. When he realized the room was waiting for his attention, he set down his pen and nodded for the Defense to proceed while the boy squirmed in his chair and his mother fumed behind him.

Continuing, the Defense asked, "Why didn't they sign it for him too because it certainly wasn't his confession? They should be the ones to go to prison, not my client. These despicable officers made a promise to this poor boy that if he would admit to the crime, he could get back home to care for his sister.

"That was a horrible lie, so please, your Honor, fix that mistake. My client is innocent, and the only reasonable choice is to find Leroy Jones, Jr. not delinquent."

Impressed with the Defense's appeal, Judge Doyle tilted his head towards the young lawyer who hadn't been the boy's attorney during the fact-finding hearing. The original attorney was dismissed due to incompetence. Prior to the detention hearing, the new defense argued the charges should be dropped based on the facts. However, it was an election year for Judge Doyle, and he couldn't publicly appear soft on violent crimes in addition to his other outstanding commitments.

Judge Doyle steepled his hands underneath his chin and then folded them on top of his legal pad. The only noise in the room was from the court security officer shifting his sizeable bulk from foot to foot next to the judge's bench. The fluorescent lights reflected off his polished dome. A second officer monitored the door while he stared out a back window at the sunny afternoon.

"I'd like to thank you both for your compelling arguments. They have brought all the facts of the case to light and made this decision, though difficult, an obvious and evident one for the court," Judge Doyle said with a measured voice.

The attorneys leaned forward in their respective chairs. The boy looked up meekly while his mother chewed on her lip. The court recorder's fingers hovered over her keyboard. The tension in the room was palpable, even for the veteran judge.

"So— it is with a heavy heart that I find the defendant, Leroy Jones, Jr., delinquent. Thus, Mr. Jones will be remanded to the Cook County Juvenile Detention until his sentencing hearing."

Faces froze mid-expression. No one moved. The room appeared stuck in amber.

Then everything happened at once.

The Defense gasped, and the State's Attorney nodded happily. The mother sucked in her breath while the color drained from her boy's face with the bad news. But most importantly, the principal jumped to his feet like a kangaroo on meth.

His calm appearance fell away to reveal white-hot rage. With surprising athleticism for someone so big, he hurdled the wood railing and sprinted towards the judge's bench. The large security officer rushed to intercept him as the court recorder dove for cover, and the mother laughed at the chaos.

Judge Doyle sat dumbfounded, unable to move a muscle. This couldn't be happening. Never in all his years on the bench had someone tried to physically attack him. Verbal assaults occurred sporadically but never had someone dared to assault him in his courtroom. It was simply unfathomable. Didn't this man know how much good the judge did for this community?

The principal leaped at the judge as the bailiff dove for his waist. The guard was able to wrap a hand around his belt, and the pair crashed into the front of the raised desk. Their combined five-hundred pounds threatened to knock it off its base. The sound echoed through the nearly empty room like a shotgun blast. Judge Doyle almost tipped over in his chair as he subconsciously jumped away.

Quick as a whip, the principal untangled himself from the officer's grasp and clawed at the desktop. The Judge's water glass was knocked over and shattered on the floor, and papers were ripped from files and fluttered down amongst the broken glass. The second bailiff lunged for his knees and held onto the flailing administrator until the first officer pounced on the man's back, pinning him to the carpet.

With crazy eyes, he fought them with the strength of a panther. Spit flew from his mouth as he shouted at Judge Doyle. "That boy's innocent, you crooked son of a bitch. You will rot in Hell for this."

An arm snaked around his neck to choke him into submission, but he bit down on the tensed bicep. A guttural scream escaped the lips of the wounded officer, yet he didn't release his hold. The first officer extracted a Taser from his belt. He stuck the prongs deep into the man's ribs and pulled the trigger.

A rapid electrical ticking sound emitted from the device, followed by a high-pitched squeal from the man. He twitched violently, his back arched, then he fell limp, any hope of retribution lost. More security officers flooded into the room from surrounding courts. Some secured the judge while others detained the delinquent.

Judge Doyle screamed, "Get that animal out of here."

With his voice barely above a whisper, the defense attorney said, "What did you expect to happen? Your verdict was a complete travesty of justice."

"What did you say?"

"You heard me. You're the only monster here today."

Judge Doyle couldn't believe his ears. He'd almost been killed over a brat destined to be a career criminal, and this man dared to call him a monster. It was for this reason that Doyle wouldn't lose any sleep over his backroom deal. He's sworn an oath to administer justice faithfully, and God damn it, he would, but why shouldn't he be thoroughly compensated as well? This town was being torn apart by druggies, rapists, and gang bangers, and the only thing standing in their way were men like Judge Doyle.

Banging his gavel with such force, Judge Doyle almost snapped it into two pieces. "Officer, remove the Defense from my court. I find him in contempt."

As he was escorted out, the mother got up from her seat and smoothed out her red dress. She met her scared son's eyes and used a finger to cross her heart. He nodded his head as she mouthed a promise that was easily understood. The Judge missed it, but he would certainly come to regret this day.

Chapter 1

With the radio cranked up, Jake almost missed his daughter's phone call. His terrible singing was also to blame, but 80's power ballads were his guilty pleasure, so Sam would forgive him, even if it was her second attempt to reach him. Jake reached for the ringing phone on the passenger seat but only succeeded in knocking it to the floor. Swerving into the next lane, he finally snagged the device as a semi-trailer honked at him for his recklessness.

Turning down the music, he said, "Hi Sam."

"Hey, Dad. Where are you?"

"I'm about to cross the border into Indiana."

"So you're still in Michigan?"

"Yes."

"I thought you were supposed to be home a week ago?"

"Yeah. It took a little longer than I planned to get things squared away," Jake said, hoping Sam would never learn what had delayed him.

Jake had assassinated a man.

Murder is never the answer, but Jake's victim was a deranged biker intent on killing Jake along with his best friend's family— an innocent woman and her three children. Tom had already been killed by the psychopath during a supposed road rage altercation. But after the American justice system had failed them, it was literally kill or be killed, and Jake was not going to allow Tom's family to die. No way, even if he ended up blackmailed by the biker's gang for his crime. Tom's family was as close to him as his own family. The kids called him Uncle Jake.

In fact, all of Jake's friends and family were back in Michigan except for Sam. Jake and Sam's mother had divorced years ago, and Chicago was Kate's hometown, so if Jake wanted to be a part of his daughter's life, he was stuck in the Windy City. However, Sam was in her junior year of high school, and she would be off to college in a year. He hoped she'd attend the University of Michigan; it was one of the places she'd applied, but ultimately it would be Sam's choice. Jake would not try to manipulate and control her like his ex-wife.

Sam said, "I'm really sorry, Dad. I know Tom was your best friend. Are Mary and the kids doing Ok?"

"Yeah. I think so. It'll be tough for a while, but I think they'll be all right."

"That's good. I guess."

An awkward silence followed, which was understandable given the topic. Still, Sam was usually great at filling voids in the conversation. Definitely better than Jake.

He asked, "Is something wrong, Sam?"

"Kind of. I need to ask you a question?"

The apprehension in her voice was palpable. Sucking in a breath, Jake said, "Sure."

"But I can't do it over the phone."

"Fine. Do you need me to swing by your mom's when I get to town?"

"No. I'm already at your apartment."

"You are?"

"Yes," Sam laughed nervously.

"How did you get there?"

"Umm . . . Robert drove me."

"Did he?" Jake couldn't be sure that Sam's stepfather hadn't dropped her off at his place. Sam was a better liar than Jake too.

"He did. I swear."

"Good. Because my neighborhood is not the best. You could get mugged. Or worse."

"I know. Which is why I didn't walk," she said, sounding annoyed.

"I'm glad," he said, almost positive he'd been lied to.

Sam asked, "So, you'll be home soon?"

"Yes. It should be about two hours if I don't run into traffic."

She laughed. "There's always traffic in Chicago."

"You got that right. Are you sure you can't tell me what the problem is over the phone?"

"I'm sure. Love you, Dad."

"Love you too." They ended the call, and exactly two hours later, Jake entered his apartment building.

The place was nice but a little old and rundown. It was all he could afford on his paltry salary. After leaving the Chicago PD, Jake's father-in-law, a prominent local judge, had Jake blackballed for every job in the city, down to a department store security guard. Jake found work in a small factory making car parts, but most of his paycheck went towards child support. Kate insisted that she didn't need his money, but Jake had his pride. Though that may change depending on how quickly he found another job. His last boss was not happy over Jake's extended stay in Michigan and had fired him.

As Jake ascended the stairs to his second-floor apartment, a short dark figure wearing jeans and a hooded sweatshirt pushed past him going in the opposite direction. They bumped shoulders, almost toppling Jake over backward. The person didn't slow down or offer an apology.

"Excuse you!" Jake shouted.

"Go screw yourself."

"What did you say?"

The individual bounded down the steps and ran out the door, a backpack slung over one shoulder. Jake thought about going after them but knew it was pointless; confronting a jerk wouldn't change their attitude. He took a second to collect himself and continued up the stairs to his apartment, where he found the door ajar.

That wasn't good.

Hadn't Jake just lectured Sam about the neighborhood? He pushed open the door and stepped inside. "Sam?"

No response.

He called out louder. "Sam!"

Nothing.

Frowning, he put the unused keys back in his pocket and dropped his suitcase at his feet. He closed the door behind him.

The first thing Jake noticed was the apartment was eerily quiet. The only sound he heard was his heart beating against his rib cage. The small living room and dining area were empty. It was a long shot, but he stepped across the room and separated the blinds to check his tiny balcony. Two cheap green plastic chairs and a propane grill filled the space, but no Sam.

Turning back, Jake examined the small kitchen, and his jaw dropped. Fuck! Bright red droplets littered the floor, and a bloody handprint was smeared across the countertop. More blood sat congealed in the sink. This was not good. Not good at all.

His mind raced through different scenarios as the pounding in his chest matched the beat of a bass drum. The deadbolt had been intact, so had Sam forgotten to lock the door? Or had she answered it without the chain and got ambushed? Or did she know her assailant, a friend or neighbor perhaps? Any were possible with the evidence he had before him, or was it related to Sam's problem? Why hadn't he pushed her harder for answers? Was Sam in real trouble?

The one thing he did know was the person on the stairs had acted guilty. Was his daughter lying in a back corner of the apartment raped, stabbed, and bleeding to death while he stood here playing detective?

"Sam!"

In the short hallway, all three doors were open. First, he ran to Sam's bedroom and found the comforter pulled tight across the bed, and nothing of Sam's on the desk or floor. The room appeared untouched, so he moved across the hallway to the bathroom and flicked the switch. Light flooded the small room, bouncing off the white walls, the tiles, and the checkered shower curtain. Good. Everything looked normal, but he had one more room to check.

Sweat beaded on his forehead as he turned the corner to the master bedroom, half expecting to see Sam's mutilated body on his bed. It wasn't; however, the mattress was askew. He frantically searched the room but saw nothing else out of place. Which meant, if Sam was still in the apartment, the last place she could be was in his walk-in closet. The idea was crazy, but he had to check.

Jake ripped open the door and turned on the light, scanning the cramped space. Shirts and pants were arranged neatly on their hangers, and his shoes lined the floor. A firebox for his important documents sat untouched on the floor next to his secured gun safe. Luckily, no Sam.

Sitting on the corner of the bed, he nudged the mattress back into position. Interesting. It must've been knocked out of place as he hastily packed for his trip. Yet it was a dumb thing to worry about with his daughter missing? All his brainpower should be spent on finding Sam. With the apartment searched and blood in the kitchen, Jake had to consider the possibility she'd been kidnapped? Chicago was a hub for the sex-trade, and Sam was a gorgeous young girl, so it was a distinct possibility.

He rested his head in his hands and rubbed his temples. The process jarred loose a simple solution to this mystery. Jake was mad at himself for not thinking of it in the first place. He would just call Sam. It was probably a simple misunderstanding. Maybe, she had stepped out for a minute. This didn't explain the blood, but rather than waste more time, Jake pulled his phone from his pocket. It almost slipped from his sweaty hands before he found Sam's number. He stabbed at the screen and placed the call, but it went directly to voicemail.

Damn it! Sam always answered his calls.

The cop in him was gone; only the frantic father remained. He cursed and threw the phone on the bed. Staring at the carpet, he contemplated his next move. Should he call his ex-wife, Kate? That would be a fun call. She'd blame him for living in a crime-ridden neighborhood, for leaving her alone, for the divorce, for everything. No. Time was of the essence. He'd call the police first and then Kate.

As Jake reached for his discarded phone, he heard a noise at the front door. Had the kidnappers returned to clean up the blood? Maybe. Probably. Without time to get his gun from the safe, he raced to the kitchen to grab a knife from the drawer. With the weapon in hand, he pressed himself next to the front door and turned off the lights.

Every muscle in his body tensed as the door swung open.

Chapter 2

A small figure entered the apartment.

Jake turned on the lights, the knife poised to strike. The girl screamed, clutching her chest. The plastic bag she was holding fell to the floor.

"Sam!" Jake quickly lowered the knife.

"Dad! You scared the crap out of me."

"What the hell is going on?" Jake asked, realizing his daughter was unharmed.

Sam shook her head. "Exactly! What is going on? You were about to stab me with a knife."

"Sorry, honey, but I thought . . ."

"Yes?" She looked at him quizzically.

"Well, never mind what I thought."

He returned the knife to the utensil drawer and then embraced his daughter. She softened in his arms as he squeezed her tight. He missed this; he'd been gone too long. After a few seconds, he released his hold on Sam and asked, "Why is there blood in the kitchen?"

"I was emptying the stupid dishwasher for you, and I dropped a glass. I cut myself on one of the pieces, and you didn't have band-aids, so I had to go out and buy some."

"Ohhh."

"You didn't see all the broken glass in the garbage?"

Jake shook his head. "I always check my garbage first thing when I get home, but I forgot this time."

Sam laughed. "What did you think happened?"

"Truthfully?"

"Yes."

"I thought someone had broken in and hurt you."

Sucking in a breath, Sam said, "Boy, if that happened, you'd kill the guy."

It was Jake's turn to laugh, but it came out as a nervous chuckle. Sam went to the door to retrieve her bag from the local drug store. She looked exactly like her mother when Jake and Kate first met with red hair, alabaster skin, sparkling blue eyes, and a smile that could light a stick of dynamite. Kate had been gorgeous, a fact that clouded Jake's judgement because the woman had some personality flaws. Luckily or unluckily, Sam had Jake's temperament, which meant she was caring and kind but impulsive.

"Could you help me?" She sat down at the table and fumbled inside the bag. Her left hand was wrapped in a paper towel. Blood seeped through the white cotton.

"Sure." He grabbed the first aid cream and squirted some on a piece of gauze, dabbing it gently on the cut.

She flinched. "At least, it wasn't my right hand. It would have made painting hard."

"Good thing. Did you finish that portrait you were working on? You never told me what it was about."

"I had to start over. I'll show it to you when I'm done."

"Fair enough." Taking the box from the bag, he removed a bandage from its wrapper. He placed it over the wound and tenderly pressed down.

Wincing, she said, "You need to do a better job of stocking this place."

"I know. I will. I tried calling you before you got back. Why didn't you answer your phone?"

"It's dead, and I forgot my charger. Can I borrow yours?"

Jake finished applying the bandage. "Sure."

"Where is it?" She stood up and pulled the device from her pocket.

"First, ask me your question."

"Can't I do it later?"

"Samantha Marie, is it really that bad?"

"Kind of . . . I got a 950 on my SAT."

Jake couldn't recall, but he didn't think he scored that high when he took the standardized test, not that it made a difference. Kate had high expectations for their daughter. "Didn't you take one of those prep classes?"

"I did, but it didn't help."

"Shit! Your mother is going to be mad."

"Mad. That's an understatement. She destroyed my painting when she found out."

Jake did a double-take. "She did what?"

"Mom poked her finger through the canvas."

Shaking his head, Jake asked, "Has she finally lost her mind?"

"Oh! You know her. She's worried that I'm putting my art or a boy before my studies."

"Nice. Is your mother still blaming me for the way her life turned out?"

"No— or it sounds like having me was a mistake, but she does want me to achieve everything she didn't."

"She's a district attorney, for Christ's sake, what more does she want?"

Sam shrugged. "She won't even listen to me when I bring up art school."

"Art school?"

"Yes. I've been giving it a lot of thought, and I think I want to apply to School of Art Institute here in Chicago."

Jake was caught off guard, but he shouldn't have been. Sam loved to paint. It wasn't what he'd pictured for his daughter, but it wasn't his choice. With a straight face, he said, "It's your life. If you don't shoot for your dreams now, it only gets harder."

She smiled, "Good. Because I need to make a decision quick. If I have to study for another SAT, I won't have time to work on my portfolio. And I can't get into the School of Art Institute without a good portfolio. As it is, I'll have to work around the clock to finish a new painting by the deadline."

"Can't you fix the old one?"

Biting her lip, Sam said, "Maybe I could, but truthfully it was pretty childish. I can do better."

"All right. Just don't kill yourself."

"I won't," she said. "Do you think I'm making the right choice?"

Jake rubbed his chin. "Only time will tell, but I think you'll regret it if you don't give it a try."

"Mom is going to be pissed. She had plans for me to go to law school."

"Screw your Mom. No one should have to do something they hate."

"But you work at a job you don't like?"

"Not anymore. I quit last week."

Sam's jaw dropped. "No way."

"I did. I should've done it a long time ago."

"Do you have anything else lined up?" she asked, sounding very adult-like.

"No, but I have enough money saved to last me a little while."

She said, "Maybe I should go to a regular college."

"Why?"

"Art school tuition is not cheap, and they don't give out scholarships. And I doubt Mom will pay for it."

Jake hadn't considered the price, but it didn't matter. He'd work three jobs if he had to cover the cost; he wouldn't allow Kate to bully Sam. "You only need to worry about getting into that Institute. I'll handle the rest."

"How?"

"I started a savings account when you were born," Jake lied.

Beaming, she hugged him. "Thank you, Dad."

"What do you plan to do with your Mom?"

"Lie to her until it's too late for her to do anything."

"Like tonight. I'm guessing your Mom doesn't know you're here," Jake said.

"I shoved some pillows in my bed. Hopefully, she thinks I'm sleeping."

"Ahh. The classics never die." Jake had pulled that trick a hundred times. "So Robert didn't drive you over?"

"No. I scheduled an Uber to pick me up around the corner."

"And what happens if your Mom finds your empty bed?"

Sam sighed. "She'll go crazy calling everyone looking for me."

On cue, Jake's phone rang. He checked the caller ID. It was Kate.

Chapter 3

Jake let his ex-wife's call ring five times. Before he answered, Jake moved into the living room and took a seat on the couch; Sam joined him. With as much pleasantness as he could muster, he said, "Hi Kate."

"Jake?" She sounded out of breath. "I don't have time to explain. Sam is missing. I doubt it, but have you heard from her?"

"She's at my apartment."

"What?" Kate screamed through the phone.

Sam flinched. He waved off her whispered apology and said, "Kate, calm down. She's fine."

"Don't tell me to calm down, Jake— you lost that right a long time ago.

It was a stupid thing to say, he knew, since she'd never taken his suggestion to relax. Ever. "You're right."

"Of course, I'm right. Did you know she snuck out of the house?"

"No. I just got back home from Michigan and found her sitting here." Jake could picture Kate at the other end of the phone, pacing around her exquisite kitchen with the butcher block and the designer pots and pans that she never cooked a meal with. He asked, "Was Sam grounded again? You punish her for any little thing. It's no wonder she sneaks out."

Silence.

"Hello?"

Kate said, "Put Sam on the phone."

Jake looked to Sam, who shook her head and silently mouthed the word, NO. Jake said, "She's in the bathroom. I can drop her off later."

"I'll come get her now."

"Really. I can do it."

"No. We need to talk too, and I'd rather do it at your place." The phone beeped.

Kate never came to his apartment, which could only mean that she had things to say to them that she didn't want her new husband or stepdaughter to hear. Great. This night couldn't get any worse. Sam slumped deeper into the couch like all the bones had been removed from her body. Jake patted her leg. "Don't worry. We'll get through it together."

She laid her head on his shoulder. "Thanks. You're a good Dad."

"No. I should have done better by you. I should have . . . "

"Dad, stop."

"No." Jake blinked away his tears. "When Tom was murdered, I did some serious thinking. Too much, probably. And I came to the conclusion that things shouldn't go unsaid because sometimes you don't get a second chance."

"Dad— "

Undeterred, he said, "Sam, I'm very proud of you. You're growing into a wonderful young woman. You're strong, smart, beautiful, and you can do anything you set your mind to, so if you want to be an artist, then God damn it, you should."

"I love you." Sam hugged him. He didn't cry, but he could have. They released their hold and smiled at one another. She fidgeted with the hem of her shorts. Hesitantly, she asked, "Do you think . . . Do you think that I could come live with you full-time?"

He sat up straighter. "Seriously?"

"If it's not too much trouble, I was hoping that you would let me live here. I could keep the place clean and cook for you if you bought real food."

Gripping the arm of the couch, he asked, "Was that your big question? Was that the one you were afraid to ask?"

"Yes." She nodded her head slowly. "No pressure. I'll understand if I can't."

"Sorry, Sam. I got lost in all the talk with art school and SAT scores, but I'd love it if you stayed here."

"I won't cramp your style?"

"My style? Yeah, right. I eat carryout every night, watch cable because my TV is too old for Netflix, and then fall asleep on the couch. It's not a pretty picture—are you sure you want to live with me?"

"Definitely."

Jake would have to increase his security, add a second deadbolt and a heavy-duty chain. And whatever job he found would have to be on days so that he could be here every night with Sam, but he could make it work. There was no way he'd miss this opportunity to be a bigger part of her life.

Sam said, "There's only one problem."

"Let me guess. Your Mom doesn't know you want this either?"

"No."

"When you were young, I never wanted to put you in the middle of a legal battle that I'd probably lose anyway," Jake said. "However, now that you're almost an adult, I don't think there's anything she can do about it."

"You really think so?"

"Last time I looked into it, you had to be fourteen years old to make your own choice on where to live."

"Wow. Then you think we can do it?"

He tried to sound confident. "I do."

Chapter 4

Twenty-three year old, Trent Morrison juggled a pizza box as he kicked the door closed behind him. It rattled in its cheap frame. A flickering television cast shadows across the dirty apartment. The place reeked of rotting food and sweat. Trent gagged but managed to keep down his lunch.

In front of the television, a large man slept in a recliner. His sweaty scalp shined through his thinning hair. The man's snores drowned out ESPN's SportsCenter with a racket that sounded like a tired table saw in need of new bearings. If not for the sound, Trent would have thought he'd walked into Seven's first murder scene.

Trent flipped on the light, but the obese man didn't stir. Annoyed, Trent kicked the back of his chair, and the man jumped, nearly tipping over backward. His flabby arms pinwheeled to keep him upright.

"What the hell?" Tiny shouted.

Tiny rotated his body from right to left, never succeeding in spotting Trent, who purposely moved behind the big man. The exertion caused his breathing to grow raspy and labored. It was disgusting. Trent hadn't let his injury drive him to such a pathetic existence. In fact, except for the slight limp, he was still a good athlete. His teams always won the pickup basketball games at the gym.

Trent stepped into view. "Hey, Tiny."

"Morrison, you scared me. And you know I don't like it when you call me that." Springs groaned as Tiny relaxed back into the chair, scratching his stomach with a meaty paw.

"Sorry, you left the door unlocked. This isn't the greatest of neighborhoods— I'd be more careful."

Trent flopped down on the ratty sofa and made room for the pizza box on the crowded coffee table. A glass with a congealed liquid tipped over and rolled to the floor. Gross. Trent couldn't tell if the smell came from Tiny, the leftover food, or the couch. It was so bad, Trent would swear an animal had died in the upholstery, but more likely, it was Tiny's inability to perform basic hygiene.

Tiny eyed the cardboard box. "Did you bring me dinner and my money?"

"Depends. Do you have my pills?"

Lifting a huge thigh, Tiny dug around the cushions of his chair. He retrieved an opaque bottle and tossed it across the room. Trent poured the contents into his hand, counted the pills, and slipped the bottle into his bag. He threw a roll of cash back; it hit Tiny in his massive belly. Trent took pride in his accuracy from his day's playing quarterback in college.

The big man removed the rubber band and leafed through the bills. "Hey, this isn't enough."

"Exactly. You shorted me pills last time."

"My back was killing me. I needed to keep a few for my pain."

Trent shook his head. "Not my problem."

"Come on! I need the money to cover my rent."

"Again. Not my problem." Trent frowned. This was a business, not a charity. "Too bad you don't have any Ritalin or Adderall. Kids pay top dollar for that stuff."

"But I don't have ADHD."

"Neither do these kids, but it helps the overachievers study all night and get all A's— that way they don't end up like you or me."

Tiny shrugged. "My life isn't that bad."

"Mine either," Trent lied. He stood up and slung his bag over his shoulder. He needed to get back to the store to pick up his next delivery. Pizza's provided an excellent cover for him to buy and sell illegal prescriptions.

On the television, a football highlight drew Trent's attention to the screen. A heavily muscled linebacker knocked a ball carrier clean off his feet. The poor guy's helmet flew five yards back, most likely resulting in a concussion.

Tiny howled with delight. "Did you see that?"

Trent recognized the defender and looked away as bile rose in his stomach. The player on the television was the one responsible for Trent's current situation. If not for him, Trent would be a starting quarterback in the NFL with a mansion and a model girlfriend. Not sitting here in the shithole dealing pills to opioid addicts.

Trent turned to leave, and his knee creaked. "No, I missed it."

"That's him, isn't it?"

"Who?"

Tiny shifted in his chair, eyeing the pizza box. "You know who."

Looking back at the screen, Trent's mouth twisted in disgust. "Yeah. That's him."

"Damn, did you see how much his new contract is worth? It has to piss you off. You would've been a first-rounder if not for him."

"Fuck you."

"Don't be that way."

Trent snatched the pizza box off the table and headed for the door. "Whatever."

"Come on, Trent. You know I was a big fan of yours. What you did in that Illinois game was incredible. Six touchdowns. And that Hail Mary against OSU. That was a one in a million pass."

"Great. Do you want me to autograph a fucking ball for you?"

Tiny rubbed his hands together. "Would you do that?"

"No way. You'd sell it online for rent money and then keep all your pills for yourself."

Tiny grimaced. "I don't think your autograph would cover the rent— even this place."

Trent closed his eyes and nodded. "I suppose it wouldn't. I have to go."

"Wait! Aren't you going to leave me the pizza?"

Trent dropped the box on Tiny's lap with a thud.

Tiny licked his lips. "Thanks, man. How about your brother, Austin? I read every college in the nation wants him. Has he accepted an offer yet?"

"Not yet."

Trent twisted the knob and headed into the drab hallway, slamming the door shut behind him with a chuckle. Through the hollow metal door, Tiny screamed, "Hey, this is vegetarian."

Chapter 5

Someone knocked on Jake's door, fast and loud. Sam sat up straight in her seat as she wrung her hands nervously in her lap. Jake opened the door, and Kate tried to walk by him, but he blocked her path.

He gave her his best smile. "Hi, Kate."

"Jake."

Her cold stare attempted to cut him off at the knees. A tailored cream suit accented Kate's fit body. Expensively cut, wavy red hair fell above her shoulders. The only sign of age was the start of crow's feet around her dazzling blue eyes, but she had no laugh lines around her mouth. She spotted Sam huddled in the corner of the couch, and her pupils narrowed on her errant daughter.

Jake didn't step aside. "Like I said on the phone, I just got back from Michigan when I found Sam here. I swear I would have called you after I told her about my trip."

Kate did her best to look respectful, though she had never liked his friends, especially Mary. "Yes, I was sorry to hear about Tom. I know how much he meant to you. How's his family?"

"As good as can be expected."

"Did they find who did it?"

Jake looked down at the floor, afraid the prosecutor would read the guilt on his face. "No. The police thought they had a lead, but it didn't pan out, so it looks like they may never find the killer."

"How terrible? I can't even imagine. Be sure to tell Mary that my thoughts and prayers are with them."

"I will," he lied. His friends had never liked Kate either.

With the pleasantries out of the way, Kate pushed past Jake. She stopped in front of Sam, hands on her hips. The taunt muscles stretched her linen pants in all the right places. "Young lady, do you mind explaining yourself?"

"Mom. I . . . didn't mean to scare you." Sam stuttered, visibly shrinking.

Leaning forward, Kate said, "Well, at least you came here. I thought you ran off to see that boy. He's a bad influence on you."

Sam pushed herself deeper into the couch. "He is not. Austin is the reason I scored as high as I did on the SAT. He helped me with the practice exams."

"So you could have actually done worse than a 950?"

Sam's nostrils flared. "Thanks!"

"How about we all settle down?" Jake sat next to Sam and put an arm around her.

Kate turned on him. "Do you understand how serious this is? This is her future, damn it. Sam's grades aren't the best, so a high SAT score was her ticket to a good college and then law school."

Jake shook his head. "Listen to yourself. Those are your dreams, not hers. She's almost eighteen, and we need to start letting Sam make her own decisions, like applying to Art school."

Kate snorted. "Art school. Did she sucker you into that crazy idea?"

"It's not crazy. She should follow her passion."

"Passion doesn't pay the bills. We'll be supporting her for the rest of her life."

"You don't know that."

"Who do you know that became a successful artist? Tell me, who?"

Jake rubbed his face in frustration. "Nobody."

"That's what I thought. She doesn't know what is best for her, but I do— I can be the adult."

"Seriously. Your dad gave you that same speech nineteen years ago. Did you listen?"

Kate pointed a finger at him. "I should have, which is why I won't let her make ALL the same mistakes that I made!"

Sam shot up from the couch with a look of terror on her face. "Mom! You promised— "

"What?" Jake asked.

Kate waved him off and turned back to Sam. "Am I that unreasonable that we couldn't have talked about this at home? That you needed to run over here?"

"Ummm . . . " Sam looked down at her feet.

Kate sat down on the other side of Sam and rested a hand on her daughter's shoulder. "Now, honey. Once you're at college and start taking classes, I know that you'll love it. Besides, you can take art classes for all your electives, right?"

"I guess."

"Good. Because the next SAT test date is in six weeks, and I found the perfect tutor that promises he can get your score up by 300 points."

Jake exhaled loudly. "Kate, you're not listening to her."

"I'm listening to her, Jake. But I can help her make the tough decisions. That's what a good parent does; they don't try to be their child's friend."

"Excuse me!" Jake shouted.

Kate made a sweeping gesture at Jake's economy apartment. "Yes, excuse you. You could've been so much more, but your mother coddled you. And look where you ended up, Jake."

"I'd rather be here than another of your father's pawns, like Robert."

Kate closed her eyes. "I'm too tired for the same old arguments. Sam, get your stuff. We're going home."

"Wait a minute. I'm not letting you take her away from me so you can bully her into getting your way. Not this time. You're so much like your father; it makes me sick."

If looks could kill, Jake would be dead. Through tight lips, she said, "You wish you could be half the man he is."

His vision clouded, and he fought to maintain control of his temper. He lost that battle. "You know, Sam asked me something before you got here."

"She did?" Kate turned to her daughter, but Sam avoided her gaze.

"Yes. Sam wants to move in with me,'" Jake said.

Kate's eyes nearly bulged out of her head. "You're kidding me, right?"

"No. I'm not. I think it's what Sam needs right now." He couldn't help himself by adding, "Besides, you have your new family. This will give you more time to focus on them."

Kate grabbed her daughter's hand. "Sam? Tell me this isn't true."

Still not looking at her mother, Sam croaked, "I'd like to try living with Dad for a little while. I'd still come home on weekends."

Shaking her head, Kate said, "I don't believe it. This is insane. Sam couldn't possibly move in here."

"It's not insane. I'm her father."

Dropping Sam's hand, Kate paced around the cramped room. "Hell, you can barely take care of yourself, Jake. And you work nights. There's no way Sam can be left in this dump alone."

"Well, to be completely honest, I quit my job, so when Sam lives here, she won't be left alone."

Kate snorted. "Of course. Do you have another one lined up?"

"No."

"That figures. Whatever, it doesn't matter. She's not living here."

A vein pulsed in Jake's temple. "It's her decision."

"You pushed her into this. You're trying to turn her against me."

"I didn't do that. I'm not like you."

Kate's lips pressed to a thin line. "No. You'd just sit in this crappy apartment and feel sorry for yourself— poor little Jake. Life is so unfair. Do you want me to fix you a drink? Or do you want to go to the bar and get it from your little floozy?"

"Fuck you, Kate." His hand clenched into a fist. How dare her bring that up in front of Sam.

Smiling wide, Kate said, "Come on, Jake. I know you want to. Do it. Hit me."

"Stop it," Sam shouted.

"Why don't you give me another black eye?" Kate asked. "How about a fat lip too? That'll teach me to shut my mouth. Come on. You've done it before."

A puzzled look crossed Sam's face. "Dad?"

"Tell her, Jake. Tell her that you hit me."

Jake shook his head. "I pushed you."

"Same thing."

"No. It's not. And I only did it after you hit me."

Kate laughed. "I did not. You were stinking drunk. How do you remember anything?"

"I remember."

"Really? Because I have pictures of my injuries. Do you have pictures, Jake?"

"No."

"Good. So, the second you think about going to court to get custody of Sam. I'll destroy you. Try me!"

Sam looked at Jake with sad eyes. He looked down at the floor as his heart splintered into a thousand pieces. Kate was right. There was no way he'd ever beat her in court. He'd failed Sam yet again.

"Come on, Sam. We're leaving." Kate practically dragged her daughter from the apartment; the door slammed shut behind them.

Chapter 6

The next morning, Jake crawled out of bed. It had been a long night as he counted his many regrets. His back ached from tossing and turning on the lumpy mattress, so he twisted from side to side to loosen up. The vertebrae popped like popcorn in a microwave. Afterward, his stomach gurgled, so he went to the kitchen and got a glass of water.

Looking in the fridge, he confirmed Sam's earlier assessment. The shelves were almost bare, and what was there was spoiled. He'd need to go to the store today. He tossed the rotten stuff in the garbage with the shards of glass. All that remained was baking soda, a jar of olives, and a carton of questionable eggs. He scrambled two eggs and took a tentative bite while he considered the recent turn of events.

Getting revenge for Tom's death had brought Jake great satisfaction, and then Sam asked to live with him, so Jake dared to think his luck had turned, but he should've known better. Kate would never allow it; she'd never forgiven him for his past indiscretions. She'd made mistakes too. Why should Jake's haunt him forever? Jake prayed Sam would believe him. He'd only pushed Kate.

Jake finished his meager breakfast and flopped on the living room couch. Too quickly, the walls closed in on him like the trash compactor from Star Wars, so he decided to go for a walk before he went stir crazy. His neighbor's door opened a crack as he approached the stairs.

A pair of oversized glasses peeked out, forcing Jake to pause. "Hi, Mrs. Goldstein."

"Jake, is that you?" She opened the door wider to reveal a smiling wrinkled face.

"It is. I got back last night. Thanks for keeping an eye on my place."

She tucked a strand of white hair behind her ear as a pair of cats wound around her legs. "Please come inside. I have all your newspapers collected in a bag."

"I don't want to bother you. I can get them later."

"Nonsense. I've been up for hours, and I have a pot of coffee ready. Let me pour you a cup."

Jake hesitated with his decision. He wasn't sure he'd make the best company right now, but Mrs. Goldstein had never invited him inside her apartment before, and he didn't want to appear rude. She was one of the few residents he knew, along with the Indian family on the other side of the hall. Still, he'd been surprised Mrs. Goldstein offered to get his newspapers when she saw him with a suitcase. Jake guessed everyone wanted a purpose, however small.

"All right. One cup."

"That's a good boy."

The elderly woman turned and shuffled towards the kitchen while the cats darted to the living room. He followed them inside, closing the door behind him. The apartment was a mirror image of his own, familiar but eerily different in its color and decoration. Mrs. Goldstein motioned for Jake to take a seat at the table as she went into a cupboard. She extracted a white mug and poured him a cup of coffee from the percolator on the counter.

"Cream? Sugar?"

"No, thanks. I take it black."

"My Ira took it black too." She handed Jake his cup and sat down opposite him.

"Aren't you having any?"

Shaking her head, she said, "I've already had my fill. Any more than that, and I'll be piddling all morning."

He blew on the hot liquid. "Thank you for getting my papers."

"No problem. I'm glad I caught you. In the old days, people had time to share a cup of coffee and shoot the breeze."

"True. Now everyone is rushing around with a phone at the end of their nose."

Mrs. Goldstein cackled as a black and white cat jumped into her lap. "You got that right. I don't have one of those gosh darn things, and I wouldn't know how to work it if I did."

"There are times I wish I didn't have one either," Jake said, taking a sip from his cup.

She bowed her head. "I don't mean to pry, but it was very busy at your apartment last night."

"Yeah. Sorry about that, my ex-wife and I don't always see eye to eye."

"Ira and I never fought. The man was a saint, so gentle and kind; he'd never yell or raise a hand to me."

"Well, I don't think it will happen again."

She raised an eyebrow. "Oh?"

Not wanting to air his dirty laundry, he changed the subject. "This is excellent coffee. What brand is it?"

"Folgers, nothing fancy. It's all I can afford on a fixed budget. Let me get you a second cup."

"You don't have to."

She brushed the cat out of her lap and grabbed Jake's cup. "Tut tut, it's my pleasure. Plus, it'll finish off the pot."

"All right."

Pouring the last of the coffee into Jake's cup, she set the pot in the sink. "However, I wasn't talking about the yelling. I was talking about all the comings and goings. I didn't notice it so much until Mr. Bigglesworth pointed it out."

Mr. Bigglesworth? Did his neighbor have a gentlemen friend? Good for her— everyone needs somebody. Mrs. Goldstein returned to the table with Jake's cup. The black and white cat jumped back in her lap.

Jake said, "I don't believe I've ever met your boyfriend."

"Boyfriend? I could never love another man after my Ira."

"Then is Mr. Bigglesworth just a friend?"

She scratched the head of the feline in her lap. "Oh no, Mr. Bigglesworth is one of my cats."

At the mention of his name, the tawny Siamese cat jumped up on the table to sit next to Mrs. Goldstein with a regal air, tail twitching like a whip. It yawned and licked a paw with a pink tongue.

"And the cat pointed it out?"

"Yes. Mr. Bigglesworth can communicate with me, and he told me to look out my peephole to see her leaving your apartment."

Jake nodded his head. "Interesting."

"He doesn't believe me, Mr. Bigglesworth," Mrs. Goldstein said, scratching the regal cat between the ears.

"No, it's just that I've never heard a cat talk before. Could he do it right now?"

The cat stopped licking its paw and stared at him intently. Jake waited, but no audible speech came from the cat as he expected. Mrs. Goldstein giggled. "Mr. Bigglesworth says that he's not sure he can trust you. Maybe, he'll do it later."

"But he can do it?"

"Of course, Mr. Bigglesworth is special."

"And he talked to you just now?"

"Yes, he talks directly inside your head. It's like there's a microphone in your mind."

He took a sip of his coffee. "So with this microphone, Mr. Bigglesworth told you to watch the hallway, and you saw my ex-wife leave my apartment?"

"Not your ex-wife. This woman was younger."

"My daughter?"

"No, it wasn't her either."

He leaned forward. "Are you sure it wasn't my daughter, Sam? She went in and out of my apartment a few times last night."

"I know what your daughter looks like. This was the short African American woman from the grocery store down the street."

"Packard's Market?"

Mrs. Goldstein nodded. "That's the one. I almost didn't recognize her out of her uniform."

It had to be the same person Jake had seen on the stairs. Shit! Jake's worst fears could've been realized if Sam had still been home. He asked, "Are you sure it was my apartment?"

"Oh, you don't have to feel guilty if you asked her to water your plants. She's such a hard worker, and after that trouble with her son, I bet you wanted an excuse to give her a bit of money. You're such a sweetheart."

"That's me. A big ol' sweetheart."

"I try to tip her when she waits on me at the deli counter, but she says it's against store policy."

Jake winked at Mrs. Goldstein. "Why you're a bigger sweetheart than me."

"Stop." She playfully slapped the table.

Jake finished his coffee and carried his cup to the sink. "Well, I should get going now. I need to go to the market and settle up with my friend."

Mrs. Goldstein held up a finger, stopping Jake in his tracks. "What's that, Mr. Bigglesworth?"

Feeling silly, he waited for the cat to answer her. After a few seconds, she turned back to Jake. "Mr. Bigglesworth says that you should be careful."

"He does? Why?"

"Mr. Bigglesworth says he can't tell you— that it would overstep his bounds on this planet."

Jake studied the cat, and the feline met his gaze. Uneasily, Jake said, "I met a fascinating man back in Michigan that had a whole house full of cats. He must have had ten of them that he used for protection."

Mrs. Goldstein said, "Cats for protection? Wouldn't a gun work better? I have a little .45 in my nightstand."

"Well, he said aliens visited our planet and used mind control on us, but it didn't work on cats, so they were his shield."

Mrs. Goldstein frowned. "Cats can't act as shields."

Jake shrugged. "It sounded crazy to me too."

"Your friend may be crazy, but he doesn't understand how it works. They can't protect me from aliens."

"They won't?"

"No. Mr. Bigglesworth is the alien."

Jake pointed at the cat. "He is?"

"Yes, Mr. Bigglesworth comes from a star in Orion's Belt. His kind sees potential in the human race, so he was sent here to make sure we don't destroy our planet before we reach enlightenment."

"I wish him luck." Jake eased himself towards the door. "I should really be going now."

Mrs. Goldstein hopped up, knocking the other cat from her lap. "Wait! You almost forgot your papers."

"Thanks." He tried to take the bag, but Mrs. Goldstein didn't let it go.

"Last thing. Can I get your phone number in case Mr. Bigglesworth decides he can trust you?"

"Sure." Jake gave her his cell and retreated from the apartment slowly as Mr. Bigglesworth watched him leave.

Chapter 7

Skipping his walk, Jake returned to his apartment and set the newspapers on the table in chronological order. Most of the news was too old to be useful, but he still scanned them anyway. One item, an attempted rape, mere blocks from his apartment caught his eye. Jake could get his news online like everyone else, but there was something about spreading out the sports page under a bowl of cereal that a phone or computer couldn't match; call him old-school.

However, he couldn't focus on the papers with all his fears bouncing around his head like pinballs. What scared him the most was Sam may never talk to him again. But he couldn't forget that on any given day, Sonny, the leader of the motorcycle gang, could show up and demand Jake repay his debt to them, and now he was burdened with alien cats watching him too. His life was insane; he wanted to scream.

Yet Jake tried to keep his head. Sam was a smart girl. She knew her mother was a difficult person. Hadn't she'd come to him with her dream to go to art school instead of Kate? He sent her a text.

Hi Sam. We need to talk. There's more to the story. Please call me

He hit send and waited. And waited.

After a minute without a response, Jake decided to take his walk. Mrs. Goldstein said his mysterious intruder worked at the corner grocery. Perhaps he should pay her a visit. Grabbing his keys, he pulled the door shut and locked it. He kept his head down as he passed Mrs. Goldstein's door, but he couldn't shake the feeling of being watched.

On the street, he turned right and walked two blocks to the corner store, Packard's Market. Jake usually shopped at Strickland's, the grocery store three blocks in the other direction since their prices tended to be cheaper. However, he had been in Packard's a handful of times when it was convenient, so he knew the store did have a deli counter where his suspect supposedly worked.

The automatic doors slid open with a mechanical hiss. He scanned the three checkout lanes. Only one was in operation with a woman at the register; a teenaged boy was bagging for her. The deli counter lay in the back corner, away from the registers. Before he made his move, Jake wanted to get a lay of the land. He went to the far side of the store and made his way back slowly, checking each aisle. An employee restocked shelves in the canned food section while the rest of the aisles were empty except for the random customer.

Finally arriving at the meat counter, a teenaged boy, slightly older than the bagger, sliced ham for a mother with two young girls hanging on her legs. That was it. No other employees were waiting on customers, especially a short African American woman. Dejected, he considered leaving and trying again tomorrow when he remembered he had nothing to eat in his apartment. Cold cuts would be easy and within his culinary abilities, so he pulled a number from the red ticket dispenser. Maybe, Jake could prompt the kid to tell him when her next shift was.

After the ham, the woman made requests for exotic cheeses and meats from the back refrigerator. The teenager became flustered with the complicated order and looked to Jake, who gave him a sympathetic shrug while the two girls ran circles around their mother and screamed. She ignored them as she requested a half-pound of potato salad.

The worker exhaled loudly. "Tasha! I need your help. We have a customer waiting."

"Be out in a second," a voice yelled from the stock room.

As he scooped out potato salad, the boy said, "She'll be right out."

Jake smiled. "No problem."

He moved off to the side, hoping Tasha was his intruder? He was pretty sure he'd be able to tell by height and body type unless more than one woman fitting that description worked here. He ran through potential lines of questioning but knew once the conversation started, he'd have to improvise to keep her talking since she'd be under no obligation to answer anything. God, he missed being a detective.

Eventually, an African American woman in her late twenties appeared from behind the swinging door. She wiped her hands on a green apron and scanned the room until her eyes fell on Jake. Recognition flashed across her face, but just as quickly, it returned to what must be a practiced look of congeniality. Jake maintained a neutral face himself, though inside he was smiling. Tasha was about the right size and shape. It had to be her.

"Can I help you?" she asked.

"Yes, a pound of smoked turkey."

"Is pre-sliced all right."

"That's fine."

Jake watched her travel from the counter to the scale. He was even more convinced that she was the woman from the stairs based on how she moved. She weighed out the meat, slipped it into a bag, and attached the price sticker.

Handing him his order, she asked, "Anything else?"

"A half-pound of Swiss cheese?"

"How do you want it sliced?"

"For sandwiches," he replied.

The suspected intruder grabbed a block of white cheese from a waist-high refrigerator. She studied Jake out of the corner of her eyes as the machine whirled and cut the wedges of Swiss onto white wax paper.

Jake asked, "Do I know you? You look familiar."

She angled herself towards the large shiny machine. "I don't think so unless you've shopped at this store before."

Jake nodded though he could've sworn he'd seen Tasha before this week, but he couldn't place where. "I guess not."

She handed Jake his cheese. "Can I get you anything else?"

"Thanks. I'm good." He tossed the packages into his cart.

The woman spun on her heels and headed for the stock room. Over her shoulder, she said, "Have a good day.'"

"You too," Jake called after her.

Damn! He didn't get as far with Tasha as he wanted, but Jake had a plan to get her information without alerting her. Taking a meandering route, he picked up a loaf of bread, a bag of chips, coffee, and several frozen dinners. Afterward, he went to the checkout, where he waited behind two people with way more items than him.

Eventually, it was his turn. The cashier didn't look at him as she began ringing up his food. "Did you find everything you were looking for?"

"I did. The woman in the deli department was very helpful."

"Tasha is awesome. She's been working here longer than me."

"She looks very familiar, but I can't place her?"

Leaning in close, the woman whispered, "Did you see her on the news last week?"

Jake snapped his finger and lied, "That's it."

"It's so sad. I don't care if his father was the silkworm rapist—that boy wouldn't harm a fly. And how could he commit the crime when he was watching his sister? You tell me how they could find him guilty?"

Shit! Tasha was Leroy's baby-momma. She'd been in the apartment that fateful day along with their two kids. Jake couldn't believe he hadn't recognized her, and now Leroy's son had been convicted of rape. He must have missed the story in his cursory scan of the papers, but he didn't think the news would tell him why Tasha had been in his apartment yesterday? Nothing had been missing or damaged, and Jake had nothing to hide. Outside of the events of Tom's death, Jake was an open book. Even his internet browser history was boring, so what had Tasha been looking for? It made no sense. Not until he recalled his night of restless sleep on a lumpy mattress.

The cashier cleared her throat, and Jake realized she was waiting for a response, but he'd forgotten the question, so he threw out a generic reply. "It's a God damn shame."

"The courts in Chicago are a joke. The judges are as crooked as our politicians."

"Crookedier." Jake laughed, thinking of Kate's father. He wouldn't be surprised if Judge Doyle was crooked, on top of being a son of a bitch.

The clerk handed him his bag. "You have a nice day."

"You too." He left the store with his heart thumping in his chest, anxious to search his bed.

Chapter 8

Later that evening, Trent parked in front of his parent's house, a large two-story colonial. He remained behind the wheel, massaging his bad knee after a long day of delivering pizzas. The song on the radio wasn't one he particularly liked but waiting for it to end delayed Trent having to see the disappointed look in his father's eyes. At least Austin would fulfill Bo's dream of one of his offspring playing professional football, just like his old man.

The song ended as long shadows stretched across their manicured lawn. With a sigh, Trent gathered up his belongings and unfolded himself from the driver's seat. He slammed the rusty door shut and headed up the walk. His mother had left the porch light on for him like she'd done since he was twelve.

In the kitchen, he found his dad and brother at the table. Dirty plates and finished glasses of milk were pushed aside. His mother stood at the sink, elbows deep in sudsy water, washing the night's pots and pans. An old-fashioned apron protected her floral print dress. His parents were a throwback to a by-gone era. Their home life was oddly comforting and simple, which was probably why he'd never moved out. Sleeping in his parent's basement was lame, but it had to be better than living in a cheap apartment with disgusting roommates.

"Hi, Mom." He gave his mother, Barbara, a kiss on the cheek.

A smile spread across her face as she set a pot in the drying rack. "I thought you were working late. I can pull the left-overs out of the fridge and warm them up for you."

"That's all right. I ate at work."

She shook her head. "All that pizza is not good for you."

"I eat salads too."

"Good boy," she said, putting her hands back in the suds.

Trent carefully set his bag down on the floor and pulled out a chair at the table. Deep in conversation, Bo and Austin didn't acknowledge him as they debated the various football camps that Austin could attend this summer. Bo's barrel chest pressed against the table, the edge cutting a line across his thick midsection. Bo pushed for the traditional powerhouses, while Austin wanted ones near the coast for a little fun in the sun before his career got serious.

The debate went on for a full five minutes before Austin elbowed Trent playfully. "Will you tell Dad I don't need to go to Alabama's camp? The number one recruit in the nation is already verbally committed to them. It would be a waste of time."

Bo said, "But then we can see what promises the Big Ten coaches make to keep Austin out of the SEC. It's the smart thing to do, right, Trent?"

He shrugged, "I think you both have valid points."

Bo waved a thick arm at him. "What good are you?"

Barbara set a large pot in the rack. "Bo!"

"Oh, honey. He knows I'm joking. Don't you, Trent?"

"It's fine, Mom."

Bo shook his head. "See, you're too protective, always babying these boys."

Trent pushed his chair back and gathered up his bag. The legs squeaked on the spotless kitchen floor. To Austin, he said, "Maybe you should go to the Bama camp. Another SEC school might extend an offer if they think you're interested in playing down south."

Bo slapped the table. "Listen to your brother. He knows what he is talking about."

Austin's face scrunched up like he'd smelled something bad. "But I want to play in the Big Ten like you and Dad. If Wisconsin wasn't going through a coaching change, I'd follow after you."

"You should keep your options open. You never know what the future holds," Trent said. The irony of the statement was lost on his father.

Trent stomped down the stairs to his finished part of the basement. The living room consisted of a hand-me-down leather sofa and a flat-screen TV that Trent had bought himself. Bo's framed Packer's jersey was prominently displayed above the couch. Trent's college jersey was in the bottom of his dresser. His dad had spent seven years in the NFL as a tight end. The experience hadn't made him wealthy, but he'd parlayed his fame into a respectable mortgage business.

Pulling his bedroom door closed behind him, Trent fell face down on the bed. The sheets smelled like lavender-scented detergent. His bag bounced off the mattress and landed on the floor. He rolled to his back and noticed the room was freshly cleaned. His dirty clothes were laundered, furniture was dusted, and the floor was vacuumed. However, there was no need to get excited; his stash was in a trunk with a combination lock at the end of his bed. His parents were so naïve they probably assumed he hid girlie magazines inside the footlocker.

Trent kicked off his shoes, and they thudded to the floor haphazardly. Staring at his phone, he scrolled aimlessly for the next half-hour. The time went by in a mind-numbing blur. When his eyes couldn't focus anymore, he let the phone drop out of his hand, and he turned to the fifty-gallon fish tank on his dresser. Brightly colored fish chased each other as a large Plecostomus sucked on the side of the glass. Trent spent a lot of time maintaining the tank, so the fish had a perfect little life. Unlike his own.

He knew he should stop dealing pills, but he couldn't work for his dad. The mortgage business would steal his soul, nothing but numbers and negotiating with banks all day. No, thank you. Yet, it was only a matter of time before he got caught. Every dealer did. If only he could avoid arrest until he had enough money to buy a small house and a dog. He loved animals but never had a pet growing up because of his mom's allergies, but he didn't hold it against her. She gave everything for her family.

The fish's hypnotic movement pushed him over the edge, and he rolled to his side, fluffing the pillow under his head to go to sleep when he heard a knock on his bedroom door. Rubbing his eyes, he said, "Come in."

The door opened slowly, and Austin stepped inside. "Can I turn on the light?"

"Go ahead." Trent sat up and swung his legs off the side of the bed.

The fluorescent bulbs hummed to life as Austin shut the door behind him. "Did I wake you?"

"No. What's up?"

"I have a question for you."

"Ok?"

Austin rammed his hands into his pockets. "Do you miss it?"

"Miss what?"

"Football."

"Yes and no. I liked being part of a team, but I don't love the game like you and dad."

Austin nodded; his mouth twisted to the side, but no words came from it.

Trent asked, "Did you come to a decision on which camps to go to this summer?"

"Camps? Nah! Dad doesn't know, but I think I'm ready to verbally commit."

"Where?"

"I'm thinking about maybe playing at Northwestern."

Trent cocked his head to the side. "Northwestern? Are you serious?"

"Yes," Austin said, shifting from foot to foot. "Sam will stay in Chicago for art school, and I think we have a future together. So if I went to Northwestern, we wouldn't be far apart."

"She's a cute girl. And I know you've been through some difficult stuff together, but are you sure you want to base your decision on a girl?" Trent had emphasized the word, difficult.

"You heard about the abortion?"

"It was kind of hard not to with all the yelling a few weeks back, but I knew Dad couldn't hold it against his golden boy for too long."

Austin's head dropped. "We were using protection. I don't know what happened."

"Whatever. I don't judge. So, you like Northwestern's program?"

"I like the new coach. He said they'd tailor the offense around me, so we should be able to win the West division for sure."

"If that's what you want, I'll stick up for you with dad. For whatever that's worth."

Austin tossed a glance in the direction of the footlocker. "Thanks, Trent. You're the best."

Trent laughed. "I'm definitely not the best."

"I'm serious. If my college career could be half as good as yours, I'd be happy."

"It will be better. I guarantee it, especially if you can lead Northwestern to a Big Ten championship."

"Thanks." Austin left the room, pulling the door closed behind him.

Trent remembered his bag lying on the floor and cursed under his breath. Stupid. If he wasn't more careful, his parents would discover his business, and Bo would do more than kill him. From his days in the league, Bo detested the weak players who relied on pills to play through the pain.

Trent pulled his latest acquisitions from the bottom of the bag and hid them in the footlocker. Damn. He swore that he had more pills in there. At least two more bottles of percs and some pep pills were missing from his inventory. He checked the locker's latch. There were small scratches on the metal. Had someone pried the lock open? Unlikely. No, Trent chalked it up to his bad memory and too many concussions throughout his career. He must have sold them. It was the only thing that made sense.

Still, a bad feeling grew in the pit of his stomach, but he chose to ignore it because the only other possibility was that Austin was stealing pills from him. And that was impossible. Austin was a good kid; he wouldn't do something dumb like use pills himself or sell them to his friends at school. That would be plain stupid.

Chapter 9

By the following day, Jake still hadn't heard from Sam, and it was driving him crazy. Literally. So he drove up to the high school and parked across the street to wait for her. Sitting hunched low in his seat, he felt like a creepy pedophile, but he didn't really have another choice. It isn't like he can plead his case with Sam at Kate's house.

The clock on the dashboard warned Jake that it was almost eight o'clock. Damn! School would be starting soon. He drummed his thumbs on the steering wheel and scanned the young faces hurrying up the school's steps to beat the bell, but none of them were his daughter. Had Sam gone in another door? Had he missed her? His prayers must have been answered because up ahead, a girl with red hair walked towards Jake's car. It was definitely Sam with a boy's arm slung over her shoulder. The muscular young man with the varsity jacket must be the football star boyfriend that Kate had ranted about. Atticus? Aubrey? He couldn't remember. No one was happy with naming their kid Andy anymore.

As they approached, Jake climbed out of the car. When Sam saw him, she smiled, which Jake took as a good sign. Giving her a little wave, he said, "Hi."

The boy stepped between Jake and his daughter. "Do you know this guy, Sam?"

"Yes." She chuckled. "He's my Dad."

"Oh."

"Can we have a minute, son?" Jake asked.

Sam pushed the boy towards the school. "Go ahead. You can't afford to get another tardy."

He sighed. "No. I can't."

"I'll see you after first hour." She gave him a quick peck on the lips.

The boy moved his backpack to his other shoulder and headed towards the school. Looking back, he gave Jake a suspicious look that was more cute than intimidating.

"Your boyfriend. What was his name? Abacus?"

She rolled her eyes. "His name is Austin."

"Is the relationship serious?"

"You could say that."

"And your mother doesn't like him."

"Not really..."

"Then he sounds like my type of guy."

"Austin does play your favorite sport. Football."

"Really? What position?"

"Quarterback."

Jake nodded. "I thought he looked like a pretty boy, but I won't hold it against him. Is he any good?"

"Yes. A bunch of colleges are looking at him. His dad and brother played in college too."

Jake came around the car to stand by Sam. "Really, where?"

She held up her hands. "I know he told me, but I forgot. Their last name is Morrison. Does that help?"

He shook his head. "No. It's a pretty common last name."

"Sorry."

"Why doesn't your mom like Abercrombie?"

"Austin! I don't know." She laughed nervously. "I guess Mom wouldn't like anyone that takes time away from my studies."

"Sounds about right."

"But she's hardly ever there. I swear I take care of Izzy more than they do. That's why she doesn't want me to move in with you. She'd lose her babysitter."

"No. She doesn't want you to move in with me because she blames me for everything bad that happened in her life."

"You're probably right . . ."

An awkward pause filled the space between them. He looked at her, and she studied the pavement. The conversation had been mostly superficial, but she had talked to him instead of making excuses about needing to get to school. He touched her shoulder. "Do you blame me too after what your mother said the other night?"

"No."

"Then how come you didn't return my text?"

She looked up and frowned. "Mom took my phone away."

"Figures that she'd let me twist in the wind," Jake growled.

"I thought about using Izzy's phone to send you a text, but I didn't want to get in more trouble."

"I understand. I only care that you're not mad at me. Are you?"

She ground a foot into the pavement. "No."

"Come on, Sam. Tell me the truth."

"I'm not mad. I don't think. But did you do it? Did you hit mom?"

He closed his eyes and took a deep breath before answering, "I pushed her. I pushed her pretty hard, and she hit the corner of the table. But it was the only time I ever laid a hand on her."

"Did Mom hit you first?"

He'd said as much the other night, so Jake decided to take the high road. "Your mother has a fiery personality."

"Was that the first time she hit you?"

"Umm . . . "

She brushed his leg with her fingertips. "I thought so. It's been a few years since she smacked me. I'm surprised she didn't do it the other night— she was angry enough, but I am bigger than her now. So, maybe that's why she didn't."

A pit grew in Jake's stomach; he pulled Sam into an embrace. "I'm sorry. I didn't know, but I guess I should have suspected."

She let her body sink into him. "It's fine. There were kids that got it a lot worse than me."

"But still I— "

She shook her head. "Dad, stop."

"It's just that I have so many regrets. I wish there was a way that you could move in with me, but your mother will never allow it."

"I know." The school bell rang. The street was empty, but Sam stayed put, making no effort to get to class. She asked, "Do you really think she has pictures of her black eye?"

"I'd bet my life on it, so if we challenged the custody agreement, then she'd get nasty."

"That sucks."

Jake grabbed her hand. "It does, but I still want you to apply to art school. I won't let her kill that dream."

"Should I?"

"Yes. Do you need money for the application?"

"If you have it?"

He nodded, knowing he would find it somewhere. "And your portfolio?"

"I'll work on it after she goes to bed."

"Be careful burning the candle at both ends."

"Don't worry. I've got it covered, speaking of which I should get to class before they lock the doors."

He gave her a quick peck on the cheek. "Yes. I'll talk to you later. When do you get your phone back?"

"Friday," she yelled over her shoulder as she ran up the steps.

Relieved with how things worked out, Jake watched her red hair bounce towards the front door of the school. His marriage to Kate had ended horribly. No kid should have to see that, but Sam had survived it and was a good kid. Now, all Jake wanted was for her to choose her own path in life, one where she didn't have to repeat either of her parent's mistakes.

Chapter 10

After resolving things with Sam, Jake drove back to his apartment to focus on his countless other problems. Tasha being the biggest. However, when he considered the facts, he thought it would be best to let Tasha's scheme play out on her timing. He'd look less guilty. Which left Jake to deal with his next biggest problem, finding a new job. He might be able to get his old one back, but truthfully, he didn't want it.

The job market had changed a lot since Jake found his last one in the classifieds. He guessed he should look online instead of the paper this time. He'd call Bobby; he was always hiring new employees; he'd know what websites to use. But Jake doubted he'd be able to answer the more important question. What should Jake do with his life? He certainly didn't want to operate a drill press for the rest of his life, but he wasn't qualified for much else.

Maybe Mary was right. Jake should be a private investigator. Tom's widow was smarter than Jake and probably knew him better than he knew himself. Investigative work would be stimulating and allow him to use his previous experience. It wouldn't be the same as being a police detective, but it could be a close second. He wondered how long it would take to get licensed. Maybe a firm would let him start doing leg work or surveillance while fulfilling the necessary requirements.

Pulling into his lot, Jake parked his car and went up the backstairs to his apartment. He fired up the old computer in Sam's room. It hummed to life slowly. Very slowly. Now he knew why Sam used her laptop for homework. While Jake waited, he dialed Bobby. He answered with a muffled grunt. "Hey."

"Hi, big guy," Jake said.

"Little man."

"How's the shoulder?"

"I'm still in some pain."

Bobby had been shot the night they'd gotten their revenge on Tom's killer. Jake had enlisted his two remaining friends to help in his retribution. Yet, their so-called friend, Rick, in all the chaos of the murder, had double-crossed Jake, stole the biker gang's drugs, and almost killed Bobby in the process. Now Jake owed the biker gang a favor for the million dollars in lost heroin. Jake could only assume it would be another murder, possibly Rick's, but that was a problem for another day.

From the sounds in the background, Jake knew Bobby was working on a vehicle in his service station. Jake said, "Dummy, the doctor told you not to use your arm for two weeks. Do you want permanent muscle damage?"

"I have one of the kids turning the wrench while I supervise."

"Liar."

Bobby laughed. "You caught me, but when did I ever listen?"

"Never."

"Enough about me, how are things in Chicago?" Bobby asked.

Jake found himself telling his friend an abbreviated version of the situation with Kate and Sam. He usually didn't share like this with Bobby. It was more a conversation he'd have with Tom, but Tom was dead, Rick was gone in the wind, and Mary had her own issues.

When Jake finished, Bobby said, "Kate's such a bitch."

"She's not."

"You have to say that. She's Sam's mother, so I'll say it for you. Kate is a ball-breaking bitch. Do you want me to lay a hit on her?"

Jake sucked in a breath. "We're out of that business."

After a pause, Bobby said, "Yeah, I was just joking, but that really sucks. I know how much Sam means to you."

"Thanks."

"Have you heard anything from Rick?" Bobby asked.

"No. You?"

"Nope. If he's smart, we'll never hear from him again."

Jake said, "Rick's a lot of things, but smart is not one of them."

"You're right. I don't think we've heard the last from Rick. Sonny came around when I was back on my feet, asking more questions about him."

Sonny was the president of the Devil's Hand, the aforementioned motorcycle gang. Sonny had outsmarted Jake by collecting evidence of Jake's murderous crime. It was that DNA that Sonny would use as leverage for Jake to repay his debt to the club. Jake hated him but also respected him for his cunning ruthlessness.

"What did you tell him?" Jake asked.

"I told Sonny that Rick mentioned running to New York or Los Angeles, so he said he'd have his people start there."

"They're a local club, right? Only the one chapter?"

"Yes. But he has friends everywhere. Sonny will find him."

Jake didn't doubt that. It would only be a matter of time.

Bobby said, "Well, buddy. I need to get back to supervising these no-nothing punks I call employees. I'll talk to you soon."

"Later, buddy."

They disconnected.

Jake checked his computer screen. It had finished all of its gyrations and was ready for action. Damn! He forgot to ask Bobby about job sites with all the talk on Rick and the Devil's Hand. Oh well, Jake should be able to figure it out on his own. He cracked his knuckles, grabbed the mouse, and clicked on his internet browser, but before he could start typing, his phone buzzed on the desk next to the keyboard.

Groaning, he checked the caller ID. The number had a local area code, probably a telemarketer. With some reservations, he answered it. "Hello."

"Mr. Bryant?"

"Yes, who is this?"

"Mr. Bryant, this is Ms. Sherman, the assistant principal at your daughter's school. We were unable to reach your wife, and you're the backup number. There was an issue with Samantha this morning and— "

"If this is about her being tardy, it was completely my fault. You have my sincerest apologies."

"I'm afraid it's a little more serious than a tardy," the nasally voice replied.

"Oh?"

"We'd like you to come up to the school immediately. Can you do that?"

"S . s .. sure. I'll come right down." His heart pounded like a bass drum. "But can you tell me what kind of trouble Sam is in?"

"We'd prefer to discuss it in person. When can we expect you?"

"I can be there in fifteen minutes."

"Perfect. We'll be waiting."

The assistant principal disconnected. Jake didn't bother to turn off the computer as he ran for the door.

Chapter 11

Jake got to the school as fast as was humanly possible for someone not strapped to a rocket. Twelve minutes later, he was directed into an inner office sanctum by a frumpy secretary in a navy-blue cardigan. She left him in front of the assistant principal's closed door. He took a moment to gather himself and then knocked on the frosted glass as butterflies danced in his stomach.

A muffled voice told him to enter.

Jake turned the knob to find Sam sitting in a padded chair facing a stern woman with short black hair. She didn't smile as she said, "Mr. Bryant. I'm Asst. Principal Sherman."

"Call me, Jake."

Asst. Principal Sherman didn't use his given name as she came around the large desk and extended a bony hand. Jake was always uncomfortable shaking hands with a woman. Not surprisingly, her grip was firm. She pumped his hand up and down twice before releasing it. Jake took the seat next to Sam, who avoided his eyes. He rested a hand on her shoulder, and she flinched.

Ms. Sherman smoothed out her wrinkled olive-colored pantsuit and retook her seat behind the desk. She rested her elbows on top of an ink pad the same color as her jacket and steepled her fingers.

"I'm sorry to have to call you in today, Mr. Bryant."

"Me too."

"Yes. But Samantha has gotten herself into some serious trouble this morning."

"What kind of trouble?"

Ms. Sherman opened her hands to direct Jake's eyes to the corner of her desk. A cloth purse lay on its side, partially opened. Next to the bag sat an unmarked pill bottle. Inside the transparent plastic cylinder were several orange and white capsules. Jake looked from the pill bottle to his daughter. Sam pinched her lips tight in a grimace.

Ms. Sherman cleared her throat. "Mr. Bryant, does your daughter have a prescription for those pills?"

Jake didn't answer immediately. Instead, he turned back to Sam, who almost imperceptibly twitched her head to the side, so Jake kept his mouth shut.

The administrator sighed. "A teacher found the bottle when it rolled out of her purse during a test. It doesn't have a label, and your daughter has refused to provide any information on its providence."

"Providence! That's a five-dollar word," Jake said with a whistle.

"Well, I am an educator, and you're both evading my question."

Meekly, Sam said, "Legally, we don't have to answer any of her questions."

"Samantha, you are not under arrest."

"Not yet, but my answers could get me arrested."

"Wait!" Jake held up his hands. "Let's all slow down."

Ms. Sherman picked up the bottle and shook it. The pills rattled around loudly. "I like to believe we could deal with this internally. Samantha has been a model student, but this is serious. Our school district is in a prescription pill epidemic, and we need to find the source. If Samantha would tell us who sold her the pills, then I'm sure we could come up with an amicable solution."

Sam shook her head. "No one in the school sold me those pills."

"Fine." Ms. Sherman exhaled. "The in-house officer is performing a locker search as we speak. We'll find those responsible without your help."

Sam sucked in her breath.

Ms. Sherman noticed Sam's reaction, and she gave the bottle another shake. "You're lucky these aren't opioids, young lady, but even possessing these without a prescription is a misdemeanor."

"What type of pills are they?" Jake asked.

Ms. Sherman said, "They appear to be Adderall, and we have nothing on file that Samantha suffers from ADHD."

Without warning, the office door busted open, and Kate stormed into the room. She wore a meticulously tailored jacket, a long skirt, and a frown. She stopped behind Sam, resting her hands on the back of her chair. Kate glared at the administrator. "Please explain to me what is going on here?"

It was Ms. Sherman's turn to cower under intense scrutiny. She pulled at her shirt collar as she brought Kate up to speed on the morning's events.

When she finished, Kate said, "Great. So this has been a complete misunderstanding. I don't know why Sam brought her pills to school, but she'll bring in a copy of her prescription tomorrow for your review."

"We will?" Sam asked.

"Of course, we will," Kate hissed. "Are we done here?"

"I guess so," Ms. Sherman stammered.

"Then let's go." Kate pulled Sam from her seat and steered her out the door.

The bewildered assistant principal returned the pill bottle to Sam's purse and extended the bag to Jake. He took it limply and caught up to the women in the outer office, returning the bag to Sam. They walked in silence to the school's front doors as Kate's heels clicked on the polished floor.

A young police officer walked towards them, headed to the office. He towed a large boy behind him. It was Sam's boyfriend, Austin. In the officer's other hand was a gym bag that clattered worse than a baby rattle.

Sam broke away from her mother's grasp. "Austin. I didn't say anything."

"Ma'am, please step back." The officer said authoritatively.

Austin shook his head. "It doesn't matter. They found my stash."

Sam said, "Don't admit to anything."

"Too late." Austin snorted.

After the officer and Austin entered the office, Sam whispered to Kate. "Can you help him?"

Kate shook her head furiously. "Let his big-shot father hire him a lawyer."

"Mom!"

"Don't 'Mom' me. You're in enough trouble as it is. We'll discuss this at home."

Jake stepped in front of them. "Wait, I need to be a part of this conversation too."

Kate rolled her eyes. "If you insist."

"I do."

"Well, I'm not going to your dump of an apartment again. I just had this outfit dry-cleaned."

"Fine. We'll go to your place." Jake followed them out of the school.

Chapter 12

The door to Kate's fancy townhouse opened slowly. Robert, her new husband, braced himself against the frame like he expected Jake to punch him. Jake wanted to laugh. Of all the people he'd like to hit, Robert wasn't one of them. The man was beat on enough.

"Come on in, Jake." Robert moved to the side. "Kate got here a few minutes ago."

Jake suspected she'd been home longer. Kate had run a yellow light as she pulled out of the school. And she'd probably run a few more on her route, so Sam could be properly cowed before Jake arrived.

"I'm surprised to see you. Shouldn't you be at work?" Jake asked.

"Judge Doyle wasn't in session this morning, which was a good thing given this mess with Sam. It's all-hands-on-deck, so to speak."

"You call Patrick, Judge Doyle, outside of court?"

Robert shrugged. "It's a habit."

Robert had been Kate's classmate in law school. If they'd had an affair, it had been an emotional one. Robert didn't have it in him to be an adulterer. Besides, at the time, Robert had enough problems with a cancer-stricken wife and baby. However, after his wife's death and Kate's divorce, the pair took comfort in one another. Poor bastard! And adding insult to injury, Robert went to work for his father-in-law as his aide.

"Is Patrick here?" Jake asked.

"No. The Judge had to . . . take care of something. I'm sure Kate will fill you in later."

"I'm sure she will."

Kate's shrill voice echoed down the hallway. "What were you thinking? I can't believe you'd do something so stupid."

Damn! It sounded like Sam needed him. Jake raced down the hallway towards the kitchen and slid to a stop in the doorway.

Neither woman noticed his arrival. Sam sat at the end of the table while Kate paced behind her in her business suit. Her shirt was still buttoned to the top.

Sam's jaw clenched. "I'm sorry for being a stupid kid."

"I didn't say you were stupid. But it was a stupid thing to do. Adderall? Why do you need Adderall?"

Jake took the seat next to Sam. "I'm here. Thanks for waiting."

Smirking, Kate said, "It's not my fault. Maybe if you had some of Sam's Adderall, you could keep up? Do you have some extra pills for your slow father?"

"You're not funny, Katey-Kat," Jake growled.

Kate stamped her stocking foot. "Don't you dare call me that."

"Can you two not fight for once?" Sam groaned.

Unfazed, Kate continued to pace back and forth. "You didn't answer my question, Sam. Why Adderall?"

Sam said, "I didn't want to disappoint you. I have a lot of work to do before I retake the SAT. And finals are coming up, and I have a ten-page AP English paper due on Monday."

"Are you sure?" Kate asked. "Or was it so you could paint all night?"

"No!"

Jake exhaled slowly to gain control of his emotions. "Kate, she gave you an answer. Stop attacking her."

"I don't believe her. Art should be a hobby. It certainly won't put a roof over your head, and she'll be dependent on some jerk to take care of her."

"So I was a jerk?" Jake asked.

Kate smiled. "You said it, not me."

"Please stop," Sam cried.

"Don't tell us what to do, young lady. You're the one in trouble here. Where did you get the pills? It had to be Austin, or else he wouldn't have been with that police officer."

Sam's head dropped. "It wasn't Austin."

"It doesn't matter. You're breaking up with him like you should have done months ago."

"No! I won't," Sam shouted.

"Yes. You will."

Jake coughed. "You can't do that, Kate."

Kate laughed. "I can, Jake. Have you lost sight of the fact that our daughter got busted with prescription pills? At school! She could be arrested."

"You're right."

"I know I'm right." Kate sat down at the opposite end of the table. "But I've got it covered. Tomorrow, Sam will bring in a prescription for the Adderall and— "

"You told the assistant principal that, but how?" Jake asked.

Sam looked at her mother questioningly as well. "Yes, how?"

"My Dad has close friends who are doctors. One of them will backdate a script for Sam, and she'll be covered. Thank god, it was only one bottle. What were you thinking, Sam? Well, you almost got your wish to be a starving artist."

Jake shook his head. "You're going to sweep this under the rug?"

"Yes. What would you have me do? Let Sam be arrested?"

"No," he said. "But there needs to be some ramifications."

"Don't you worry, she'll be punished." Kate turned to Sam. "You're grounded. Without a social life, you won't need pills to do well in school. And you can forget about prom— I doubt Austin will be able to go anyway."

Jake leaned forward in his chair. "Hold up a minute."

"What? You think she should go to prom?"

"Maybe... I don't know. I'd just like some say in all of this. I'm all for grounding her. She more than deserves it, but if Sam wants to go to art school, I won't let you bully her out of it. I won't."

Jumping out her seat, Kate shouted, "Why are you still talking about art school?"

"Because it is important to her."

Sam nodded while avoiding Kate's glare. "My teacher thinks I stand a really good chance of being accepted to the School of Art Institute."

"That's not what we talked about," Kate said.

Exhaling loudly, Jake said, "Let her take a chance and go for her dreams. They'll be plenty of time for school later if it doesn't work out. You didn't start college right out of high school either."

"Thanks to you."

"Me? I didn't force you to marry me."

"What choice did I have after I got pregnant?" Kate asked.

"If I remember right, it was you that seduced me that night."

"You were the one who forgot the condoms."

"You were on the pill."

Sam slapped the table. "I'm sitting right here. Can you punish me first, and then you two can argue about my conception?"

Jake said, "Fine. Consider yourself grounded until the semester is over."

"Excuse me. It's my house." Kate waited three seconds before speaking again to prove she was in charge. "Sam, go to your room and don't come out for seven weeks."

"But the semester is over in six weeks."

"I know. Now march," Kate said.

Chapter 13

Sam left the room, and Jake turned to his ex-wife and shook his head. Kate rolled her eyes. "What?"

"You always have to one-up me, don't you?"

"That's not what it's about."

"What is it about then?" Jake asked.

"Sam doesn't know how lucky she is," Kate said, looking away from Jake. "The next time she screws up, I might not be able to fix it."

"You act like she screws up all the time. Sam's a good kid."

"She's almost an adult. She needs to learn to take some responsibility for her actions."

Jake smiled. "Just like you've taken your share of the blame for what went wrong in our marriage."

Kate fell into the chair, farthest from him. "Fine, Jake. You're right. Our marriage failed because of me. You did nothing wrong. You were a model husband. Any woman would be blessed to have you. They certainly lined up after the divorce. Oh wait, they didn't."

"Forget it. But this fake prescription— "

"It's not up for discussion. The plan is already in motion."

"It's her first offense. At worst, she'd get probation and some community service."

"And a record! It's next to impossible to get into a good law school with a criminal record and forget it if she wants to run for public office one day."

"Public office? Where did that come from?" Jake ran his fingers through his hair. "Why won't you listen? She wants to go to art school."

"Are you going to support her for the rest of her life while she sells her paintings on Navy Pier?"

"Sure, if it makes her happy. I'll definitely pay for art school."

Kate laughed. "How are you going to do that? You can't afford to feed yourself right now, let alone a forty thousand dollar a year art school."

Jake tried not to choke and barely succeeded. Wasn't that twice what an average college cost? Screw it. Even if he had to sell a kidney, he'd find a way to pay for it. He stuck out his chin and said, "You underestimate me, and you underestimate Sam. Don't you see how talented she is?"

"I don't underestimate her. Why do you think I push her so hard? She has so much more potential than I did at that age. All I did was worry about boys, and you can see where that got me."

Jake considered pointing out her hundred-dollar haircut and her million-dollar townhouse, but he knew it wouldn't matter. He stood up. "I'm gonna go, but I'm not going to let you decide Sam's life for her."

Kate pulled her phone from her jacket and typed a message. God, she was frustrating. She could at least acknowledge his departure. Jake said, "Hello?"

"I heard you." She hit send. "I get it. You're Super Dad now. You care more about Sam than I do."

"Whatever. Bye, Kate," Jake said.

"Bye." The phone beeped in her hand, and she smiled.

Heading for the door, Jake said, "It's my weekend for Sam, right?"

"Yes. And I expect her to be grounded at your place as well."

"Don't worry, I'll lock her in her bedroom and only give her bread and water."

"You're quite the comedian. Maybe your new job should be down at the comedy club."

He stopped in the kitchen doorway. "Maybe I will follow my dreams too. I do like to make people laugh."

"I always said you were a clown."

"And I always said you were a . . ."

"Really? What was I?"

No. He didn't want to stoop to her level, so he left it unsaid.

Jake left, slamming the ornate front door shut behind him. Outside, a dark SUV with tinted windows idled at the sidewalk. The type of vehicle favored by drug dealers, athletes, and mob bosses. Had Kate ordered a hit on Jake from her phone? Was that why she had been smiling? That would be one way to kill the art school conversation.

Cautiously, Jake descended the steps. The passenger window lowered. He couldn't see inside the vehicle except for a dull green glow from the instrument panel. Half expecting to see a semi-automatic weapon jut from the opening, Jake took a tentative step forward to get a better look but saw nothing. He felt stupid. It was probably a lost tourist, so he moved closer.

"Can I help you?"

"Yes. Get in the car!" The gruff voice said, sounding oddly familiar.

"I don't think so." Jake didn't move, but he probably should have run.

"Jesus Christ, if I was going to kill you, I would have done it years ago, so get in the car."

The door opened, and Jake could make out a male figure in the driver's seat. It leaned forward into the light, and Judge Patrick Doyle, his former father-in-law, impatiently motioned him inside. Jake's insides twisted, not out of fear, but revulsion. He despised Doyle more than anything in the world, Kate included. Jake should be considered for sainthood for only having punched the man once in the face.

Grudgingly, Jake got in the vehicle and shut the door. "Hi, Patrick."

"You're such an asshole, Jake."

"Is that an official legal ruling or just an opinion?"

"It's a fact because you keep on causing problems in my life. I don't allow anyone else to do that."

"Then you must really love me?"

Doyle slapped the steering wheel. "Quite the opposite. But lucky for you, my granddaughter does, though I don't know why. She's a smart girl otherwise."

Jake laughed. "So Patrick, is there a point to this little meeting, or do you want to just insult me? Either way is fine; I've got nothing but time on my hands."

"I bet. Until you have to collect your food stamps at the welfare office."

"Good one. Food stamps. We used to tell that one in the schoolyard. Next, are you going to call my mom fat?"

"Shut up, you idiot."

Taking a deep breath, Doyle interweaved his fingers and brought his hands to his chin. He gazed solemnly out the windshield. Jake waited him out. If he interrupted his theatrics, it would just prolong their meeting. And despite what he said, Jake wanted to get away from this jerk before he did something that would put him in jail.

With his thumbs still pressed to his lips, Doyle said, "I hope you can keep up, but I wanted to warn you that your old partner, Steve Hill, will call you tomorrow and request a meeting."

Jake leaned back in his seat and arched an eyebrow. "He will?"

"In that meeting, Hill will offer you a position as a detective in his unit."

"What?" Jake nearly fell out of his seat.

"Pay attention. Hill is currently the commander of the South Precinct, and he has several openings in his department from attrition."

"All right?"

"And Hill convinced his superiors to get you reinstated."

Jake's mind was reeling because Doyle's announcement could be true. Hill had always liked him. He was the one person who stood by Jake after he'd been labeled a bad cop. But there had to be a catch for Doyle to be the bearer of this good news.

"Let me guess," Jake said. "You vetoed my reinstatement."

"I could have, but I didn't. I had a better idea instead." Doyle reached across the center console and popped open the glove box.

Flinching, Jake grabbed the judge's wrist with one hand and pulled back the other to strike Doyle in the face.

Doyle growled, "Let go of me. I told you I wasn't going to kill you."

Jake released the older man's wrist, and Doyle pulled out a thin brushed metal case with his initials engraved in the top. Snapping it open, he extracted a fat cigar and held the tin out to Jake, who reluctantly took one. Using a fancy cigar cutter, Doyle snipped off the end of both their stogies and lit his own before passing the lighter to Jake. Making loud puffing sounds, the end of Doyle's cigar glowed a bright red at its edges.

"What's your idea?" Jake asked, the lighter poised under his cigar.

Doyle powered down his window and blew out a plume of sickly-sweet smoke, "My idea is to let you have the job."

"Really? Let me guess— there's a catch."

Doyle laughed. "There's no such thing as a free lunch, boy."

Chapter 14

Miles away, Trent limped in the front door of his parent's house, his backpack slung over his shoulder. The house was eerily quiet. No one was in their usual spots. Austin and his dad should be at the table, debating the merits of different college programs, and his mom should be working over the stove, clanging pots and pans. The aromas of meat and potatoes should be filling the air. Darn. He hadn't eaten since breakfast, and he was starving.

"Hello."

No response, which was odd. Very odd. His mother was always home.

He called out louder. "Hello!"

"In the living room." His mother's muffled voice finally responded, more timid than usual. Plus, it sounded like she had been crying.

Hesitantly, he entered the room. She sat on the couch with her hands folded in her lap, staring straight ahead. Trent sat down next to her. "Is something wrong? You're not in the kitchen."

"I wasn't up for cooking tonight," she said, not turning to address him.

"Good. You work too hard. Have Dad order in Chinese."

"Maybe."

Trent laid a palm on top of his mother's hands to still their shaking. "So, where is Dad? Where's Austin?"

"Your father is downstairs in your room."

"My room?" Trent asked as a loud crashing noise came from the basement.

"Mom, what's going on?"

Still not looking at him, she said, "I think you should talk to your father."

"All right."

Trent got up from the couch and quickly descended the basement stairs as another heavy thud erupted from his room. He stopped in the doorway to find his dad prying open his footlocker with a large flat screwdriver. The room was trashed. Dresser drawers were pulled out with clothes strewn across the floor, and his desk chair was stuck in the drywall above his bed— a cyclone would've caused less damage. The only thing left untouched was the fish tank on the dresser. Frightened fish darted from side to side under the fluorescent light.

"Dad?"

The lock gave away with an awful screech, and the footlocker lid popped open. His dad let out a low growl as he dug around. Throwing the blankets aside, he found the pill bottles and cash.

"Son of a bitch! I knew it."

"It's not what you think." Trent took a tentative step inside the room.

Bo stood up, holding an orange-brown pill bottle in one hand and a wad of bills in the other. "What is it then?"

His lips flapped up and down like a ventriloquist's dummy. "It's ahhh . . . ahhh . . . "

"Don't bother. I don't want to hear your lies."

Snapping his jaw shut, Trent ran his fingers through his hair and yanked at the ends in frustration. How had his dad found out about his side business? This was bad. Really bad, but he could fix it. Trent would beg for forgiveness and concede to work for his dad. He was sick of dealing with the low-life druggies anyway. Maybe the mortgage business wouldn't be as horrible as he thought.

Hesitantly, Trent took a step closer to his irate father. "I know it was wrong. I'll stop."

"You'll stop?"

"Yes. Take the money and use it to fix the basement."

"It's too late to fix anything."

"What? Why?"

Bo tossed the money at Trent. The wad of cash caught him in the nose. He reeled from the sting as the bills rained down to the floor. The pill bottle bounced off his chest, adding insult to injury.

"I'm sorry," Trent pleaded.

"You're sorry?" A vein pulsed on Bo's forehead; the rest of his face was purple with rage.

"Please. I'll flush the pills."

The words were barely out of his mouth when Bo shoved him in the chest with both hands. He stumbled backward but kept his footing. Bo shouted, "You're God damn right, you're going to flush them. The police are probably getting a search warrant as we speak. One son locked up is enough. Your mother would make me get a lawyer for your sorry butt too, and Austin needs all my resources."

What? Did Trent hear his dad correctly? Austin was locked up. No. It couldn't be possible. Feeling weak in the knees, he moved to the bed and sat down on the edge of the mattress. His heart hammered in his chest.

With a voice that didn't sound like his own, Trent said, "What are you talking about? Where's Austin?"

Towering over him, Bo yelled, "He's in jail, you dumbass. The police found some fucking pills in his locker. He got them from you, didn't he?"

"Umm . . . Umm . . . "

"Answer me, you stuttering idiot."

"Ummm . . . "

A hand, the size of a Christmas ham, flew through the air. Trent tried to duck, but it landed on his temple. White stars exploded across his vision. He didn't try to strike back— guilt had taken all the fight out of him. Cowering in a fetal position on his mattress, Trent waited for the next blow. It didn't come.

"You're such a screw-up. I bet you couldn't even get rid of these right." Bo stomped around the room, gathering up the pill bottles. He dumped their contents into the fish tank. The fish nibbled at the pills, assuming they were food pellets. No. Not his little friends.

"Stop!" Trent stood up but then sat back down. His head still felt woozy from the punch.

"Shut up."

"Please. You'll kill them."

"Seriously! The only thing you ever worry about is these stupid fucking fish. You should be worrying about your brother." Bo grabbed the footlocker by its lid and tossed it at the dresser with all his might. It crashed into the fish tank.

"No!" The squeal that escaped Trent's lips made him sound like a child.

The tank's glass shattered, and the water poured out like a fountain. The fish landed amongst the mess. They flopped on the wet carpet next to the cash and empty pill bottles. Their mouths opening and closing in a futile attempt to breathe. Trent wanted to save them but knew it was useless. "You didn't need to do that?"

Bo roared. "Get the fuck out of my house!"

"Let me stay. I can help?"

"You want to help? Go turn yourself in. It should be you locked up for the next twenty years. Not your brother."

Trent shook his head. "What are you talking about? Twenty years for a few pills?"

"That's what the police said."

"They're trying to scare you."

"Well, it worked.

"If Austin didn't admit to anything, a good lawyer should get him off with a fine and probation. With his talent, plenty of good schools will still offer him a scholarship."

"And when did you graduate from Law School, Mr. Know-it-all? Oh, that's right. You didn't. You dropped out, so why don't you take your advice and shove it up your ass."

"But –" Trent closed his mouth. Bo was right. It was his fault. Austin had looked up to him not just in football but obviously in his illegal activities too. Trent had to do something. He couldn't let Austin lose everything he'd worked for; he was twice the athlete Trent had been.

"No buts. Pack a bag and leave. You have five minutes."

"I can fix this," Trent pleaded.

With murder in his eyes, Bo got inches from Trent's face. His voice grew cold, and through clenched teeth, he said, "Don't, you'll screw it up. Just get out. You've always been a disappointment. I shouldn't be surprised that you ruined Austin's life too."

"Yes, sir." Trent threw some random clothes from the floor into his bag and left without saying goodbye to his mother. He didn't want to cause her any more pain.

Chapter 15

Jake tapped his cigar out the window, and the hot ash fell to the ground. "So, what's the catch?"

"The catch is that I won't veto your rehiring if you stay out of Samantha's life. Forever."

Jake laughed, doubling over, nearly dropping his cigar. When he could catch his breath, he said, "I didn't hear you say please."

The judge ignored Jake's antics. "I'm dead serious. I won't stand in the way of your reinstatement if you walk away from Samantha and don't look back."

"Sounds like a hell of a deal."

"It is. You should take it."

Jake glowered at Doyle. "Fuck you! What kind of man do you think I am?"

"Now. Now. Jake, you need to think about what's best for Samantha. Bad enough she has half your DNA. She doesn't need your stupid advice too." Doyle blew out a plume of smoke, not bothering to aim it out the window. It engulfed both of them.

"And your solution is for me to leave and let her be manipulated by you and Kate."

"Manipulated? We're the only ones who have her best interest at heart. See."

Doyle pulled a yellow sheet of paper from the visor and waved it at Jake. He snatched it from his hand and studied the page. It was a prescription for Adderall postdated months ago, signed by one of Doyle's crony doctors. Instead of throwing it out the window, Jake set it down on the dashboard and turned back to Doyle.

"Am I supposed to be impressed?"

"You should be," Doyle said. "It will keep Samantha out of prison; her boyfriend won't be so lucky. So what do you say, Jake?"

"No way. I won't do it."

The smooth façade slipped off Doyle's face, but he quickly recovered it. "You're being short-sighted, Jake. You get a job back that you love, and Samantha gets a chance to make the most of her opportunities."

"In the South precinct? I'd have to move away from Sam unless I want to spend three hours in the car every day. Is that your angle?"

Doyle spread his arms wide. "I told you this wasn't my idea, but who am I to look a gift horse in the mouth. Being a detective is demanding, and you're no spring chicken. I'd think you want to put your best foot forward by moving closer to the job."

"Could you fit any more colloquialisms in that last sentence?"

"If the shoe fits... "

"That doesn't even make sense."

"Are you sure?"

"Yes."

"Either way, I'm prepared to set you up in a modest apartment in Roseland or Calumet Park."

"You'll set me up?"

"Yes. I've invested wisely over the years and moving you far away from Samantha would be another wise investment. For her future. What do you say, Jake? No one has to look bad here. Samantha doesn't have to know why you're doing it."

"What do you mean?"

"Take the job, and you'll be her hero, making the city safe by putting away nasty criminals, but you'll have to work weekends and be too busy to return her calls. You'll drift slowly away. It sucks, but it happens."

"You're crazy."

"Crazy like a fox, think about it, Jake, even you should see it's the best thing for everyone involved."

Shaking his head, Jake threw the half-finished cigar into the gutter. It tasted like shit, just like this proposition they wanted him to swallow. Did they think he was stupid? Nothing was worth giving up his relationship with his daughter.

"I'm not doing it."

Doyle exhaled. "Be reasonable. You need to put Samantha first for once."

"So let me get this straight. You won't stand in the way of my reinstatement as a detective in the South district for my old partner, Steve Hill. And you'll pay for a new apartment. But only if I walk out of Sam's life."

"I'll pay for half the rent as long as you hold up your end of the deal."

"That's not what you said."

"Details. Details. We can negotiate all the finer points later."

Jake laughed. "I bet."

"What? You don't trust me."

"No."

"Then you're the only one. This town loves me. Why do you think I keep on getting re-elected?"

Jake's response slipped out of his mouth before he could stop himself. "Because you're crooked."

Doyle sneered. "No. Because I'm fair and logical, and if you were half the man I am, you do the right thing here."

"Sorry. My relationship with Sam is more important than any stupid job."

Doyle took a final pull from his cigar and tossed it into the street. A passing-by car ran over the glowing red butt, making it look like a small flat turd. He said, "Fine. The least you can do is listen to Hill's offer and act surprised. I know he is very excited to work with you again. He feels bad for what happened after—"

"None of what happened was Hill's fault," Jake interrupted.

"True. And it certainly wasn't your fault either, Jake."

"Wrong. I've made mistakes. But I'm willing to own up to them. Are you?"

"I don't make mistakes," Doyle said, reaching for the metal cigar container on the center console. "And I don't like being made a fool, so I suggest you think long and hard before you make a decision you regret."

"Screw you!"

Before Doyle could close the case, Jake grabbed the remaining three Cuban cigars. They had to be worth twenty dollars apiece. He exited the vehicle and made a display of dropping them to the ground and crushing them under his shoe. The tinted window powered up as he waved like a crazed fool. Jake would show Doyle and Kate. He'd beat them at their own game.

Chapter 16

Mentally drained, Jake turned onto his street. A confrontation with Judge Doyle was like going ten rounds with a heavy-weight boxer, but his day didn't get any better. In the parking lot of his building, Jake found two police vehicles and a white crime scene van.

It was game time. He turned off the engine but remained behind the wheel. When his head was clear, he opened his door and exited the vehicle. He prayed he'd found all the items Tasha had planted in his apartment, or it would be his ass.

Inside the building, he could hear voices from the second floor. They were loud and authoritative. Cop voices. He'd sounded like that not too long ago. He trekked up the stairs and stopped at the top to take in the scene. His door was wide open. An officer and his landlord stood at the threshold, while inside the others scurried around, inspecting every inch of his place.

The landlord nodded at Jake, drawing the officer's attention in his direction.

"Mr. Bryant?" the officer asked.

"Yes."

"We have a warrant to search your premises."

Jake nodded. "May I see it?"

"That is your right."

The young officer handed over the yellow paper. Jake read it carefully. It documented a search to be performed today and covered his entire apartment and his vehicle. They were looking specifically for a silk bag, rope, condoms, and a large hunting knife— a rape tool kit. More specifically, items used three nights ago in an attempted rape a few blocks from here. And more importantly, tools the silkworm rapist had used to pull off his crimes all those years ago. Jake handed the warrant back.

The officer folded it, put it in his front pocket. "I'll need the keys to your vehicle as well as to your gun safe, Mr. Bryant?"

"No problem."

Jake knew they'd get into them one way or another, so he fished the keys out of his pocket and set them in the officer's outstretched hand. The officer went inside and came back out with a technician carrying a plastic evidence toolbox. They conversed for a second, then left Jake with the landlord to search his car while the team inside looked at the safe.

The landlord, Mr. Douglas, turned to Jake and shrugged. "Sorry. I had to let them in."

"I understand."

"Truthfully, I was surprised. You and Mrs. Goldstein are my best tenants. Are you in some kind of trouble, Mr. Bryant?"

"I don't think so."

It all depended on who was smarter, Jake or Tasha. He'd been surprised Tasha would attack someone as part of a plot to destroy Jake. Though he shouldn't have been, a parent will do anything to save their child from harm. Between the lump in his mattress and the newspaper article, Jake had pieced together her plan and removed the evidence of his supposed crime. Luckily, Tasha's victim had not been injured, only frightened to build the case for her son's innocence.

Mr. Douglas said, "Good. I told the officer that you've never caused any problems in the building."

"I appreciate that. Thanks."

"No problem." Mr. Douglas stared inside Jake's apartment. "Do you think they'll damage anything during their search?"

"Don't worry. I'll cover the repairs if it comes to that."

Mr. Douglas nodded and retreated downstairs.

Eventually, the lead officer returned from the rear lot with Jake's keys. He gave them back without a word and stepped inside the apartment. Jake leaned against the wall and studied the pattern in the hallway carpet. He'd never really looked at it before. It was hideous. So ugly, it turned his stomach. Though, it could be that he was losing patience with the invasion of his privacy.

A few minutes later, the officer came back out. "Mr. Bryant."

"Yes?" Jake forced himself to smile. "I hope you didn't find what you were looking for. Did you?"

The officer shook his head. "Your apartment and vehicle are cleared— none of the items were present. The techs are gathering their equipment now. We should be leaving soon."

Great. He'd found it all. "Thank you, officer."

"I hear you used to be one of us."

"Yes. A few years back."

The officer nodded. "It's a shame what they did to you."

"Shit happens."

"Ain't that the truth. Like today and this bogus report."

"If I didn't have bad luck, I wouldn't have any luck at all." Jake followed the officer back into the apartment and took a seat at the table.

True to his word, the officer and his team were gone ten minutes later. The kitchen cupboards and drawers had been thoroughly turned upside down as well as his bathroom. The bedroom didn't look as bad as he expected. Everything had been gone through, and his closet was ransacked. He didn't have the energy or the time to put things back together now. Besides, he had a strong feeling that someone would be outside that he'd like to have a discussion with.

Tasha would be disappointed that her plan failed, but he couldn't care less. He needed to make sure she didn't try something stupid like this again because the next time someone may get hurt, and Tasha would end up in jail alongside her son.

Chapter 17

When Jake got downstairs, both police cars and the van were gone. However, as he expected, an African American woman stood outside. If she could have shot daggers with her eyes, Jake would have been dead on the spot. With a mixture of pity and disdain, he marched across the empty parking lot.

"Hi, Tasha."

"Hey," Tasha replied, keeping up the tough veneer. "I remember you. Weren't you in my store the other day?"

"That's me. What are you doing here?" Jake asked.

"I saw all the police cars and wanted to see what was going on. Are you here for the same thing?"

"I live here. All the commotion was for me. Somebody reported me for an attempted rape."

She pointed a finger at him and smiled. "I knew there was something suspicious about you. I hope you have a good alibi."

"You know I live alone, so no one can vouch for my whereabouts."

Looking indignant, she asked, "How would I know that?"

"Because you broke into my apartment the other day to plant the evidence against me."

"What are you talking about?"

He shook his head. "Stop with the lies, Tasha. You know exactly what I'm talking about. You hid the rope, the knife, and the silk bag under my mattress. Good thing I found it after we talked at the store— I made sure to throw it in a dumpster miles from here that was picked up this morning."

Tasha cursed under her breath, not appearing to care that Jake saw her disappointment.

"Too bad it took so long to get the search warrant, or I'd be in jail right now."

"Screw you."

Jake stepped closer to her. "I bet it was a lot tougher than you thought to attack someone, an innocent girl, even if it was just to cut her on the arm."

She glared at him. "Fuck off."

"It wouldn't have worked, anyway. My touch DNA wasn't on your evidence."

"They didn't need DNA on my son."

"True. It's a shame what happened to him."

Sneering, Tasha said, "Don't patronize me. You were a part of it."

"I don't know what you are talking about."

"The hell you don't. First, you execute Leroy for no reason, then you have Junior locked up for a crime he didn't commit. What do you have against my family? What's next, you going to rape my daughter?"

"I'm not a rapist."

She pulled her arm back to hit him. "But you are a thief and a murderer."

If he hadn't ducked, her hand would have smacked him across the face. She tried to catch him on the backhand, but he grabbed her wrist. She struggled to break free, but he held her arm tight. "Stop."

"No." She screamed at him. "I know you had your people take it to cover your tracks."

"Take what?" Jake released her hand.

Rubbing her wrist, she said, "Don't act dumb. You know what I'm talking about."

"I don't. So you're gonna have to help me."

"The letter, stupid! The one that got shoved in our door the morning you killed Leroy."

"A letter?"

"Yes. It was typed and in a plain envelope. One of you must have took it so Leroy would look guilty. Your crooked partner or some other cop."

"I swear to you that I don't know anything about a letter."

Tasha rolled her eyes. "Then you must be their patsy."

"I'm sorry." Jake sighed. "Leroy's death wasn't a conspiracy, and I'm not Lee Harvey Oswald."

Nodding, she said, "You are Oswald. That explains why they didn't stick up for you over Leroy's gun. Because Leroy did have a gun that day."

Jake's hands balled up into fists. "Fuck. I knew it."

Tasha smiled. "And the joke's on you, white boy. I wasn't going to let Leroy get busted on some stupid weapons charge, so I hid it."

"But he shot at me!"

"You killed him."

"It was self-defense," Jake shouted.

"It was murder."

Jake forced his hands open. Tasha had her version of the story, and Jake had his, but they both could agree Jake had knocked on their townhouse door to question Leroy's involvement in a string of violent rapes in Chicago. But what had been disputed was whether Leroy pulled a gun on Jake before it disappeared in the chaos. It had been unlucky for Jake since he'd been reassigned to desk duty for his actions, which ultimately made him quit the force. But much worse for Leroy because he'd died before he could answer for his crimes.

"We'll have to disagree, but I am curious. Where did you hide the weapon?"

Tasha looked down her nose at Jake. "In my baby girl's diaper."

"You put a loaded gun in a baby's diaper? She could have died."

"The safety was on."

"And now you're trying to frame me for rape? There's something wrong with you."

"Of course, there is. I lost my husband, and now they have my son. Both of them were innocent, and I'll do anything to clear Junior's name before he dies too."

Jake was pretty sure that Leroy was the Silkworm rapist. The crimes had stopped after his death. But how could no one have searched Leroy's baby before they cleared the scene? Was Tasha right? Had Jake been used by the brass? And to what ends? Everything he thought was being turned on its head.

He asked, "And you think this letter that disappeared would have proved Leroy's innocence."

She shrugged. "Probably not. The system is out to get my family."

"I don't know about that."

"It is. The whole system is crooked. It was your uncle, Judge Doyle, that put Junior away."

"Judge Doyle is not my uncle," Jake hissed.

"Whatever. I know you're related, and word on the street is that he's taking bribes to fill the prisons with our kids."

"Seriously?" Jake knew there was no point in arguing with her about his relationship to Doyle.

Tasha nodded. "Dead serious."

"Do you have any evidence of that?"

"No."

"Well, rumors won't get us anywhere."

"Fuck you." She waved a finger at him. "You better hope I can get Junior out, or the next time I'll find a way to hurt you as bad as you've hurt me."

Tasha jumped into her rusted Oldsmobile and turned the key. The engine sputtered to life, and she punched the accelerator. The car came within a couple feet of hitting him on its way to the road. Jake stood there, dumbfounded. The gun hidden on a crying toddler seemed obvious to him now, but he'd never heard anything about a missing letter. Had it been a setup? Was Leroy not guilty? Could the actual rapist be someone connected to the establishment who needed to be protected?

It was too much. His head ached from all the revelations that had been thrown at him today. He needed time to process it all, so he went inside to put his apartment in order. At least that was a puzzle he could piece together.

Chapter 18

The next day, a buzzing sound jarred Jake from his fitful slumber on the living room sofa. Banging his shin on the coffee table, Jake dropped the TV remote with a curse. He took a second to orient himself while he wiped the crust from his eyes. From the sunlight streaming between the blinds, it was still morning. Good. He hadn't slept the day away.

Leave it to Judge Doyle and Tasha to turn Jake's world upside down. He was pretty sure that Tasha's threats were empty, but he should sleep with one eye open just in case. However, Doyle's promises carried some weight as he'd proven in the past— yet, it wouldn't change Jake's decision. He would choose Sam's well-being over his own every day of the week.

But damn, Jake would love to be a detective again! The job had given him a level of satisfaction and purpose he'd found nowhere else . . . short of being a dad. Still, he feared the temptation of Steve Hill's offer when it finally came would be too tempting. Working as a drill press operator made Jake feel like he was biding his time until he died.

The phone continued to shriek on the cushion next to him. Looking down, Mary's beautiful face lit up his screen. He lunged for it, answering before the call ended.

"Hello."

"Hi, Jake."

He switched the phone to his other ear. "Good morning."

"Were you asleep?"

"I think so."

She laughed. "But it's after nine, you lazy bum."

Glancing at his screen, he replied, "That's Michigan time. It's only eight o'clock here."

"Oh shoot, I always forget about that. I'd just dropped Hunter off at school and had some time to kill. You free?"

"For you, of course. How are you and the kids getting on?"

"Fine."

He made a face. "Are you lying to me?"

"No . . . Maybe." She sighed. "We're all having a hard time still. Over the kid's protests, I signed everyone up for individual therapy sessions. I think it will help to talk about Tom's death instead of ignoring it. We've each only had one session, but the therapist says we're off to a good start."

"Sounds like you're on top of it."

"I hope. I know it will be a long road."

"I bet."

"And the kids still have typical kid-problems."

"Anything I can help with?"

"No. It's just lately that Lindsey is pushing all my buttons. She's being a real pain-in-the-butt."

"I never went through that with Sam. Maybe she did it to Kate, but not with me."

"And she's been texting some boy too. I'm not sure I'm ready for that— she better not be sending him pictures."

Whistling, he said, "I doubt it, but better you than me."

"Shut up!"

There was a pause, and then her words gushed out like a fountain. "And Hunter hates little league. Tom signed him up before all this happened, and I thought it would be a good distraction. But it's his first year of kid pitch, and he hasn't got a hit yet. He says the kids make fun of him, and he wants to quit."

Jake sat forward on the couch. "I could free up some time this weekend to come work with him."

"Seriously? You'd do that."

He hadn't really thought about it before he made the offer. His life was a mess, but he could make it work somehow. Tom's family needed more from Jake than a revenge killing.

"Yes. I'm serious."

There was a longer pause than before. Mary said, "No. I can't let you do that. I talked to the coach and explained the situation. He's going to spend extra time with him after practice until things turn around."

Dejected, Jake slumped back into the couch. Helping Hunter to hit a baseball was a manageable task compared to the problems in Jake's life right now.

"Does the coach know what he's doing, or is he some beer-bellied Dad that got roped into it because everyone else was too busy?"

"I think he used to play for the Detroit Tigers. Does the name Kirk Gibson ring a bell?"

Snorting, he said, "You're lying!"

"Maybe I am, but just because he has a big belly and wears cargo shorts doesn't mean he can't teach an eight-year-old how to hit a baseball."

"If you say so— "

"I do."

Jake always felt weird asking about Emma since it might cross a line set by Mary. After all, Emma might be Jake's daughter. A bad decision by them both— it happened only once, and they swore to never speak of it again. But it would also be peculiar if he completely ignored Emma too. When Jake had left town, Emma was having more trouble than the other kids coping with Tom's death. He swallowed his guilt. "Emma, how is she?"

"Not good. She's been really depressed — she always was a Daddy's girl."

The way Mary said it so casually, Jake knew it wasn't a jab at him. Mary had no doubt that Tom was Emma's father. Jake wasn't so positive, given the timing of the pregnancy.

"I'm sure she'll come around with therapy. How about you?"

"Some days are good, and some days are bad. I never know when it is going to hit me. They say time will heal all wounds, but I don't know . . . But enough about us, I called to see how you were doing. Any luck finding a job?"

Standing up, he paced around the living room. He wasn't sure he should drag her into all his problems, but he really wanted her opinion. "Funny you should say that. My old partner, Steve Hill, who is now the commander of the South precinct, is going to offer me a job as a detective."

"He is?" Mary squealed.

"I heard about it through the grapevine, but it hasn't happened yet."

"That's incredible. I'm so happy for you."

"But there are strings attached."

"Like what?"

Jake ran his fingers through his rumpled hair. "My ex-father-in-law won't block my reinstatement as long as I agree to stay out of Sam's life. Apparently, I'm a bad influence."

"He can't do that," she yelled. "You're her father."

Worried that he'd wear holes into the carpet, he flopped back down on the sofa. The old couch's springs groaned in protest. Jake said, "He can. And he will. You know how much power he has in this town."

"That's terrible. You know you can't do that to Sam."

Not responding, he scratched his head and stared at the opposite wall.

"Jake!"

Sam was his top priority, but Mary was the one friend he could voice his darkest thoughts to, even if he didn't plan to act on them. He groaned. "I know. I know . . . but being a detective was the only thing that made me happy."

A car horn beeped over the phone. Mary yelled, "You need to pull your head out of your butt."

Jake asked, "Crazy driver?"

"No. I'm talking to you. Kids always come first. Do I need to come to Chicago and knock some sense into you?"

Jake laughed. "Don't worry. I was counting on you to set me straight, though it may be mute if I wind up in jail."

"What? Don't tell me they found out about Caleb."

"No. Not that. Tasha Pittman is out to get me."

"Who?"

"Leroy's baby momma. The man that I killed in the line of duty."

"Why is she out to get you after all these years?"

"She had a stupid scheme to frame me for rape to get her son out of jail."

"You have to be joking."

"I wish I was," Jake said before giving Mary an abridged version of foiling Tasha's plot, the police search, and their confrontation.

"Wow!" Mary gasped when he was finished. "I'm surprised, but I'm not. When it comes to your kids, a mother is capable of anything. If someone hurt one of my kids, I'd rip their face off."

"I bet you would."

"So what do you think was in the mysterious letter?"

"I don't think there was a letter. It's probably an invention of her own mind to justify Leroy's actions."

"Maybe. At least you know for sure there was a gun. That should be a relief, less guilt for you to carry around."

He shrugged. "I guess."

Regardless of what anyone else had thought, Jake had always been confident Leroy had a weapon that day. Still, his death had been incredibly hard on Jake. Caleb's murder had been easier, which worried Jake— was he turning into a psychopath? No, he wouldn't kill again, unless someone tried to hurt Sam, or Mary and the kids . . . or Sonny called in his favor. Shit!

Mary broke him out of his musings. "Well, it's time for my first appointment, so I need to let you go."

"No problem. I should take a shower."

She sighed. "Hang in there. It will get better."

"Thanks," Jake said. "But it should be me trying to lift your spirits."

"You did. Just by being you, Jake."

"That's me, good ol' Jake," he said, his voice sounding flatter than he intended.

"Are you all right?"

Trying to sound more convincing, he said, "I'm fine."

"Are you sure? I can't afford to lose anyone else in my life."

"Positive."

"You promise?"

"I promise. Bye, Mary."

"Bye."

Jake flopped down on the couch for a minute to gather his thoughts. Before he could muster the energy to shower, his phone buzzed again. The number had an area code from the South side of Chicago. He accepted the call. "Hello."

"Jake, you'll never guess who this is."

"Steve Hill?"

His old partner said, "Son of a bitch! How did you know?"

Chapter 19

That same morning, but across town, a loud ringing stirred Trent from his slumber. He banged his knees on the steering wheel as he fumbled for his phone. With nowhere else to go, he'd spent the night in his car. Trent's friends disappeared after his career-ending injury— the hot girls too, assuming his bad luck was contagious. An all-American linebacker was not a virus. Not that it mattered. It only proved they weren't real friends, only acquaintances who split when the promise of a pro contract and all its millions were gone.

Answering the buzzing phone, he lifted the phone to his ear. "Hello."

A mechanical voice asked, "Will you accept a collect call from an inmate at the Cook County juvenile temporary detention center?"

The question was followed by his brother saying his name— Austin Morrison.

"Yes. Yes. Yes." Trent repeated into the phone.

The voice prompted him to provide his credit card information. Once processed, the two brothers were connected.

"Austin!"

"Trent, I screwed up bad."

"What the hell happened?"

"Dad didn't tell you?" Austin asked.

Trent tried to stretch out his long body in the small car, but it was an impossible task. "No. Dad just yelled at me while he trashed my room, then he threw me out of the house."

"Wait! What?"

"Yeah. He blames me for your arrest."

"That's stupid. It's not your fault. I stole the pills from you."

Trent punched his leg in frustration. "Damn it! Watch what you say over the phone. I'm sure this conversation is being recorded."

"It doesn't matter. I confessed to everything."

"Please tell me you didn't."

"I did. Sorry."

"You did screw up bad, little brother."

"I know."

"But why? Why would you deal?" Trent asked.

"There is a huge demand in my school. A bunch of kids wanted them. I figured once I showed you how much money I could make that you'd cut me into your business."

Trent growled. "But you don't need to do this stupid shit."

"You do it. It can't be that stupid."

"Wrong. It is stupid. But I don't have a future, and you do."

Austin laughed. "Dad's lawyer is not so sure after my confession."

"It's not funny," Trent said.

Austin's voice cracked. "If I don't laugh, I'll cry. I'm so fucked."

"Then why did you confess?"

"It wasn't my fault. The stupid detectives tricked me. They promised it was all no big deal."

"And you believed him?"

"Yes. He told me that they don't put future Hall of Famers in jail. I didn't know they could lie to you to get a confession."

Trent shook his head. "Didn't you watch *Making a Murder* on Netflix?"

"You know I only watch sports."

"A fat lot of good that will do you now. What were you thinking? In the documentary, they promised that poor kid that he'd be home in time to watch *WrestleMania*. And he's been in jail for over ten years now."

"Shit! Are you serious?"

"Bet your ass. I should've hidden my business better. Damn it! You heard me talking on the phone that one night and then go into the footlocker, didn't you?"

"Yes. But don't blame yourself. It was my decision to sell the pills."

"Shut up. Didn't I say this was being recorded?"

It suddenly felt very stuffy in the little vehicle. He rolled down his window and reached across to get the passenger side window too. The faint breeze did little to quell his anger. He wanted to scream. Instead, Trent took a deep breath and exhaled slowly. "This is all my fault."

"Not that I'm pointing fingers, but I'm pretty sure this mess is Sam's fault. A teacher found the pills in her purse. She didn't rat me out— I know that. But Ms. Sherman still had the in-house officer perform a locker search, and he found my stash."

"Who?"

"Ms. Sherman."

"No. The other name you said."

"Oh Sam, my girlfriend.

"She did this? Man, she's getting you into all kinds of trouble. What a bitch!"

"Don't say that. She's not like the other girls. She's smart. She's going places. That's why she needed the pep pills to finish her art portfolio, but I guess a stupid teacher spotted them in her purse."

"Doesn't sound too smart to me if she got caught."

"Well, she is. The whole family is smart. Her mom is a city prosecutor. If she wanted to, I bet she could get my case thrown out."

"She could? Would her mom do that?"

"I doubt it. She hates me for knocking up her little girl."

"But what if I —"

Austin cut him off. "Hang on a second."

Trent heard another voice in the background, gruff and forceful. His brother came back on the phone. "The guard says my time is up. I have to go."

Gripping the steering wheel with his free hand, Trent said, "Wait. Maybe I could talk to Sam's Mom."

"Good luck with that. She's a stone-cold bitch."

"I have to do something. I can't just sit here in my car all day."

"Ok. Try it."

"I will. And call me tomorrow, or I won't know what is going on with your case."

The line went dead.

Trent had no idea whether Austin heard him or not. The phone slipped from his hand as his head hit the center of the steering wheel. The horn bleated weakly like a sheep. Trent felt worse than he'd ever had. It should be him locked away, not Austin. He had to get his baby brother out of jail any way he could.

Chapter 20

Jake pushed open the heavy wood door to O'Malley's Bar, a local watering hole where he agreed to meet Steve Hill. Jake was early since he had nothing else on his calendar this morning. He took a long look around the place. It was like he stepped out of a time machine. Nothing inside had changed, not the décor or the patrons.

Wearing a crisp white apron, the owner filled drinks from behind a polished oak bar. The same drunks sat in the same plush red stools they'd occupied for years. The familiar smell of beer, salty snacks, and loneliness hung in the air. The only change was a new flat-screen television, silently playing a Cubs game in the far corner. Jake's old stool stood empty, welcoming him to the past. The chair sighed contently when he plopped down.

Shane, the owner, placed a shot glass in front of Jake. "It's been a long time since you darkened my doorway."

Jake put his hand over the empty glass. "Yes. It has."

"Not having your usual?"

Jake shook his head no.

Shane swept the small glass off the bar. Jake and Shane had a complicated relationship. He'd been Jake's friend and pseudo-therapist during one of the roughest spots in Jake's life, but you'd never know it from the ruthless insults Shane would hurl at Jake. He liked to think it was Shane's unusual way of showing affection. However, the man could just as easily be a sarcastic jerk who took pleasure from Jake's problems.

"I'd like to say I'm happy to see you," Shane said. "But then I'd be lying."

"You never lied to me before."

"I see you haven't gotten any smarter, either."

"And you haven't gotten any prettier?" Jake quipped.

The bartender grinned. "That's not what you used to say to me when you were blind drunk, but I guess I won't have to worry about that today. What can I get you? A diet soda? You're looking a little fat."

"How about water and an order of French fries?"

"Sure thing." Nodding, Shane scooped ice into a tall glass and added water from a dispenser. He set the glass in front of Jake and headed towards the kitchen.

After he left, Jake looked awkwardly around the bar as he sipped on his water. The men drinking around him were no one he cared to talk to, so he picked up his phone and checked the time. Still another thirty minutes before Hill would arrive. Scrolling through his news feed, he killed time until Shane slid the basket of fries in front of him. Jake liberally applied salt to his food while Shane leaned against the bar, watching him.

Tired of all the unanswered questions in his life, Jake asked, "So Shane, back in the day, was I your friend or just a good customer?"

"Neither." The bartender busied himself by refilling Jake's water. "I took pity on you— ten thousand sperm, and you were the fastest?"

"I'm serious." Jake retrieved a couple of napkins from a shiny silver dispenser one stool over.

"Me too. You're two letters short of being an asset."

Annoyed, Jake made to get up and leave, but Shane motioned for him to sit back down. He rubbed his chin as he pondered Jake's question. "Well, you always tipped well for a cop. And you never caused no trouble inside these walls. But all kidding aside, I think what you're really asking is, do I like you well enough for a guy who was screwing my sister."

Jake's chin dropped. Their affair was another of his many regrets. "You knew about that?"

"Yes. You two weren't as secretive as you thought."

"Sorry. If it's any consolation, I wasn't using her. I liked her."

"She should have known it never would've worked. You were a married man. Truthfully, I was happy after she broke it off with you. But I was a little surprised you didn't act like a fool afterward."

Jake bit the inside of his cheek— it cost him nothing to let Shane believe what he wanted to believe.

"I mean, you were always an asshole, but you didn't turn into a bigger asshole, and that's saying something."

"Thanks. Can I ask if Maureen still works here?"

A frown was Shane's only response.

Jake held up his hands, the palms out. "Don't worry, I'd just like to say hi for old time's sake."

Shane shook his head. "I haven't talked to her in over a year."

"Really?"

Shane leaned his elbows on the bar. "Yes. She hooked up with some new guy. He must be rich because he set her up in a fancy penthouse in Chestnut Towers. The one that looks like the roof is wearing a hat. And he gives her money. Lots of it, I think. Probably a professional athlete or someone famous. She told me she didn't need this crap job anymore."

"I'm sorry to hear that."

Shane shook his head. "It's not right, I tell you. Mo should have a proper relationship. If she ever has a kid, it'll be a bastard, and we were raised better than that. My dear Mother would roll over in her grave."

Jake opened his mouth and closed it. There was nothing he could add to that statement. Shane left Jake to his food to go serve other thirsty patrons. Jake finished the fries quickly, not realizing how hungry he'd been. He pushed the basket away and wiped his mouth off on the paper napkin, scrunching it into a greasy ball.

If Jake knew anything about Maureen, she'd agree with her brother. She'd always wanted to be married with a house full of kids, but she had poor taste in men, obviously since she'd chosen to be with Jake. However, working in a seedy bar didn't help her cause either. It was a shame. She was a wonderful woman. Which was why Jake had broken up with her, she deserved someone better.

Their relationship ended the same night Jake's marriage had officially imploded. He showed up at Maureen's doorstep unannounced with a duffel bag filled with his clothes and Judge Doyle's tax documents. It was an odd combination of items, but surprisingly, it was the tax documents that had initiated his divorce and not his indiscretions.

Judge Doyle had asked Kate to pick up the documents, so he could give them to his accountant after his party. It was Judge Doyle's 50th birthday gala, an indulgent affair held at a fancy downtown hotel for three hundred of his closest family and friends. Forgetting the task amongst Kate's other responsibilities, she'd asked Jake to retrieve them from the courthouse on his way to the party. Jake had a hard time finding the correct files and showed up late. To endure the extravagant show of power, Jake had too much to drink at the party. And true to form, Doyle chose to belittle Jake for his tardiness in front of his cronies.

What neither of them had counted on was Jake still having part of his spine. It cost Doyle a straight nose and Jake his marriage.

Kicked out of his house and looking for comfort, Jake had gone to Maureen's apartment. It would have been simple to jump into a new life with her, but it wouldn't be fair to Maureen. He was a hot mess. Their relationship would end in a ball of flames too. As trite as it sounded, Jake knew he needed to spend time on himself, or he'd only succeed in ruining more lives.

In his haste to leave, he'd forgotten his bag, and he didn't have the heart to go back and cause Maureen more pain. And he certainly couldn't tell Kate that he'd left them at his girlfriend's apartment, so Jake claimed they'd been stolen from his car. Ironically, Judge Doyle had been angrier over the lost documents than his broken nose. Jake could only assume that it wouldn't look good for his constituents to know how much he made while they lived in poverty. Maybe he should give more to charity.

Shaking his head to get out of the past, Jake finished his water and checked his phone. Hill should be here any minute. He'd lost more time reminiscing than he'd thought. Swiveling in his bar stool, he checked the entrance as the heavy bar door opened, and his old partner walked in.

Steve Hill spotted Jake and made a beeline for the bar. Deep wrinkles lined his face, making him more distinguished, more commander-like. Hill stuck out his hand. The grip was still as firm as a vise.

"Jake, you ol' son of a bitch."

"Hill, you, older son of a bitch. How are you?"

"Great. You?"

"Great."

"Good. Enough of the chit-chat. I bet you'll never guess why I asked you here."

Jake smiled. "You're going to offer me a job as a detective in your department."

Arching an eyebrow, Hill said, "How the hell did you know that?"

Chapter 21

Trent rode the elevator to the third floor of the Federal building downtown. His heart hammered in his chest. Austin's future depended on Trent's ability to negotiate, which didn't bode well for Austin. Trent had been known to trip over his own tongue, so Austin's only hope was Sam's mom would listen to reason.

The secretary was not at her desk, so Trent cautiously entered the inner sanctum and found the mother's office. He wrapped his knuckles on the frosted glass pane. From behind it, he heard a muffled voice calling him inside. He did as he was commanded, stopping just inside the threshold. The office was intimidating, with book-lined shelves stretching from wall to wall and a desk as large and menacing as the tomes behind it.

In a leather-bound chair, a woman with red hair and a form-fitting jacket scribbled furiously on a yellow notepad. A pair of reading glasses were perched atop her thin nose. She was definitely Sam's mom. The two could pass for sisters. Though the lady in front of him would undoubtedly be the older and crueler of the siblings.

"Yes?" she asked, not looking up from her paperwork.

"Can I come in?"

"Didn't I just tell you that you could?"

"Sorry. I guess you did."

Trent stepped fully inside the office and shut the door behind him— there was no turning back now. He took a seat across from her and set his rattling bag at his feet. Sweat erupted from every pore, and his hands twisted in his lap like a pair of fighting snakes. Grabbing the armrests, he fought to control his nerves.

With white knuckles, he said, "I appreciate you seeing me, Ms. Bryant."

She looked up at him and frowned. "It's Ms. Doyle-Martinez."

"Sorry. I just thought since . . . "

Raising an eyebrow, she asked, "Who are you?"

"Trent. Trent Morrison. I'm Austin's brother."

"Oh! I should have seen the resemblance."

"And you're Samantha Bryant's mother, correct?"

"Yes. But more importantly, I'm the assistant district attorney for Cook County, and given your brother's legal issues, I'm not sure it's in his best interest for you to be here."

Trent squirmed in his seat. "You think so?"

Sam's mom smiled. "I do, so if you'll excuse me."

"No. Wait! I have evidence that will clear Austin's name."

"Evidence? You don't want legal representation?"

"No."

"I strongly warn you that the State will use whatever you hand over as it sees fit. It could possibly harm your brother."

He clutched the chair tighter. "I understand."

"Fine." She held out a hand. "What do you have for me?"

He retrieved his backpack from the floor and dumped the contents on her desk. Opaque pill bottles and wrinkled bills spilled out everywhere. Sam's mom gasped in either surprise or dismay. Trent tried to push the items into a neat pile, but the orange cylinders resisted his efforts. She picked up a random bottle and removed the lid. It was empty.

She held it out to him. "What is this supposed to be?"

He took a deep breath and said, "This was my stash. I was the drug dealer, not Austin."

She picked up a second bottle and shook it. "But there's nothing here."

"I know. I'm sorry. My dad fed all my pills to my fish, but the bottles should be enough proof, right?"

She shook her head. "How do I know that you didn't pick these bottles out of the garbage?"

"Because I didn't. And there's all that cash too. You could trace it to the people who bought drugs from me."

She pushed the dirty bills around with one finger. "It looks like there's not even three hundred dollars here."

Trent grimaced. "There used to be three hundred, but I spent some of it on food."

Leaning back in her chair, she sighed heavily. "All of this proves nothing."

"What are you talking about?"

"Did someone put you up to this? It has to be a joke."

"It's no joke. I could tell you who my suppliers are."

She leaned forward in her chair. "You could? Who?"

"I have a bunch. There are a whole lot of people you could take down. It would be a big bust for your office— they're all on my pizza route."

"Your pizza route?"

"Yes. Delivering pizzas is my cover. I get the pills from some of my customers."

"You can't be serious," she groaned.

"I'm dead serious. You need to arrest me and free Austin."

"I can't do that."

His temper got the better of him. He stood up so quickly he nearly toppled over his chair. "Why not?"

"Because any idiot can scrape together some money and empty pill bottles and call it evidence, but it's not."

"Are you calling me an idiot?"

"You said that, not me."

He banged his fists on her desk. "I swear I had a bunch of pills. You have to believe me."

She glared at his hands until he removed them. "It doesn't matter what I believe. It only matters what we can prove. And the State can prove that your all-star brother brought opioids on to school grounds with the intent to distribute."

"So that's it. I'm a washed-up has-been, but my brother's name is in all the papers, so if you take him down, then you'll get re-elected."

"You're wrong. His fame has nothing to do with us pursuing a case against him."

"Then it must be because he knocked up your daughter."

She gritted her teeth. "I'm more professional than that."

"How can you even try this case? Isn't it a conflict of interest?"

"I'm not trying his case. I've passed it off to an associate."

"Good. Can I speak with him or her?"

She shook her head. "It won't do any good. The evidence against your brother is strong. The pills were in his locker, and he confessed. Unless he takes a plea, we'll be taking his case to trial."

"What kind of plea are you offering him?" he asked.

"I'm sorry, but that is privileged information for your brother and his lawyer. Now, if you'll excuse me, I have more important things to deal with."

She turned his nose up at him, and it pissed him off. Under his breath, he muttered, "Bitch!"

Her eyes pinched tight. "What did you say?"

"You heard me."

"I'm going to ask you to leave." She pushed back her chair while maintaining her glare.

Blood pumped in Trent's ears, and his whole body tensed. She knew Austin. He was a good kid. It should be obvious to anyone that Trent should be behind bars, not his brother. But he'd failed, and Austin was still screwed, which pushed Trent past his breaking point. Puffing out his chest, he leaned over the desk, getting as close to Sam's mom as he could.

"If you don't drop the charges against Austin, you'll regret it."

Ms. Doyle-Martinez cocked her head to the side. "Are you threatening me? You should know threatening a government employee is a federal crime."

Trent was too angry to back down. This bitch was going to ruin his brother's life out of spite and personal gain. "It's not a threat."

"Then what is it?"

"It's a fact, and don't say that I didn't warn you."

Ms. Doyle-Martinez picked up the receiver on her desk phone and tapped a key. "Security."

"Forget it. I'm leaving."

She ignored him. "Yes. I have someone in my office that needs to be escorted from the building."

Trent limped quickly out of her office.

Chapter 22

Steve Hill squinted at Jake. "How did you know I was going to ask you that?"

"Lucky guess?" Jake replied.

"Bullshit. It was that bastard, Doyle, wasn't it?"

"Maybe."

"Maybe, my ass." Hill directed him to a booth in a dark corner.

They settled into the plush leather seats facing each other. A plump waitress approached their booth, smiling widely. The new waitress was half as pretty as Maureen and twice as old. From her bangs, jet-black wisps of hair fluttered in an unseen breeze.

She leaned against the table. "What'll it be, boys?"

"Whiskey rocks for me," Hill said.

"Just a water."

Hill smiled at Jake. "Still on the wagon? Good for you. My doctor would like me to cut back, but at my age, I figure the damage is done. Make mine a double. I'll drink his too."

"Sounds good, Sweeties. Be right back."

Steve waited until she was out of earshot. "Doyle is a son of a bitch. It's a wonder you didn't kill him by now for all he's done to you."

Jake laughed. "Are you trying to drum up business for the homicide division?"

"No. But every good detective should be able to commit the perfect murder, right?"

Jake chuckled nervously; no murder is perfect. He'd found that out the hard way with Caleb. Avoiding the question, Jake winked and said, "It's been too long, buddy."

"It has." Hill slapped the table for emphasis.

"I'm surprised you were free. Shouldn't you be sleeping for your afternoon shift at the stamping plant?"

"I quit that stupid job."

"How long ago?"

Jake waved off this question too. "Enough about me, what about you? Do you like being a commander?"

"It's not bad. It's the same shit as before, but now I'm a babysitter and shrink to a bunch of middle-aged men and women."

Jake nodded. "It looks like it's taking a toll on you."

Snorting, Hill said, "Yes, I'm tired when I wake up in the morning and dead tired when I go to bed at night."

"How was the drive coming over from the South side?"

"It wasn't that bad in the middle of the day, it only took me a half-hour, but at night it would be a killer."

The waitress arrived with two glasses— one short, one tall; one with amber liquid and one without. Hill raised his glass and looked expectantly at Jake, so he did the same. Their glasses clinked together. Hill toasted, "To us working together again."

"I didn't say I'm taking the job."

"Please, Jake. I know you want to be a detective again. I can see it written all over your face. Not to mention, you could restore your good name."

Jake shook his head. "I still don't get it. I've been gone a long time, and as you pointed out, I didn't leave on the best of terms."

"It's a funny story. HR was reviewing old files, and it turns out there was a mistake on your paperwork. You were never formally discharged. When I heard about it, I insisted that you be considered for one of my open positions."

"Why me?"

"You're doing this backwards, Jake. Shouldn't you be convincing me to hire you?"

"Just humor me."

Hill rubbed his chin. "Fine. I want you on my team because I think you're smart and have good instincts. You used to be one hell of a detective, and I think you could be one again, but mostly I'm doing it because I feel guilty."

"Guilty?"

Hill said, "The department should have had your back. You were not at fault that day— no way you should have you went in that front door alone. You should have had backup. It was chaos in there. No lights, people screaming everywhere, the baby crying. You thought he had a weapon. I would have done the same thing."

Jake drummed his fingers on the edge of the table. "Tasha came to see me the other day."

"Who?"

"Tasha Pittman, Leroy's girlfriend."

"What did she want?"

"To watch me get arrested after she planted evidence in my apartment for that attempted rape the other night. Luckily, I removed it before the search warrant was served."

"You're kidding me! Did you report her?"

"It wouldn't do any good."

"Probably not." Hill shrugged.

"But I did get her to admit she hid Leroy's gun in the baby's diaper that day."

Hill considered it for a second and shook his head. "Bullshit. Someone would have found it before they cleared the scene."

Jake said, "You said it yourself. It was total chaos."

"I can't believe she wanted to protect that rapist scumbag."

"She still thinks he's innocent."

"Then why did he act guilty?"

"Tasha said he got a letter shoved in the door that morning."

Hill paused. "What letter? What did it say?"

A letter proving Leroy's innocence had never been part of this story's narrative, so he didn't make anything of Hill's hesitation. "I don't know. I was hoping you knew something about it."

"I'm sorry. I don't."

"But you did hear that Leroy's son was convicted of rape in Judge Doyle's court?"

"I did, and I heard his principal attacked Doyle when he found him guilty."

Jake smiled. "I would've liked to see that."

"Me too."

"Doyle should have recused himself, given the complicated family history with the participants."

"True. But there aren't many juvenile judges."

"It's still bullshit," Jake said.

"The man is bulletproof."

Slumping in his seat, Jake exhaled loudly. "That's for damn sure. You know he's blackmailing me over your job offer."

Hill pulled his head back in surprise. "How?"

"He says he will block my reinstatement if I don't walk out of Sam's life."

"He can't do that."

"Are you sure?"

Hill scratched his head. "Pretty sure."

Jake wasn't; Doyle had friends in high places. Superintendent O'Shea had been the Assistant Superintendent at the time of Jake's resignation. He hated Jake. Doyle and O'Shea were thicker than thieves, and he'd been standing next to Doyle at his 50th birthday party when Jake flattened the judge's nose.

"That's what I thought."

Hill reached across the table and touched Jake's arm. "Take the job, Jake. Realistically, how will he keep you out of Sam's life with social media and all the other crap that's out there."

"You have a point," Jake said.

"God damn right that I have a point. Besides, I can cover for you with whatever lies you need to use."

"Thanks." Taking a sip of his water, Jake asked, "Can I have some time to think about it? I mean about taking the job."

"You've got three days before I have to turn my decisions into HR. I have two openings, one in violent crimes and one in gang."

"I'd prefer the one in violent crimes."

"I'll see what I can do." A phone chimed loudly in Hill's pocket. He checked the caller ID and shook his head. "No rest for the wicked. Another problem that can't wait."

"I bet."

Hill pulled a ten from his wallet and tossed it on the table. "You'll cover for me if that's not enough? We can catch up when you accept the job. Don't let that asshole win."

Jake smiled. "I won't."

Hill gave Jake a hearty slap on the shoulder and exited the bar.

Jake looked around for the waitress and their check, but she was nowhere to be found. Sitting in the silence, he considered his future— going back and forth on what he should do. Eventually, he reached an answer. Sam would have to understand it was the best choice for both of them. He hoped.

The waitress finally came over, and Jake paid the bill. However, he didn't leave. Instead, with his stomach churning, he dialed Sam. It rang and rang before going to her voicemail. Shoot! He forgot Kate had her phone.

Chapter 23

A beautiful little girl with thick black hair opened the door to Kate's townhouse. Wide-eyed, she stared up at Jake; a gap in her front teeth added to her charm. Leaning against the door, she said, "Hello. How may I help you?"

Jake knelt down. "Hi, Izzy."

"Wait. Are you Sam's daddy?"

"I am. Is your step-mommy home?"

Heels clacked down the hallway. Jake wondered if Kate ever took them off, or were they a permanent part of her armor? The little girl flinched as Kate yelled, "Isabella, how many times have I told you not to answer the door. It could be a not nice person."

"Sorry."

Putting a hand on her shoulder, Kate guided Izzy out of the entryway. "Why don't you go find your father."

"All right." Izzy sprinted away.

Kate turned to find Jake. However, from the look on her face, it was like she'd found a rotting skunk carcass instead. "Oh, you're early."

"Hello to you too, Kate."

"Was it your idea?"

"What are you talking about?"

Jake shook his head. "You know what I'm talking about."

Smiling, Kate said, "No. It was my Dad's plan, but I approved it. This is a critical time in Sam's life, and we know what is best for her future."

Jake clamped his jaw shut to keep his venomous quip unsaid.

She eyed him warily. "Did you make your decision?"

"Yes."

"And?"

"I've decided to take the job."

She smirked. "I thought you'd do that."

"You did? Why?"

"Just that you usually put your desires before your family's."

His fists clenched. "Really? Because I thought I was putting Sam's needs first this time by walking away."

Kate opened her mouth and then closed it. Jake took pride in besting her for once. It killed her not to have the last word, but she should know she'd already won the war. There was no need to worry about this verbal battle.

"Do you want to come in?"

He shook his head. "Thanks, but I'd prefer to break the news to Sam out here where she can't make too much of a scene."

"And you're done pushing for art school?"

"She can play with her paintings after she gets a real degree."

Nodding, she said, "It's for the best. I'll go get her."

With the door ajar, Jake took a seat on the top step and waited. Through his jeans, the concrete felt cold on his backside. Cars drove by, and the first mosquito of the night buzzed in his ear. A minute went by, then two. Eventually, the door creaked open behind him.

"Dad, what's going on?"

He looked over his shoulder. "Hi, Honey. Why don't you take a seat?"

Hesitantly, she sat down next to him, and he placed a hand on her shoulder. "Is the pill-thing taken care of?"

Rolling her eyes, she said, "The school has my fake prescription."

"That's a good thing, right?"

Her mouth twisted up. "I don't even know anymore."

Checking over his shoulder, he cleared his throat and said loudly, "I have something important to tell you."

"You do? What? There's been a lot of whispering around the house today."

"Yes, there's something more important than your drug problem."

"Dad!"

"Don't dad me, we still need to have a serious discussion about that, but that is not what I need to tell you."

"What is it, then?"

Sweat broke out on his forehead, and he took a deep breath. "All right, it won't be easy for me to say, so please don't interrupt me. It's about my future, not yours."

"You're starting to scare me."

"There's nothing to be scared of. This is for the best."

Putting everything in the best possible light, he told her about the job offer and what it meant to their relationship. How he should move closer to the job since he'd already be working long hours and the commute would kill him. When he finished, he studied her expectantly.

Sam stood up slowly and moved towards the door. "Are you serious?"

He pursed his lips. "Yes."

"You're giving up on me?"

"That's not it."

She crossed her arms in front of her. "Will you at least keep your promise and pay for art school?"

Peeking over his shoulder, Jake saw a shadow matching Kate's shape by the window. He said, "Sam, I think your mother is right. Art should be a hobby."

Chapter 24

Jake held up an index finger to pause the conversation. He chanced another glance over his shoulder. The shadow moved away from the window. He counted to twenty in his head before he said, "All right, I think your mom's gone."

"Do you think it worked?" Sam whispered.

He pulled her in for a hug. "I hope so. That was quite an act we put on."

They released, and he looked back to make sure Kate was truly gone. She had. The shadow hadn't returned.

Sam said, "Good thing, I heard my phone ringing in Mom's room. You're the only one who calls, all my friends text."

"I know— my plan wouldn't have worked otherwise. Izzy won't tell on you for using her phone?"

"No, I told her that I was texting Austin. She thinks he's cute, so she'll cover for me."

He rolled his eyes. "Great."

"But what happens if Mom and Grandpa find out that we double-crossed them?"

"They can make your life hell for the next year, but then you'll be eighteen and an adult. They can't legally stop you from going to art school."

"I guess not."

"And it's your dream, right?"

"Yes!" she squealed.

"Shhh. We don't want your mom to hear." Jake held a finger to his lips. "Now, you have to do the hard part and get accepted."

She sat back down on the step. "It's going to be so hard."

"And I don't want you using pills to stay up all night and work on your portfolio."

"Yes," she replied meekly. "It was stupid. I know. And I'll never forgive myself if Austin gets in real trouble."

"Wasn't he trying to sell pills to other kids too?"

Grinding a toe into the pavement, she said, "I don't know, maybe."

Sam's fidgeting told Jake he was correct. He rested a hand on her leg to save her shoe. "If I've learned one thing in my life, it's that you need to focus on things you can control."

"Ok. I will, but how will you pay for art school if I get in? Because Mom certainly won't do it."

"While we're pretending to go along with their plan, I'll work a lot of overtime."

"And when they find out, Grandpa won't pay for your new apartment."

"He was never going to do that anyway. I'll keep my old apartment, so we can sneak in a visit now and then."

She touched his arm. "Awesome. Not seeing you was the only part of this plan that I didn't like."

"They are not as smart as they think. You could tell your mom that you joined an SAT study group or something."

"I guess that would work. Can I still come over this weekend?"

"I'm sure your mom will be fine with one last visit since she thinks she's getting her way. We can finalize our plans then."

"I can't wait."

He checked over his shoulder; the window was still vacant. "We've been out here long enough for what should be a tense conversation. Can you go inside and act upset?"

"No problem. I'll just pretend that I'm going to follow their stupid plan and ruin my life."

"You're a good kid."

"Not really. I've done some pretty stupid things lately."

"We all make mistakes, but I better never hear that you took Adderall. Got it?"

"I won't. I promise."

"Good girl."

"Wait, won't you get fired once I go to art school in a year and a half?"

"Chicago PD is union. I'll be off probation in twelve months. Your grandfather can make my life a living hell, but as long as I don't do something stupid like assault him again, I should be fine."

She offered up a weak smile as she stood up. "Are you sure?"

"I promise. Now get inside, and I'll see you this weekend."

Giving him one more hug, Sam transformed before his eyes. She worked herself into a frantic state, her eyes red, her face blotchy. Flinging open the door, she rushed down the hallway, crying. He stood there in genuine amazement. With him, what you saw was what you got though he liked to believe he was capable of a good lie when required, but women could take it to another level.

Standing up, Jake leaned against the ornate railing and waited for Kate to come out and gloat. He wasn't disappointed. The door cracked open, and Kate sidled up next to him.

"So you told her?"

"Yes. Didn't you see her crying?"

She nodded. "You know I'm doing this because I love her."

"That's why I'm doing it too."

He knew both statements were true. Kate would crush anyone that got in her way. She was very much like her father in that regard. While Jake would give up everything for the ones he loved since he'd watched his mother do it her whole life. Hadn't she let him move away without a word after raising him nearly single-handedly for eighteen years? Her example had stuck, but he wasn't sure if it was for the best. Unhappiness followed him around like a bad smell, while men like Patrick always seemed to have a smile on their faces.

She touched the back of his arm. "I'm proud of you, Jake."

Resisting the urge to pull away with disgust, he said, "Can Sam still come over this weekend? Kind of like our last hurrah."

"I don't see why not, but she's still in trouble. Don't let her go out."

"You think I'm going to give up a minute of my time with her."

"I suppose not."

"Goodbye, Kate." He stepped off the porch.

"Jake, wait a minute."

"Yes?" He turned back to her.

"My dad would like you to come by his office tomorrow."

"Why?"

"To sign a document formalizing our little agreement."

Not thinking they'd take it to that extreme, he asked, "Is it a legally-binding document?"

"Yes. You'll be giving up your parental rights."

His jaw dropped as part of his act, but he'd been expecting that. After all, they were a family of lawyers. It was part of his plan to let them think they had the upper hand. For now. Taking a deep breath, he replied, "I guess I'm free. What time?"

"It's Friday, so court will end early. Say about three o'clock."

"Fine."

Kate smiled. "Sam will thank you one day."

Jake suppressed a laugh. "I'm sure she will."

Chapter 25

The next day, Trent knocked on the apartment door. As he waited, his heart pounded in his chest. This man had to help him. They'd found a way to get his daughter off the hook, so they should be able to get Austin out too before formal charges were filed against him. Then none of the big programs would have to know, Austin's future could be salvaged, and Bo would forgive Trent.

Damn! Trent heard nothing from inside. Desperation itched at every fiber in his body. This man was Trent's last hope, and time was running out; Austin would be arraigned on Monday.

He knocked louder.

The door rattled in its frame, and he heard a muffled voice. Seconds later, the deadbolt slid in its chamber, and the door opened. Trent smiled. Sam's dad stared back at him, a look of puzzlement on his face.

"Hello, Mr. Bryant."

"I didn't order a pizza."

Trent nervously pulled at the only clean shirt he could find in his car. "Sorry. This isn't a delivery, but I really need to talk to you."

"Me? Why?"

"My name is Trent Morrison," he said, sticking out his sweaty hand. "I'm Austin's brother."

"Austin?"

"Umm . . . your daughter's boyfriend."

"Austin. That's right. How can I help you?"

"Can I come in, Mr. Bryant?"

"Sure. Call me, Jake."

Stepping aside, he let Trent pass and closed the door behind him. He motioned to a dilapidated couch and took a seat in the opposite chair. The couch protested more than Trent's knee as he sat down. Taking a quick look around the apartment, Trent felt sorry for the guy. The furnishings appeared second-hand at best. Sam's mom obviously got the better end of the divorce.

Jake asked, "So, how is Austin? Is he still in . . . "

Trent nodded. "Yes, he's still in the Cook County Detention Center. His court date is set for Monday."

"I'm sorry. Your brother seemed like a nice kid. We only met once. I hear he was one heck of a quarterback."

"He IS one heck of a quarterback who will be in the pros one day," Trent said through clenched teeth.

They looked at one another uncomfortably. Trent put aside his own feelings of anger and guilt, knowing it would only hurt his cause. He shifted in his seat and rubbed the back of his neck, unsure of how to proceed. The truth was he hadn't expected to make it this far.

As he was finding his words, Jake cleared his throat. "Ahh, so what brings you here . . . Trent?"

"Umm . . . So . . . I was hoping you could help Austin."

Leaning back in his seat, Jake crossed his arms in front of his chest and drew in a breath. "How do you expect me to do that?"

"Like I said, on Monday, Austin could be charged with a felony drug possession with intent to distribute. It could put him away for a long time. And ruin his football career."

"That sucks."

"Yes, it does," Trent said, deciding to lay his cards on the table, no matter how clumsy and desperate it sounded. "I hear you were a former cop, so you have to know the system. Could you talk to the Assistant Prosecutor and get him to drop the charges? Austin doesn't deserve this. Please! I'll do anything."

Jake sighed. "I'm a former cop, 'former' being the key word. What little influence I had is long gone."

"But what if you talked with Sam's mom. She's a prosecutor."

A low whistle escaped Jake's lips. "She doesn't like me very much. If I talked to her, it would probably make things worse. I'd suggest asking her yourself?"

Trent studied his shoes. "I did. It didn't go very well."

"I'm not surprised. Didn't your family hire a lawyer?"

"They did. But I don't think he'll be able to keep Austin's case from going to trial. And if that happens, Austin can kiss his football career goodbye."

"I'm sorry."

Trent nodded. "I hear Sam's grandfather might hear the case. Couldn't he tell the prosecutor to drop the charges?"

"He could, but Judge Doyle is up for reelection next year. No way is he going to appear lenient on a drug case."

Trent wrung his hands. "Do you have any other ideas? Please. I can't let Austin go to prison."

"Why doesn't his lawyer cite a conflict of interest and get a new judge?"

"Would that work?"

"I would think so, but I'm not a lawyer."

"I'll try that if I can find a way to talk to Austin's attorney."

Jake ran his fingers through his hair. "Excuse me for asking, but where are your parents in all of this? Shouldn't they be the ones talking with your brother's lawyer?"

Trent grimaced. "I'm sure they are, but I'm out of the loop. My dad kicked me out of the house. Austin got the pills from me."

"I see."

"That's why I'm doing whatever I can do to get Austin out. I need to make this better. Do you think you could tell him about the conflict of interest thing?"

"His lawyer? He should have already filed the motion if he was any good."

"Oh. I was thinking about my dad. Could you tell him, anyway? Let me give you my dad's number."

Jake shrugged. "If you think it will help, son."

Trent read it off. Jake typed it into the contact list and said, "I'll call him later, and I wish your brother the best of luck."

Jake stood up. Trent found himself involuntarily standing up as well. A cold sweat broke out on the back of his neck. He'd hoped for more, but what did Trent expect? That Mr. Bryant would have the keys to Austin's cell in his pocket, and the two of them could skip down to the jailhouse to let Austin out, followed by a big release party with balloons and streamers.

Putting a hand on his shoulder, Jake nudged Trent towards the door. "I hate to be rude, but I have an appointment that I can't be late for."

Trent resisted his efforts. "Is there anything else you can tell me about Sam's grandfather that might help?"

"No. Just that he's a son of bitch who only cares about his legacy."

"Legacy?"

Yes. His judicial record and his family. He'd do anything to protect them."

"Got it. Thanks."

Trent limped out of the apartment and down to the street. The building's metal door slammed shut behind him. He collapsed into the driver's seat, feeling exhausted but with the niggling feeling in the back of his head. Trent was scheduled to work, but he didn't think he could deal with that tonight. It was a stupid job anyway. Let them fire him.

Seconds later, Jake turned out of the rear parking lot and drove past Trent. At least, the man wasn't a liar; he did have an appointment. So few people could be trusted to tell the truth.

Chapter 26

The courthouse appeared menacingly on Jake's left with its white face and thin black windows for eyes. He turned into the parking structure opposite the building, finding an empty spot several levels up. Slightly dizzy from driving in circles, he took a second to collect his thoughts. He had to be on top of his game for the meeting. The devil could leave without his shirt after a negotiation with Patrick Doyle.

When he got his head on straight, Jake walked across the street and entered the courthouse. Inside the door, an armed officer stood in front of a metal detector. Jake checked the directory, trying to recall Doyle's office number.

The rugged man smiled widely at Jake. "Good afternoon. Where are you headed?"

"Judge Doyle's office."

"Is he expecting you?" The officer asked. He was a dead ringer for Jeff Bridges in *The Big Lebowski*. A graying goatee surrounded his mouth. Wavy brown hair touched the collar of his tan uniform, and a flat black revolver sat in a holster of his thick leather belt.

"Yes." Jake wondered why the man wasn't out looking for his rug. "I'm his son-in-law. Well, his ex-son-in-law."

The man grinned. "I've heard about you."

"I'm sure you did."

The officer stuck out his hand and whispered, "Judge Doyle's an asshole. It must have felt so good to break his nose."

"It did feel pretty good," Jake admitted.

"I bet, but I will need you to go through the detector. I can't have you doing anything on my watch. I value my job too much. I'm only a year away from retirement."

Jake nodded. "I understand. There's a lot of nut jobs out there."

"I can't tell you how many weapons I've confiscated from family members with a vendetta."

As he emptied his pockets, Jake said, "Well, I can promise you that I don't have anything illegal."

"Are you sure?"

"What?"

The dude pointed to the tray holding Jake's belongings. "Your cell phone."

"I can't take a phone inside the building?"

"Correct. The ban has been in effect for a few years now."

"Could you hang onto it for me?"

The officer shook his head and pointed to a row of coin-operated lockers. "I'm sorry, son. I can't."

"No worries."

Jake looked at his watch and cursed; it was already five minutes to three o'clock. Doyle would scold Jake for his tardiness, and he didn't want to give the bastard an edge. Knowing he didn't have any loose change, Jake jogged back to the parking structure. However, before he reached his car, he got a text from Sam. She must have gotten her phone back.

Working on my painting while Mom is at work. Be over in a couple hours. I'll grab Chinese from our favorite place

He replied. **How are you getting there?**

Walking

You know I don't like that

With a smiley face emoji, Sam responded. **It is the middle of the day. I'll be fine**

Be careful. I should be done with your grandpa soon. Love ya. Dad.

I will. Luv U 2

Tossing the phone in his car, Jake ran back to the courthouse. The officer chuckled when Jake returned sweaty and slightly out of breath. He probably saw this same routine every day before he punched out and went bowling. Dabbing at his forehead, Jake successfully traversed the metal detector and watched as his wallet, belt, and car keys traveled through the scanner.

"Judge Doyle's office?" Jake asked as he slipped his belt through the loops on his pants.

The officer pointed up the marble stairway. "Second floor. Number 202. It's down the hall and to the left. You can't miss it."

"Thanks."

It sounded like the same place, but it'd been years since Jake's last visit. He raced up the stairs and down the hall, his shoes squeaking on the polished linoleum. Light oak doors were set along the pale-yellow walls. The monotony of the corridor was only broken up by oil paintings of long-dead magistrates. He found Doyle's office door ajar and poked his head inside. The room looked exactly as he remembered it.

The outer office was empty except for the secretary's desk and rows of gray file cabinets. On her desk was a stack of files and an ancient phone with an excessive number of buttons. A person should be able to call the International Space Station with that many buttons. Doyle's door was closed, but the clerk's office stood open, and the lights were on. For the life of him, he couldn't understand why Robert agreed to be Doyle's aid. Jake wouldn't wish that on your worst enemy. Being married to his ex-wife should be punishment enough for whatever wrongs Robert had done in his life.

"Hello?" Jake called out.

He stepped inside.

"Robert?"

A secretary didn't pop up from behind a file cabinet or stack of papers, so Jake tentatively walked to Doyle's door. With his knuckles poised to knock, he heard muffled voices from inside and pulled his hand away. Assuming it might be Robert and Doyle, he put his ear to the door to listen to their scheming against him.

The voices grew louder.

"I'm not happy."

"I know, but I'm doing the best I can."

The first voice was unfamiliar to Jake, but the second voice was Doyle's, which was surprising. Jake leaned in closer, wondering who could make Doyle sound subservient.

"Your best needs to be better."

Doyle answered, *"There's only so much I can do. I can't make them commit the crimes."*

"That's not good enough. What good is a half-full prison?"

"I understand your frustration."

"Do you?"

"I do."

"And do you know how much I've donated to your campaign?"

"You never fail to remind me," Doyle said. *"And I'd prefer to have these discussions at your office."*

"I don't care what you like."

A stern-looking woman with a helmet of graying hair strode into the office. Wearing a blue cardigan with a gaudy pin on the lapel, she set a new stack of files on her desk while eyeing Jake. In a no-nonsense tone, she asked, "Who are you, and what are you doing in here?"

Jake knew if he gave the wrong answer, she would drag him out of the office by his ear, but before he could stumble over his answer, Robert lumbered through the outer door. He wore a stupid-looking bow tie and round glasses. He stepped between them. "It's all right, Alice. It's only Jake. He has an appointment with Judge Doyle."

Turning her nose up at them, she returned to her mountain of files. "If you say so."

Robert said, "Why don't we wait in my office? The Judge had something come up with an . . . important guest."

"Sure." Jake followed him into his tiny room that was and took the lone chair facing the small desk. Leaving the door open, Robert shuffled around the perimeter of his office and sat down. He said, "Truthfully, I'm surprised you took the offer."

"It's what's best for Sam."

Wrapping his arms around his torso, Robert rocked back and forth in his chair. "It's just not like you to be so agreeable with them."

"I really want my old job back."

"Then staying on Judge Doyle's good side is essential."

Jake looked around the office that was no bigger than a coat closet. "It looks like it worked out for you."

Doyle's door slammed open, and a large man with slicked-back hair and a tailored suit stormed out. The vintage gangster was not the least bit intimidated by Alice. Instead, she shrunk behind her desk like a little girl hiding from the boogeyman. He slammed the hallway door shut behind him with a bang. A few seconds later, Doyle sheepishly appeared in the outer office. He spotted Jake, and his face reddened.

"How long have you been here?"

"I just got here." Jake would keep what he heard under his hat for now.

Doyle turned to Robert, who nodded in agreement.

"Fine," Doyle growled. "Step into my office. We have something new to discuss."

Chapter 27

Trent was still in front of Jake's apartment, piecing together his ill-conceived plan when he got a call from his brother. He brought the phone to his ear. "Austin, please tell me it's good news."

"It's not."

"Damn it!"

"Dad and the lawyer just left— "

"And?"

"Monday morning, they're going to charge me with felony possession with intent to distribute. And since I was selling to minors, it'll be a Class 1 Felony."

"Class 1. Is that bad?"

"The worst you can get."

"You've got to be shitting me."

Austin's voice cracked. "I wish I was."

"But you're a first-time offender. Can't your lawyer bargain it down to a misdemeanor and get you off with some community service or something?"

"No. That's not even close to the deal they offered me. With my confession, he says it's an open and shut case for the State. They want to make an example out of me."

Trent pounded the dashboard with his fist, shaking the whole car. "God damn it."

Austin started to cry. "I'm scared, Trent."

The guilt grew in Trent's stomach like a tapeworm. Eating his insides, it got so big he thought it would punch through his chest. He almost wished it would because he deserved to die in a pool of his own blood in a tiny little car in front of a crappy apartment building. Austin's sobs brought him back to reality.

"Stop! It's not your fault."

"What do you mean it's not my fault?" Austin cried.

"It's my fault. You never would have had the pills if it wasn't for me."

"Maybe."

"Shut up. It's true. What is the plea deal that they offered you?"

With a hitch in his voice, he answered, "If I plead guilty, they'll knock it down to a class B felony... 5-8 years."

Trent's world crashed down on him. "No. That can't be right."

"The lawyer says I should take it."

"He's an idiot. What did Dad say?"

Austin laughed weakly. "He didn't say a word."

"Really?"

"Yes. It's the first time I saw Dad speechless. I didn't know if he was about to have a heart attack or rip someone's head off. Probably both."

Austin continued to cry. Clenching his fist into a ball, Trent punched himself in his bad leg. Repeatedly. When he couldn't take the pain anymore, he moved to the other thigh. Afterward, he felt more in control. More focused.

Trent said, "You can't take the deal. Your career would be over by the time you got out."

"And if I don't, and it goes to trial, I could get fifteen years. I don't want to spend half my life in prison. I can't—"

"Austin, listen to me. I'm going to fix this. Come Monday morning, you'll be a free man."

"How?"

"I have a plan. But the less you know, the better."

"I don't understand. What can you do?"

"Plenty. You forget I almost graduated from college with a degree in general studies. Just hang in there for three more days, and I swear we'll be home together laughing about all this."

"I hope so."

"You don't have to hope. That's a promise."

"Ok, Trent. Bye." Austin disconnected.

The phone slipped out of Trent's hand and tumbled to the floor of his car. He didn't bother to retrieve it. Trent felt as useless as the g in lasagna. His plan was stupid and depended on a lot of luck, something Trent didn't have. There had to be another way.

Resting his head in his sweaty hands, he thought harder than he ever had before. What else could he do to keep his promise? Finding Austin a new lawyer wouldn't do any good, his dad had probably hired the best lawyer in town for his favorite son. And talking to Sam's mom again would get him nowhere. As well as Jake, both of them were dead ends, which left Trent with only one choice. He wasn't excited about the plan, but he was out of options, and the clock was ticking.

But how to start?

Trent had no idea. He was about to punch his leg again when he spotted a gorgeous red-headed girl walking down the sidewalk towards him.

Maybe today was his lucky day. Laden down with a backpack and a large plastic food bag in her hand, the girl still managed to have a bounce in her step. When she was twenty feet from his car, Trent was positive it was Sam, Austin's little girlfriend.

A short black woman followed close behind her.

Chapter 28

Doyle marched into his office and pointed to the smaller chair facing his desk. "Take a seat, boy."

Rolling his eyes, Jake remained standing in the doorway. The power play was already starting. "No, thanks."

Shrugging at Jake, he pushed several documents and a gold pen across the desk. "Suit yourself. Here. Sign these."

"Hmmm . . . in a minute."

Jake took his time strolling around the room. He inspected the bookcase and the view from the window while Doyle scowled at him. When he'd proven his point that he wasn't anyone's boy, Jake sat down to inspect a copy of the contract. Of course, Jake's chair sat several inches below Doyle's throne.

Jake read the top page but quickly got lost in the legalese. "What does this say exactly?"

"It's a standard contract whereby you forfeit all your parental rights to Samantha."

"What does that include?"

"The typical clauses. You'll have no privileges or access. And absolutely no legal rights regarding Samantha."

Jake played his part and overreacted by throwing his hands in the air. "Oh, that's all. Do I have to sign in blood?"

Doyle shook his head. "Come on. You agreed to this arrangement. This document just ensures you won't double-cross us."

Scanning the rest of the contract, Jake said, "I worry that you're double-crossing me. Did you slip in anything extra to screw me over?"

"No, I didn't. But if you'd like a lawyer to review it, I have some acquaintances that would be glad to offer their services?"

"I bet you do." Jake snorted.

Doing his best, he checked for any blatant red flags and saw none, which was a red flag in itself. It appeared to be a standard contract forfeiting his parental rights. He picked up the pen but let it hover above the pages to stretch out the tension. Doyle leaned forward in his seat with his lips slightly parted, eyes staring intently on the line where Jake should sign.

Setting the pen down on the desk, Jake leaned back in his chair and stared at the ceiling to buy some time. Maybe Doyle would tip his hand if he got frustrated enough. Some form of treachery had to be buried in a clause. Whatever the deceit was, it shouldn't affect Jake's plan, but it would be good to know what Doyle was scheming.

Doyle pounded the desk with his fist. "Sign the damn thing."

"I need a second."

"Why?"

"You're asking me to give up my daughter. That's not an easy thing to do."

"Let's be honest, Jake. You lost Samantha a long time ago."

"I did?"

"Yes— right around the time you cheated on her mother, lost your job, and became a drunken loser."

The bile rose up in his throat. It took every ounce of his willpower not to punch the pompous asshole again. "Fuck you!"

"Fuck me? Sign that damn contract and the will I made out for you, or you can forget all about the detective job."

"Will?"

"Yes. A will. You'll have a sizeable life insurance policy with your new job. God forbid something should happen to you. but if it did, you want Sam to be taken care of, don't you?"

"Of course."

"Good because I took the initiative of making Kate the executor of your estate."

"Kate! No way."

"You can't leave it to Sam. She's a minor. Your affairs will be eaten up in probate."

"You're right." Jake scribbled his signature on the contract giving up his parental rights but tore up the other document, sprinkling the pieces over Doyle's desk. Laughing, he said, "But I'll draft my own will with an executor of my choosing."

"Fine."

"Fine! See you around. I'm leaving."

"No, you're not."

"Excuse me?"

Doyle shook his head. "God, you're stupid. Sit back down, Jakeass."

Jake remained on his feet.

Doyle threw his tasseled shoes up on the polished oak. Frowning, he asked, "How much did you hear of my previous conversation?"

"What conversation?"

"I'm not stupid, so stop your lying. How much did you hear?"

Jake sat back down. "Enough."

"I thought so."

"I know you and your Mafioso-friend are getting rich by filling his prison with innocent kids."

"Please. They're far from innocent."

"And I knew you were a world-class bastard, Patrick, possibly the biggest asshole to ever walk on two legs. But it wasn't until today that I learned you're truly evil. How do you live with yourself?"

"At least I've never killed an innocent man."

"What?"

"You heard me. There was never a gun. You overreacted and killed an innocent man while the real rapist is still out there. Why do you think it was so easy for me to get you fired?"

"There was a gun. I have a witness."

Waving his hand in the air, Doyle brushed aside Jake's claim. "It doesn't matter. You should have had an attorney review that contract for you. Buried down on page six is a clause that penalizes you severely if you reveal any privileged information. You can't do anything to me without destroying yourself too."

Jake sniffed. "I don't have anything."

"And you won't have anything until the day you die."

"Wait!" Too many gears were in motion to follow all the schemes, but one thing stood out to Jake. "Why would you put that clause in the contract? I didn't know about your scheme until twenty minutes ago."

Doyle shook his head. "Jakehole, I told you to stop your lying."

"I'm not lying."

"You are. You knew about my scheme before today."

"No. I didn't."

"Of course, you did. Kate should have never asked you to pick up my taxes before that party. She was supposed to do it herself. Afterward, I didn't think you were smart enough to know what you had, but then why else would you keep them?"

Bluffing, Jake said, "I don't care about any penalty. I'll turn them over to the papers and expose you for the monster that you are."

Doyle laughed. "If you still had the undoctored tax statement, I'd be worried. But we both know they were destroyed in the fire."

"Fire?"

Doyle looked down his nose at Jake. "It was so simple for my associate to rent the storage locker next to yours and start a fire."

The revelation hit him like a cold shower. The fire wasn't an accident. If he hadn't been so depressed and drunk at the time, he'd have put things together. However, the joke was on Doyle, though it was in Jake's best interest to let Doyle believe the files were destroyed.

Jake hissed, "Why did you have to burn everything? Couldn't you have just stolen them?"

"And miss out on the pleasure of watching all your stuff burn?"

"You bastard. I lost everything."

Doyle laughed. "You deserved it for what you did to my little Katey."

"Speaking of Kate. Does she know about your prison scheme?"

With his lips pressed tight, Doyle shook his head. "Despite all the rumors, she thinks that I'm a saint."

"Robert?"

Doyle gazed beyond Jake. "He might know, but don't get any ideas. He's too spineless to help you."

Continuing his act, Jake hung his head in defeat. "Well, it looks like you outsmarted me, but I'm still getting my old detective job back and the apartment, right?"

"Yes, it's a cheap price to pay for your silence."

As Jake stood up to leave, a phone rang on Doyle's desk. Looking a little surprised, Doyle snatched up the receiver. The tone of his voice changed quickly with each passing second as his face grew ashen.

"Kate, slow down. What about Sam? Was she hurt? When? ... Was there a description? ... He's with me now. I'll call you back."

Setting the phone down, Doyle came around the desk and pushed Jake with two hands. Jake didn't respond; he was more concerned with Sam. She should be at his apartment by now since their meeting had run much longer than he'd planned.

Red-faced, Doyle shouted, "Do you think I'm stupid?"

Unsure how to answer, Jake responded honestly. "Yes."

"Well, I'm not. And if you think having Sam kidnapped while using me as your alibi is the perfect crime? It's not. The only thing you've accomplished is committing a felony, and I'll see you locked up forever."

"I don't know what you're talking about. What happened to Sam?"

Doyle gritted his teeth. "Don't act like you don't know. A 911 call just came in. It was reported that a black woman kidnapped Sam right in front of your apartment. Her purse and ID were left at the scene."

Jake quickly processed the information.

A black woman. It had to be Tasha. She'd told Jake she'd hurt him. Kidnapping his daughter would certainly hurt Jake. God knew what Tasha would do to her; the woman was crazy. It was up to Jake to save Sam. The police wouldn't understand the complexity of the situation, but Jake did. It was a matter of life and death.

Jake ran from the office with Doyle still screaming for answers.

Chapter 29

Jake checked both sides of the hallway for potential witnesses but saw no one. It was empty except for cigarette butts, fast food wrappers, and a stained pair of pants near the elevator. Luckily, Jake had the forethought to get her address off the internet after Tasha tried to frame him. With her threat of violence, it seemed like good information to have. Though Jake never dreamed Tasha would abduct Sam.

Jake removed the pistol from his pocket, the one he'd retrieved by sneaking up the back stairs of his apartment. He gripped the weapon firmly as he listened through the thin apartment door. From within, Jake heard a television loudly airing an infomercial on weight loss. He prayed he'd arrived in time to thwart Tasha's crazy scheme, but he'd wasted precious minutes avoiding the police at his building. However, the alternative was showing up to a gunfight empty-handed.

Jake took short deep breaths to clear his head, but it did little to control his nerves. Damn it. For Sam's sake, he couldn't afford to make any stupid mistakes today. He'd die if something happened to her. Fuck! Why had Tasha put him in this predicament? Why? To save her own son, but Jake wouldn't allow her to harm Sam in the process.

Pressing his back against the wall, Jake took one more deep breath and lunged forward. He lifted his knee waist high, and his foot shot out like a rocket. The heel of his shoe landed to the side of the knob. The door crashed open with a shriek of broken pine.

Jake rushed into the apartment, his weapon level, scanning the room. Tasha lay on the couch, her phone resting on her chest. A full ashtray sat on the floor next to her. Studying the room quickly, his eyes travelled from the living room to the kitchenette and down the narrow hallway, but Tasha was the only soul in sight.

"Where's my daughter?" Jake shouted.

Tasha sat up with a start. "Who?"

"Sam. My daughter. Where the fuck is she?"

Going from zero to ten, she yelled back, "Fool, I don't know what the hell you're going on about."

She made to stand up, but Jake stuck the gun in the middle of her chest and pushed her back down, pinning her to the cushion. "Don't mess with me. Tell me what you did with her."

"I don't know what you're talking about."

He pressed the barrel in harder. "Liar!"

"I'm not. So shoot me if you're going to shoot me."

From the set in her eyes, he wondered if she was telling the truth. He pulled the weapon back a few inches. "You didn't take her?"

Rubbing her sternum, she glared at him with hate-filled eyes. "That's what I've been trying to tell you since your white ass broke in here."

"Whatever." He moved towards the hallway. "I need to search your apartment to be sure."

"The hell you will, and you're paying for my door."

"The hell I am. That's payback for you framing me."

She jumped off the couch. "Fuck you. We're a long way from even— not until someone you love is dead."

A veil of red fell over Jake's eyes. He aimed the gun at her chest. "You better hope Sam is fine."

Her nostrils flared. "Or what. You'll kill me. Go ahead. You got away with murder once, and I'll bet you do it again."

"It wasn't murder." He shouted, "Leroy had a gun. He was going to shoot me."

"Only to protect himself. That letter warned him that the police were coming to kill him. I didn't believe it, but he did. Lot of good it did him."

"Mommy, who's here?"

A plump little girl stood at the threshold of the living room. She was wrapped in a towel; water droplets clung to her bare legs. Hastily, Jake lowered the pistol, but the girl still noticed it and screamed. Tasha ran to her, wrapping her arms around her daughter.

"Don't worry, baby. Everything will be all right."

"I'm scared, Mommy. Why does that man have a gun?"

Tasha shouted at Jake. "Just get out! Your damn daughter ain't here."

Jake shook his head. "I'm not going anywhere until I search this apartment."

"Fine, you crazy cracker. Look all you want. Then get the fuck out."

"Fine."

"And my daughter stays with me."

"Suit yourself." Jake didn't want the girl dialing 911 while they were in another room anyway. He said, "Lead the way."

Tasha strode down the hall, followed by her daughter, who cast a wary glance at Jake. He was pretty sure Sam wasn't here, but he needed to see this through. First, they led him to the girl's bedroom. Jake peered in from the doorway. The girl sat on the bed, clutching the towel close to her round dark body. Tasha hovered next to her. The room was small, with only space for a queen-sized mattress and a dresser with a television and gaming system across from the bed. Sam was nowhere in sight.

Tasha rested a hand on her hip. "Told you, yo' little girl ain't here."

"Open the closet."

"This is stupid," Tasha said as she opened the folding doors and stepped aside. The space was filled with pants, shirts, dresses, and shoes but not his daughter. The same was true for the other two bedrooms.

"Good. Now the bathroom," Jake said, backing down the hallway.

Reluctantly, the pair moved to the tiny bathroom, and Tasha pulled back the shower curtain, revealing a moldy shower with missing tiles. To keep a safe distance, Jake retreated to the adjoining living room while motioning them into the kitchen. "Show me the pantry."

Tasha pointed at a narrow door. "That closet. She don't fit in there."

"It's the last place she could be. So show me."

Tasha ripped the door open. "See. It's empty. Now leave us alone."

Jake did need to leave, but he didn't think he'd get another chance to question Tasha either. "Tell me more about Leroy's letter."

"Screw you."

Shrugging, Jake lied, "I might be able to help your son."

Tasha smiled a toothy grin. "All right, I'll tell you then— Leroy got a letter from a man saying he's the real silkworm rapist. But the police wanted to pin it on Leroy for some damn reason. So they were coming to murder him, and they's could blame the rapes on him, and he'd be dead and couldn't tell anyone the truth."

"Seriously?"

"Yes. But it made no damn sense. Then you pounded on the door, and we all know the rest."

During her speech, Jake had studied Tasha's body language closely. She didn't appear to be lying, but she was right; it made no damn sense. The letter would've cast doubt on Leroy's guilt, yet it was never cited amongst the evidence at the internal inquiry. Jake would've remembered. However, he believed that Tasha believed it existed.

Leaning against the counter that separated the two rooms, Jake asked, "What do you think happened to the letter?"

"I told you. They must have took it."

"Who's 'they'?"

"They is the old white rich dudes that are pulling the strings, keeping us in our place."

Thinking of Doyle and his benefactor, Jake nodded. "You could be right."

"I know I'm right." Tasha ripped open a kitchen drawer and pulled out a large shiny knife. She took a wild swipe at Jake. Her actions were crude. He easily jumped back; the blade missed him by a mile.

"That was stupid."

"All of this is stupid," Tasha growled, taking a step towards him. "I just want my son out of jail. And you're a liar. You can't help me."

Jake raised his gun, aiming it at the advancing woman. "Stop right there."

"Fuck you!" Tasha yelled, still waving the knife.

She was right. Jake couldn't help her. Besides, Tasha's stupid letter should be the least of Jake's worries. Sam was missing, and now he had no idea who took her and why. Without another word, he turned and ran out the broken door while Tasha screamed profanities, and her daughter silently cried.

Chapter 30

Sam woke up to a throbbing head. Groaning softly, she opened her eyes to find herself in a strange place— one she didn't recall entering of her own free will. How she came to be buckled into the passenger seat of a tiny car speeding down the freeway was a mystery to her. The last thing she remembered was picking up Chinese food for dinner at her dad's apartment.

Behind the wheel, a large man listened to a rock station while focusing on the road. The hem of Sam's dress had ridden up her leg, so she pulled it back down before bringing her hand to her head. A large bump protruded from her temple. When she pulled it away, luckily, there was no blood on her fingers. Luckier still, the driver didn't respond to her movements.

In the dim evening light, she could make out that he was a twenty-something Caucasian with short brown hair. He looked vaguely familiar, but she couldn't place him. It didn't matter; she didn't ask to be in this serial killer's car. He was probably taking her back to his lair, so he could make a costume out of her skin.

The car was moving pretty fast. She wasn't sure she'd survive if she jumped, but she had to take the chance. Quickly undoing her seatbelt, she tried to open the door. Damn! It was locked. She fumbled at the mechanism, but the driver grabbed her arm, pulling it away from the latch.

"Please, Sam! I don't want you to hurt yourself," the man said, turning to face her.

"How do you know my name?"

"It's me, Trent. Austin's older brother."

Trent? She'd only met him once or twice; he seemed like a normal guy who wouldn't kidnap someone. Obviously, she'd been wrong.

"What the hell, Trent? Where are you taking me?"

"Someplace safe."

"I was someplace safe. I think I was at my Dad's apartment."

"You don't remember what happened."

She searched her memory. "No."

He released her arm and turned his attention back to the road. "Well, you tripped off the curb and hit your head on my bumper."

From the road signs, she knew they headed out of the city. "And . . . you're taking me to a hospital?"

Staring straight ahead, he answered, "Not exactly."

The tiny hairs on her arm stood on end. Trent was really freaking her out. All she knew about him was that he'd been a football star himself until some horrific knee injury ended his career. Now he lived in his parent's basement, worked a dead-end job delivering pizzas, and kept odd hours. Which all added up to him being a serial killer.

Inching away from him, she asked, "Trent, did you help me hit my head?"

"No way," he answered too quickly.

"Can you please let me out of the car?"

His hands tightened on the wheel. "I can't."

This was insane. Sam had to do something. She lunged for the gear shifter, trying to knock it into neutral— like her dad had taught her. Trent snatched her small hand from the knob before she succeeded. Struggling against him only caused her knuckles to grind together. She cried out in pain but refused to give up the fight. With her free hand, she threw wild punches, hitting Trent in the face and shoulder. Their vehicle swerved out of its lane. Horns honked. She prayed people were copying down his license plate while dialing 911.

"Stop," he shouted.

"No."

"Please."

"Then let me go," Sam pleaded.

"I told you, I can't."

"Why are you doing this?"

"I'll explain, but I want to wait until we get there."

"Where, Trent? A secluded cabin in the woods where you'll rape and kill me."

He grimaced and let go of her hand. "No, I won't do that. Do you think I'm a monster?"

"You did kidnap me!"

"Not on purpose." His face contorted as if he was the one in pain. "Can't you trust me until we get to the cabin?"

Cabin! Sam had been right, but she had no intention of dying tonight. Diving at the gear shifter a second time, she managed to knock it into neutral. He cursed as the car lost momentum. With one hand still on the wheel, he locked onto the wrist closest to him before she could open her door and jump to freedom. Cursing, she jerked and twisted the limb but couldn't break free of his grasp. So she clawed at him, screaming, "Let go of me, you freak!"

"No." He steered the car into the breakdown lane. "You'll run away."

"Exactly. I won't let you kill me without a fight."

"Oh, Christ! Fine! I can see you won't stop until I tell you." He brought the car to a stop but kept a hold of her so she couldn't escape. "I have a plan to get Austin out of jail, and I need your help."

"Austin?" Pangs of guilt stabbed Sam in the gut.

"Yes. And if you still want to go after you hear it, then I'll drive you back to your dad's apartment."

Frowning, she said, "You swear?"

"On my mother's life." Trent ran a finger over his heart.

"All right. You have two minutes."

He heaved a sigh of relief and released her hand. "Thank you."

"But I don't see how I can help Austin. I'm not a lawyer."

"But your mom is one, and your grandfather is scheduled to be the judge at his trial."

"He is?"

"Yes." Trent shifted the car into park. "Austin said you were different than other girls. I hope so because he needs someone special right now. He called me this afternoon. His lawyer said they plan to charge him with a Class 1 Felony on Monday. If he's convicted, he'll be locked up for twenty years."

Sam gasped. "You're lying."

"I wish I was."

"I didn't know. No one told me anything," Sam said, slumping into her seat.

Trent's thumbs tapped the steering wheel with a jittery beat. "They offered him a plea deal. If he takes it, he could be out in five to eight years."

"That's too long. He can't take that deal."

"I know. His career would be ruined."

"Screw his career. A felony will ruin his life."

Fighting back tears, Trent punched the steering wheel, nearly ripping it from its base. "And it's all my fault. He got the pills from me. It should be me behind bars— not him. Austin has the future, and I'm the washed-up nobody. Just ask my dad."

Sam had been so preoccupied with her own problems that she assumed she hadn't heard from Austin because he'd been grounded after his release. At most, she thought he would have gotten community service and a hefty fine. Playing with the hem of her cotton dress, she said, "It's my fault too."

Trent nodded. "I heard that. But what I didn't hear was why you're not also in jail."

"It's kind of a long story."

"Let me guess. Your family got you off?"

Her voice was barely above a whisper. "Kind of."

"Figures."

She shifted uncomfortably in her seat. "I didn't ask them to do it. My family can be . . . over-bearing. I would gladly switch places with Austin if I could."

Trent's voice went up an octave. "Good. Then you'll help me?"

"It depends." Sam suspected Trent was a few sandwiches short of a picnic, and Austin's situation was not something you could wish away. "What do you have in mind?"

"Could you talk to your grandpa? Maybe he could convince the prosecutor on Austin's case to drop or reduce the charges. He's learned his lesson. There's no reason to destroy his career over some stupid mistake."

"I don't think he'll do that— Austin is not family."

Trent nodded in agreement. "I expected you to say that. Then we'll have to get more extreme."

"Extreme?" She felt guilty, but she wasn't sure Trent's scheme would get Austin released. And how would he react when she told him, no? Not well, she assumed.

"Yes. We have two days before Austin's hearing. How do you feel about putting the screws to your grandfather? I'm pretty sure one of your dad's neighbors saw us drive away. We could let them believe I kidnapped you, and I'm ransoming you for Austin's charges to be dropped. What do you say?"

Sam looked out her window at the growing darkness as a sense of dread crept up her spine. They didn't have to make up some story that Trent had kidnapped her. He had kidnapped her. However, she didn't want Austin's life to be ruined. They'd both had made mistakes, and Austin shouldn't have to pay for them all. She'd never forgive herself if he got sent to prison for twenty years. What Trent was asking her was absurd, but what choice did either of them have?

Needing more time to decide, Sam said, "Your plan sounds pretty half-baked."

Trent nodded. "True, but you could help me improve it."

"How? I'm just a kid. Where are we going to hide out while we wait to see if Austin will be released? You talked about some cabin in the woods."

He leaned towards her. "I did. My family's vacation cabin is perfect. No one will think to look for us there, and we're miles from anyone."

Her hand inched closer to the door latch. "But what if this plan doesn't work? What if Austin is still charged?"

"What do you mean?"

"Won't you be angry?"

"Yes. Definitely . . . " He scratched his head. "What? You'll think I'll hurt you."

"Well, you did knock me out and kidnapped me for real."

Trent threw his hands up in the air; they bounced off the roof of the small car. "I told you that you tripped. I freaked out when your neighbor started screaming, and I threw you in the car and drove away."

"So you didn't plan this ahead of time?"

"No. I swear."

"Then why were you in front of my dad's apartment?"

"Because I'd come to talk to your dad to see if he could help me, but he couldn't. Then I was just sitting there because I had nothing else to do since I got kicked out of the house. That's when I saw you. I figured it had to be fate."

Something about Trent's story sounded off to her, but Sam chose to ignore it. She really wanted to help Austin. She owed him. Austin stood by her when she'd gotten pregnant, and he'd never pressured her, even though he had more to lose than her. The decision had been hers to make, and now she made the decision to help Austin.

Sam was pretty sure Trent hadn't considered what would happen to the two of them when this was over. How would they cover up their lie? They couldn't. There would be consequences. Sam was willing to pay them, and she thought Trent was too, based on his earlier statements. But she still needed to know if she could trust him.

Sam took a deep breath and got ready to flee if he didn't respond correctly. "All right, your two minutes are more than up, and I'd like you to take me home."

"Really?"

"Yes. Sorry."

Trent sighed, "Ok. Buckle up." He started the car and looked over his shoulder to merge with traffic.

"You're really going to let me go? You could get into trouble."

"I know."

She laid a hand on his shoulder. "Trent, I needed to know if I could trust you, and you passed the test. Let's go to this cabin. I think your plan will work with a few modifications."

He pumped a fist in the air. "Thank you, Jesus."

"Save your prayers for later. We may really need them."

"You're probably right."

"And we should get this car off the road soon in case they have an Amber alert out on me. How soon until we are off the highway?"

"A little less than an hour."

Attaching her seat belt, she said, "Then you better step on it."

Chapter 31

Jake dropped behind the wheel of his car. He'd been so sure that Tasha had taken Sam to punish him. So sure, he'd kicked in her door, but obviously, he'd been horribly mistaken. But if not Tasha, then who? A random sociopath? Jake's insides turned to ice with that thought. Because they wouldn't find her alive if that was true.

Before he could plot his next move, his phone buzzed in his pocket. Hoping it was good news about Sam, or Sam herself, he answered it without looking at the caller ID. "Hello."

"Where the hell are you?" Doyle shouted through the receiver.

Jake cursed under his breath. "I'm in my car, driving to the scene."

"You should have been there an hour ago."

"I got stuck in traffic," Jake lied.

"Sure! What are you really doing?"

"I'm looking for my daughter. What the hell do you think I'm doing?"

"I don't believe you," Doyle yelled. "You think you can move Sam to another state and change her name, so we can't find her? Well, I tell you it's not going to work. I've got friends everywhere. We will find you."

"You're an idiot, Patrick. I wouldn't kidnap my own daughter."

"I'm not falling for your stupid act, Jake. This idiotic scheme has your desperate fingerprints all over it."

Jake groaned. "If I wanted to take Sam, I would have drugged her tonight and slipped away when no one was looking. You might think I am stupid, but I'm not dumb."

"Uhh . . . If you're not responsible, then who is?"

"I don't know. But after you get your foot out of your mouth, Patrick, could you tell me if the police still think an African-American woman abducted Sam?"

Doyle stuttered, "N . . . No . . . I just spoke with Katey. The police have another witness. Now they believe it was a tall Caucasian man driving a compact."

Jake's eyes went wide as he shifted the sweaty phone to his other ear. "Did he have a limp?"

"Yes, he did. How did you know that?" Doyle demanded.

"Sorry. I just arrived at the scene. I'll tell the detectives on-site."

"Jake! Don't you— "

"Bye, Patrick."

Jake disconnected and quickly processed this new information. A tall Caucasian man with a limp had kidnapped Sam. Trent fit that description to a tee, and he'd been hanging around Jake's apartment earlier in the day. Which left only one logical conclusion.

Trent had taken Sam.

But why? Was it a misguided attempt to save his brother by using Sam as a bargaining chip? The kid was stupid if he thought that would work. The system didn't work that way. The only thing he'd accomplish was getting himself killed. Who knew what he'd do to Sam in the process?

With that thought, Jake made a snap decision. He needed to find Trent and Sam before the police did. Like with Tasha, he couldn't trust his daughter's life to anyone but himself. Only he knew the people, the personalities, and the stakes involved. Jake was Sam's only hope.

Actually, Jake may get useful information from the detectives at the scene, but he couldn't stop. They'd want to question him. It would take hours before Jake would convince them he wasn't involved. That was not an option. Sam didn't have that kind of time.

At least, Jake should be one step ahead of the police with his ID of Trent. The boy couldn't have that many resources, and he seemed heavily influenced by his dad. Could the old man be involved too? It was plausible; he'd want Austin released as well. Which meant Jake needed to get to his parent's house as soon as possible.

With the phone number that Trent had given him, Jake hatched a plan, but he needed to remember Trent's last name to implement it. Jake racked his brains for the answer. What was it? Smith? No. Johnson? No. Wilson. Close. Pounding his forehead with his knuckles, the answer fell out like a brightly colored piece of bubble gum from a candy dispenser. Morrison. That was it.

However, before he could pull up Bo's phone number, Kate rang him. Against his better judgment, he accepted the call.

"Jake, what in the absolute fuck is going on?" she yelled into the phone.

"I wish I knew. What have the police told you?"

"They've told me shit."

"It's probably too soon. There's nothing to tell."

"Jake, tell me that you didn't have anything to do with it."

He exhaled loudly to keep himself from screaming.

"Jake?"

"I'm not going to waste my breath answering that."

"Did you!" Kate demanded.

"No!"

"Then tell me where you are at?"

From his parked car, Jake said, "I'm on my way to the crime scene now to see how I can help. Where are you, Kate?"

"At home. And it is killing me. But the detective told me to stay put in case Sam shows up here."

Jake ran his fingers through his hair. His scalp was damp with sweat. "Have you tried to call Sam?"

"Yes. A dozen times. Her phone must be turned off. It goes straight to voice mail."

"Figures."

Stifled sobs broke through the connection. "Jake, I don't know what I'll do if something happens to her."

"Don't talk like that. I'll bring our daughter home. I promise."

Between more tears, she said, "Thank you, Jake."

She ended the call. Jake held the phone at arm's length. He wasn't sure if he'd ever heard Kate cry before. But their daughter was in mortal danger. Kate's icy personality would return when Sam did. With the clock ticking, Jake hurriedly found the Morrison's number. It picked up after several rings.

A quiet voice, barely above a whisper, answered, "Morrison residence."

Jake cursed the time he wasted coming up with their name. "Hi, Mrs. Morrison. My name is Officer James of the Cook County District Court. I have some court documents that need your immediate attention. However, the clerk who wrote out the address made it impossible to read."

"Documents? Our address? One minute while I get my husband."

A gruff voice came on the phone. "Hello. Who is this?"

Jake repeated his made-up story in an *Aww Shucks* demeanor, but it did little to crack Mr. Morrison's tough facade.

"I don't understand. Why this isn't going through our lawyer?"

Nervously picking lint off his shirt, Jake said, "Sir, a copy is going to his lawyer, but a set needs to be received by you as well."

"What's in this document?"

"I'm not allowed to look at it. My job is only to deliver it."

"You sound a little old for a delivery boy."

"The truth of the matter is that I mistakenly let him go home early. And then I get stuck with this hot potato to deliver. Can't you help me out?" Jake asked.

"Fine. It's 740 Evergreen Terrace."

"Thank you."

"Thank me by getting here at a reasonable hour. We go to bed early in this house."

"I'll be there in twenty minutes." Jake disconnected and started the car.

Chapter 32

With the battery out of her phone, Sam fidgeted in the passenger seat like an addict craving her next fix. It had been her idea to remove their batteries, so they couldn't be tracked. However, now she wished she had the device to occupy her mind. Instead, she used the time in the car to think of ways to improve Trent's half-ass plan. Sam thought she could manipulate her family enough to pull it off, but it would require her to be at the top of her game.

Trent stole the occasional glance her way but mostly kept his eyes on the road. Subconsciously, she touched the bump on her head. The headache had faded to a dull throbbing. Checking the rear seats, she didn't see any of her stuff.

"Where's my bag? Or my purse, for that matter?"

He grimaced. "I think they got left on the sidewalk in front of your dad's apartment."

"You think?"

"I did leave them." He nodded. "In all the confusion, I must've forgotten to grab them. Did you need something out of them?"

"Yes. My head hurts, and there was Advil in my bag."

"Sorry. But I'm pretty sure there are some at the cabin."

She pulled at the hem of her short summer dress. Goosebumps raised on her legs; the material barely reached the middle of her thigh. It had been warm and sunny when she left the house, and she'd planned on changing into a comfortable pair of leggings and a t-shirt at her dad's place.

"My bag also had a change of clothes," she said, sounding whiny. "I doubt this is the best thing to go traipsing around the woods in."

Trent cast a sideways glance in her direction. "My mom has clothes at the cabin. They should fit you."

The two brothers looked very similar. After Austin filled out and lost some of his boyish features in a few years, he and Trent could pass for twins. Sam had never heard that Trent had a girlfriend, at least none that Austin ever mentioned. He was certainly handsome enough to have his pick of women.

Trent drummed his fingers on the steering wheel. "Thanks again for helping me with Austin."

"Don't thank me yet. We've got a lot of work ahead of us."

"True. But you must really like Austin to take this risk."

She thought about all they'd been through together. "I do. I like your brother a lot."

An uncomfortable silence grew between them after the declaration. Trent adjusted himself in his small seat and rubbed his knee. Stumbling over his words, he asked, "What are . . . your . . . plans for college?"

"I want to go to the School of Art Institute of Chicago."

"Art school in Chicago?"

"Yeah."

"Austin will probably be playing football for Michigan or Alabama."

She sighed, "I know. The distance will be hard."

"I'm sure you two can make it work."

Sam's head hurt too much to lie. "If I had to bet, we won't make it to Thanksgiving break our freshman year."

Trent whistled. "Wow. You're not pulling any punches."

"Sorry," she said with a shrug. "Austin and I have the perfect high school romance, but in college, our lives will go in two different directions. And there is no sense in trying to force it. I've seen it with my own parents, and there's no way I'd go through that a second time."

"Interesting."

The silence returned. Sam turned to the window and thought about love and all its complications. It seemed like it caused nothing but regret. Without asking for permission, she turned on the radio and found a station playing pop music to improve her mood. Tapping her foot to the beat, she asked, "Are we almost there?"

"Another half an hour, maybe a little more. I hope we get there before dark because the sunset on the water is breathtaking."

"Is it on Lake Michigan?"

He snickered. "The sun doesn't set on Lake Michigan— not from the Illinois shore."

"Oh, then what lake are we going to?"

"Nope. I want it to be a surprise."

"Fine. What can you tell me about it?"

"It's my favorite place on earth. When I die, I want them to spread my ashes there."

Changing stations on the radio, she said, "Let's not talk about death."

"You're right."

A new song came on. It was an older one that reminded Sam of Jake. "I wish I could call my Dad. I bet he's tearing the town apart looking for me."

"Not mine. He hasn't cared about me since I hurt my knee."

"That sucks."

"Yeah, he's kind of a jerk. He threw a footlocker into my fish tank after Austin was arrested."

Sam snorted. "That sounds like something my mom would do."

Trent said, "My dad pushed me hard to be the best. I was all-state in high school and all Big-Ten in college. There was talk that I'd go in the first round in the draft. I was so close to achieving his dream."

"His dream?"

"Did I say that? I meant my dream."

"If you say so," Sam said, picking lint off her dress. "My mom wants me to be a lawyer. That's her big dream for me. Sure, I could make a lot of money, but I don't care about that. I love painting."

"You must be pretty good at it if you're going to go to that Institute place."

"I don't know. We'll see what they think of my portfolio." Sam felt guilty that she wouldn't be working on it this weekend and more guilty for worrying about it and not Austin, so she quickly turned the conversation to Trent. "What do you like besides football?"

"Me?"

"Yes. What stuff interests you?"

Trent signaled and turned the car off the freeway as he chewed on his answer. "I've always liked animals. When I'm not working, I watch nature shows about mammals and lizards and stuff. My mom is allergic to dogs, but I guess I could get one since I'm on my own now. Maybe a black lab."

"Labs are good dogs." She committed the exit number to memory. "Did you study biology in college?"

"No. Communication."

The two lanes road was crowded on both sides with tall trees. Without streetlights, the turns were hard to see. She tried to memorize the route, but the complicated pattern of left and rights was impossible to remember. She sighed and turned back towards Trent.

"Austin told me about your injury. I'm sorry."

Nodding his head, he kept his eyes on the winding road. "Nothing to be sorry about unless you're secretly a two hundred and fifty-pound linebacker who plays for the Dolphins."

"Did you stay in classes afterward? You could have switched majors and become a veterinarian or something like that. Your dad had to have enough money that you didn't need the scholarship."

"He did. I could have . . . But I didn't. It was too depressing being around there, not being able to do what I used to do. I ended up dropping out, and one bad decision after another got me to where I am tonight. My dad didn't seem to care. He'd already switched all his focus to Austin."

"And your mom?"

"She's not that kind of mom. She worries that dinner was on the table, the house was clean, and that our clothes were washed and folded. She's not the type to cross my dad."

"My dad sticks up for me. He wants me to find my own path in life."

"Really?"

Sam said, "Yeah. Everything is black and white with my mom, which is tough. She was hard on my dad with the divorce, but he always tries to be there for me, even if I screw up."

"I'm always screwing up," Trent said with a laugh.

Sam smiled. "But things could turn around for you. My dad is getting his old job back as a detective in Chicago PD— I'm so happy for him. They never should've fired him in the first place."

"That's cool."

"It is." She laid a hand on Trent's arm. "And after we get through this, you should look into a job with animals. You could take classes to become a veterinary tech? You'd like that, wouldn't you?"

"I would, but I couldn't afford them. I'll be stuck delivering pizzas for the rest of my life."

"I bet it's not that expensive."

"Maybe," Trent said, turning into a dark driveway. "We're here."

"Now, are you going to tell me, where's here?" Sam asked.

Trent shut off the engine. "Get out, and I'll show you."

Chapter 33

Jake knocked on the Morrison's front door. He'd have expected a nicer home for someone who'd played professional football. However, in Bo's defense, he'd been in the league before the astronomical contracts of today's athletes. Still, in Jake's opinion, if Bo had invested wisely, he wouldn't have to sit at every autograph show that passed through town.

An attractive woman opened the door. "Can I help you?"

Jake gave her his best smile. "Mrs. Morrison?"

"Yes," she answered timidly.

"Hi, I'm –"

A large voice bellowed from behind her. "Is it that court officer?"

"I'm not sure."

The door was yanked out of her grasp, and a hulking brute nudged the small woman aside. "Yeah?"

"Hi Mr. Morrison, we spoke on the phone."

"Let's hurry it up. Do I need to sign for these papers or what?"

Jake took a step closer, sticking out his hand. "Sorry, Mr. Morrison. I wasn't exactly truthful with you on the phone. I'm not an officer of the court, and there are no documents, but I really need to talk to you."

He frowned. "I don't know what you're trying to pull, but I don't like being lied to. Good night."

The door started to swing shut in Jake's face, but he stopped it with the palm of his hand. "Please! Give me five minutes of your time. What I have to say could save your son's life."

Groaning, Mr. Morrison reopened the door. "How can you possibly help him?"

"My name is Jakob Bryant."

"Bryant?"

"Yes. My daughter, Sam, is dating your son Austin."

"Oh!" The big man stuck out his hand. "Bo. Bo Morrison. I've met your wife."

"Ex-wife. But I thought I would stop by and let you know I used to work with Chicago PD, and I've helped plenty of kids in your son's predicament," Jake lied.

Jake's hand looked like a child's inside his. He could feel the raw strength in his grip. Stepping aside, he ushered Jake in. The house was immaculately clean, though outdated. Bo led him onto a living room with pink walls dominated by floral print couches and Hummel figurines on every flat surface. Falling into a sofa, Bo gestured for Jake to take a seat in a chair. Mrs. Morrison hovered in the doorway, wringing her fingers into a complicated sailor's knot.

"Great. Barbara, can you get Jake some coffee or tea or a soda? What do you want?"

She smiled, turning to Jake, obviously happy for a task to perform.

Jake said, "No. I'm good."

"Fine. I'll take a cup of coffee. Decaf," Bo grumbled.

Barbara had barely left the room when Bo pointed a thick finger at Jake. "Let me start by saying, I heard your daughter got off scot-free. And truth be told, I'm pissed. Fucking pissed. Here, your daughter is bouncing around after she was the one who got caught with the pills, while my son is left to rot in jail. It's not fair. Do you realize how good of a quarterback he is?"

It wasn't fair, and Jake knew it. "Yes. I've heard Austin is a pretty good quarterback."

"Pretty good? He has pro potential, and I'm not just saying that. Scouts have evaluated him. There isn't a Division I school in the country that doesn't want him next year."

"That's impressive."

"You're God damn right it is. So, I hope you're here to tell me you can work the same magic with Austin that got your daughter's charges dismissed?"

The room suddenly felt very warm. Jake pulled at his collar. "The thing is— "

Damn it. He'd screwed up. Jake should have been more specific about which of the man's sons Jake could save. If Bo was as violent in real life as he was on the football field, this could get ugly quick. Scanning the room, Jake made a note of all the exits and potential weapons. The Hummel statues wouldn't do much damage unless Jake could throw them in the giant's mouth when he bellowed.

Bo said, "Is it a money thing? Just tell me the price. Whatever it is, I'll pay it."

"It's not about money."

"Then what is it? I might not have the legal connections your family has, but I'm pretty famous in town. Do you want Bears or Cubs tickets?"

"Sorry."

"Don't tell me you're a White Sox fan."

"God, no."

"Then out with it, Jake. What's your price?"

"I don't want anything from you."

"You're a man of honor. I like that. Not many of those around today." Bo nodded. "Good. So, how soon can we have Austin home?"

Jake leaned forward in his seat. "The truth is that I'm here to save . . . Umm, Trent."

A shadow fell across Bo's face. "Oh, him."

Barbara walked into the room with Bo's coffee and a tray of cookies. He shooed her away. "I've changed my mind. Get that crap out of here."

"Yes, dear." She turned on her heels and left the room.

Bo's brow pinched. "I don't care about Trent. He's dead to me. The boy is a stain on my good name."

"You can't be serious."

"I am. Now, if you'll excuse me, it's getting late." Bo stood up; his joints popped like popcorn in a microwave.

Jake remained in his chair. "Wait!"

"What!"

"You don't understand. Trent kidnapped my daughter, and I think he plans to ransom her for Austin's release."

"I don't believe you. The boy's not smart enough for something like that."

"It's true. An eyewitness identified him."

Bo tilted his head back and laughed. "Well, I'll be damned. Maybe he is worth something."

Jake gritted his teeth as his whole body shook with rage. "You don't get it. This isn't going to end well for him— or Sam. Do you want to lose both your sons?"

"I already have!"

"But I don't want to lose my daughter."

"That's not my problem."

Jake stood up; his hands clenched at his sides. "At least tell me where Trent might've taken her?"

Bo smiled while leading Jake to the door. "All I know is he's not here. I kicked the loser out days ago."

"You don't know where he went?"

Bo shook his head. "Nope."

"Please! Can you just take a second and think?"

"Why?"

"Because Trent's stupid plan won't get Austin out."

Bo put a hand on Jake's shoulder and pushed him outside. "We'll see about that."

The door slammed shut along with any hope of finding Sam.

Chapter 34

Mary sat on the porch swing, rocking back and forth nervously. The red wine in her glass sloshed from side to side but never spilled. An empty wicker chair stood next to her, despite the fact it was a beautiful spring evening. The kids should be enjoying it, instead of inside on their devices, but tonight she didn't mind the solitude. Mary wouldn't be able to hold up her end of the conversation; her thoughts were on Jake.

Worrying about her friend was a nice distraction from her own problems. Of which, there were so many. Bills. Upkeep on the house. The kid's mental well-being. Her own. And that nagging dread that she was missing something important— a shadow hanging over her family. But tonight, Mary couldn't shake the feeling that Jake was in serious trouble.

Mary had tried calling him, but Jake hadn't picked up. Which was fine; he was an adult. She was probably being stupid. He could be spending time with Sam, or asleep on the couch, or working at a new job. He didn't need to check in with her. She wasn't his mother.

Staring out into the night, she finished her wine and set the glass down on the porch. Her hand moved towards her phone, but she pulled it to her chest, resisting the urge to call Jake again. Two minutes later, she sighed, retrieved her phone from the seat cushion, and dialed Jake's number. It rang and rang before going to voice mail. She hung up without leaving a message. He'd see the missed call in his notifications. Besides, what would she say?

Mary considered getting another glass of wine from the kitchen when a big truck stopped in front, backed up, and then pulled into her driveway. The headlights splashed across the yard, landing on her. She froze. Her heart pounded in her chest as she jumped to her feet. She took a step towards the door. Paused. And involuntarily took another out of fright. Stop! She was acting silly. Jake had promised the motorcycle gang would leave her alone, and Mary was in arm's reach of her house. What could possibly happen to her here?

The big V8 engine shut off, blanketing the neighborhood in an unnerving silence. The truck door swung open, and a dark figure emerged from the cab. A gruff voice said, "Mary?"

"Yes?" She reached behind her for the door handle, but her feet remained rooted to the porch. She couldn't will them into motion as her brain raced through a hundred horrible scenarios.

The wide man approached her with an object in his hand. His heavy boots slapped against the pavement. He said, "I was surprised to find you out here."

"Err . . . "

Bobby stepped into the porch light, a six-pack of beer at his side. "Mary, are you all right?"

She released a breath that she hadn't realized she was holding. "Yes. Sorry. You scared me."

His mouth twisted to the side. "My bad. I guess I should've called first."

"No. I was being stupid. Who would want to hurt me anyway?"

Bobby's face stayed contorted. "Well, you are a woman sitting alone in the dark. Maybe, you should get a dog."

She laughed. "That's all I need— one more thing to take care of."

"I guess." Bobby shrugged. "Do you want some company?"

Mary returned to the swing. "I'd love some company. Pull up a seat."

"Great. I had this feeling that you needed a friend tonight." Bobby eased himself into the wicker chair.

"You did?"

"Yeah, it was weird. It was like fate was pulling me here."

"Fate . . . I've had that feeling too. Like we all have unfinished business together."

"All?" Bobby asked.

"Me, you, Jake. Have you heard from him tonight?"

"No. Why?"

Mary shook her head. "No reason."

Bobby held up a bottle of beer. "Do you want one?"

Mary looked at her empty wine glass and considered the long walk to the kitchen to refill it. She was pretty comfortable here— content enough to drink a beer. Mary took the offered bottle after Bobby twisted the cap for her. "Thanks."

"No problem. I almost didn't stop, not sure if you were already asleep, but then I saw you on the porch."

"I'm glad. We haven't had a chance to talk, just the two of us, since . . . "

". . . Since?" Bobby asked.

"Umm . . . since you got Tom's watch back."

"Yeah. That."

Mary reached over and patted Bobby's knee. "Thank you for all you did. I'd really meant to visit when you got out of the hospital, but I got . . . busy."

Bobby shifted uncomfortably in his seat. The wicker groaned underneath him. "Don't worry about it. You have a lot on your plate right now."

"And I'm so sorry you got shot."

"That was Rick's fault. Not yours."

"I know, but somebody should apologize. Has anyone seen or heard from Rick?"

"God, no. If he showed his face around here again, the Devil's Hand would put a bullet in it."

Mary took a sip of her beer. "I'm surprised they weren't mad at you and Jake as well, that Sonny seemed like a tough customer."

"Ahh . . . Jake didn't tell you about that?"

Mary raised an eyebrow. "No."

"Oops." Bobby took a big swig of his beer.

"What didn't Jake tell me?"

"Nothing."

"Bobby!"

"All right, but you can't tell him that I told you."

"I won't."

He wiped the sweat from his brow even though the night was chilly. "You see— Sonny was pissed! He'd lost over a million dollars in heroin with no way of finding Rick. Plus, Sonny had DNA evidence on Jake for Caleb's murder. So Sonny blackmailed Jake into owing the club a favor."

"What kind of favor?"

"I don't know. Just a favor."

"Would they ask Jake to kill someone?"

"Probably not."

Mary bit her lip. "But, Sonny could."

"I guess." Bobby downed the rest of his beer and opened another one.

Poor Jake. Mary wanted to throw up. The guy couldn't catch a break. No wonder he'd omitted that part of the story. She hadn't asked Jake to do what he did, but she did feel better knowing that the monster was off the streets. Yet, Jake was paying the price for her piece of mind. He should have told her, but she wasn't surprised that he hadn't. He'd always felt protective of her.

Since high school, they had a special bond, like a brother and sister— except for that one night, the biggest mistake of her life. It had been super weird for a time, but they eventually got past it. She'd almost convinced herself it hadn't happened until Jake brought it up again after finding Tom's watch on Caleb's wrist. Damn it, Jake. Why? There was no way that Emma was his; anyone who looked at her could see she was Tom's daughter.

Mary finished her beer and wiped a hand across her mouth. "Is there anything else Jake didn't tell me?"

"Umm . . . No."

"Bobby!"

"Mary. Please don't."

She held up the empty bottle. "I'll beat it out of you if I have to."

"Fine. I'm sure it was nothing, but Caleb . . ., the guy who killed Tom, said that it wasn't an accident that he ran into Tom that morning. He said that Tom had a contract out on him."

"A contract?"

Bobby shrugged. "A hit. Someone wanted him dead."

"Seriously?" The bottle almost fell from Mary's hand. Bobby's response had been the last thing she had expected. It would have been more probable if he'd said Tom was an alien.

"It was crazy talk."

"So you didn't believe him?"

"No. Caleb was trying to distract us, so he could escape. It didn't work, but you asked. And I didn't want to lie to you, but I'm positive it was a bunch of malarkey."

"Well, thank you for telling me the truth. Is there anything else?"

"No, that's it. I swear." Bobby used a finger to trace a cross over his chest.

"Good," Mary said, slumping back in her seat.

"Are you all right?"

"I'm fine."

Bobby asked, "Are you sure?"

"Yes. But I don't think I can handle anything else tonight." Her brain felt like it had short-circuited. It would be days before she could process all that Bobby had revealed.

"Can you handle another beer?"

"I can do that."

Before she could reach it, Mary's phone buzzed loudly on the swing next to her. Bobby's phone repeated the same annoying noise. It wasn't Mary's usual tone. Both phones shrieked again.

"That's weird," Mary said, checking her screen.

The alarm was an Amber alert. Mary almost tossed the phone down, but the victim's name caught her eye. Sam. Sam Bryant from Chicago, Illinois.

"Are you reading what I'm reading?" Bobby asked.

"I am." The phone shook in her hand.

Bobby said, "What the fuck?"

Mary immediately called Jake, but he didn't answer. Again.

Chapter 35

Dejected, Jake stood on the sidewalk facing the street. Night had descended on Chicago while he had wasted his time seeking Bo's help. Jake would've liked nothing better than to pound that egomaniac to a bloody pulp, but he'd have to save that for another day. Sam needed him to keep his head. Let Bo live with his regrets; Jake needed to do everything he could to save his child.

But first, Jake needed to find her.

Trent couldn't keep Sam in his car— there would be an APB on his vehicle. And he couldn't take Sam to a motel— people in neighboring rooms could hear Sam's cries for help. Furthermore, a friend wouldn't want to be a party to multiple felonies, so that was out too. Besides, Jake suspected from the look on Bo's face that he knew exactly where Trent had gone.

Jake could go back inside and demand answers, but Bo obviously wanted Trent's scheme to play out on the off-chance Austin would be released. Asshole. There was a lot more at stake than a precious football career with all its riches.

Riches! An idea hit Jake like a lightning bolt. Perhaps Bo owned more property than this modest home. That would explain its size as well as Bo's caginess. Maybe a hunting cabin, a lake house, or some unoccupied rental property. A place like that would be an ideal hideout for Trent.

If it existed, Jake might get the address with Steve Hill's assistance. However, Doyle had most likely steered the investigation in Jake's direction. For Sam's sake, Jake could call in old favors, but Hill may still say no, and Jake wouldn't blame him. Hill would be compromised, helping a fugitive from the law. Jake's only hope was the investigation was rightly focused on Trent and not him.

Before Jake could pull his phone from his pocket, someone called his name. He looked around but couldn't find the source in the dark. It called out again. The voice sounded feminine, definitely not Bo after a change of heart.

Like a fawn stepping out of the forest, Barbara timidly came around the corner of the house. She noted the closed front door and waved Jake over to the shadows. If not for the seriousness of the situation, the whole scene would be comical.

Jake followed her to the side of the house. "Is everything all right, Barbara?"

With her voice barely above a whisper, she said, "You must forgive my husband. He can let his temper get the best of him, but he means well."

"Means well?" Jake chuckled. "He's willing to write off Trent and my daughter to save Austin."

"I know. I'm sorry." She wrapped her arms tight around her midsection.

"And I'm sorry about Austin! But ignoring Trent's actions will only make this worse. Do you understand that?" Jake's voice had an edge sharper than a razor.

Barbara shrunk away from him. "Yes."

Cursing, Jake knew he'd screwed up. If he wanted Barbara's help, Jake would have to treat her better than Bo. He softened his voice. "You'll have to excuse me, but I guess my emotions get the better of me too."

"It's fine."

"Thank you. Did you hear my conversation with your husband?"

She nodded. "I was listening."

"Then you know Trent is in big trouble. Sam too. Will you help me?"

"I don't know how I can."

Jake touched the back of her arm. "I just need information."

Not pulling away, Barbara asked, "What kind of information?"

"Do you know where Trent would take Sam?"

She looked down at her feet. "No."

"Please. You can tell me. Bo doesn't need to know."

"He doesn't?"

"No. He doesn't. You love both your sons, right?"

She stifled a small sob. "Of course."

"I know you do. You're a great mother."

"I try."

"And I try to be a good father— I love my daughter unconditionally, no matter what she's done."

"We all make mistakes." Barbara cleared her throat. "I was pregnant with Trent before we were married too."

Barbara probably didn't get much human interaction outside of her family, so Jake ignored the weak association to Sam's problem. There was no point in correcting her and losing ground again. He said, "I can save Trent. I just need to get there before the police. They'll storm in and kill him. Do you know where he went?"

Barbara shuddered. "I might have a guess."

Jake leaned in close, their noses almost touching. "Where?"

She looked away. "I shouldn't."

"Please! I'm just so worried about Sam. She's all I have."

"Your daughter's a real sweetheart. Austin is very smitten with her."

"Then you'll tell me?"

"I don't know."

"Please! Does Bo own another home, possibly a cabin or a lake house somewhere? I could find it in the tax records, but every minute could count tonight."

The seconds ticked by as Barbara shifted her weight from foot to foot. Jake resisted the urge to shake the answer out of her. Finally, she said, "It's a cottage on a small lake. You won't find it in the records. It's not in my husband's name."

"Whose name is it in?"

"It's still in his Mother's. She passed away years ago, but he and his brother left things the way they were."

His heart wanted to leap out of his chest. "What's her name?"

"Mabel Morrison."

Committing the name to memory, he asked, "Does the lake have a name? What town is it in? Is it in Illinois?"

She looked anxiously towards the house before she responded. "I don't think it has a name. It's not much bigger than a pond, but it is near Fox Lake, just this side of the Wisconsin border. It's been in the family forever. They all love it. I hate it. It's way too buggy and dirty for me."

Forgetting himself, Jake grabbed Barbara by the shoulders and hugged her. She didn't pull away. Jake wondered when the last time she had truly spoken her mind. "Is there anything else you can tell me about the cottage?"

"Only that it's very hard to find. People get lost all the time."

"Any landmarks I can use to help me?"

Scrunching up her face, she said. "Sorry. I never paid attention."

"I get it," Jake said, turning to leave.

"Wait! You promised not to tell my husband."

Jake held up his hand, the palm out. "Bo will never know."

"Good. Can you promise me something else?"

"What?"

With eyes bigger than a puppy, she said, "Promise me, you'll bring my Trent home too."

He shouldn't make that promise. Sam was his top priority, but his mouth opened, and the words spilled out. "I promise."

Barbara smiled and fled back into the shadows while Jake raced to his car. As he put the key in the ignition, his phone chirped loudly in his pocket. Checking the screen, Jake read the inevitable message— an Amber alert for Sam. Luckily, the license plate listed was not Jake's, so he could still move freely. But unluckily for them all, the plate was probably Trent's, which would ramp up the pressure on him.

Jake wasn't lying when he said that every minute would count tonight. And now the clock was ticking. He gunned the engine and dropped the car into gear. The tires chirped on the pavement as he sped away.

Chapter 36

Moonlight reflected off the lake's surface like a funhouse mirror. The shoreline was vacant except for towering pines and the Morrison's cottage. There wasn't another building for miles. Nor a person. The frogs croaked loudly, alerting the lake's denizens of the new two-legged intruders.

Sam exclaimed, "Oh my God. It's beautiful."

"I told you."

"Does the lake have a name?"

"I don't think there is a legal name. My family always called it Morrison Lake."

Slapping a mosquito on her arm, Sam said, "Sounds a little vain. I would've called it Pretty Lake."

"Pretty Lake isn't very unique. If we were going to call it something else, we should've called it Bass Lake. Or Moon Lake for all the times I went skinny-dipping as a kid."

Sam walked to the end of the weathered dock as Trent trailed after her. The dock swayed under their combined weight. Squatting down, she touched the cool water; ripples cascaded out from her finger. Trent stayed a few feet behind her, his arms by his side.

"Can I put my feet in the water?" she asked.

Trent shrugged. "Knock yourself out."

"Are there any creatures I need to worry about?"

"No. We killed the last alligator a year ago."

"Alligator!"

She jumped back while Trent doubled over with laughter. His cackles bounced off the trees on the opposite shore. She felt stupid but could blame her overreaction on bad horror movies. Still, the thought of an alligator clamping down on her foot sent a shiver up her spine. If the reptile went into a death roll, its long jaw would rip her leg clean off.

"Jerk." She scooped up water with a cupped hand and tossed it at Trent.

Laughing harder, he wiped the moisture from his face. "Sorry. The worst thing in this lake is Walter, an old largemouth who may nibble on your toes."

"It better not, or I'll scream," she said, kicking off her sandals.

"Won't matter. We're all alone out here."

"I see that. The isolation should help with our plan." Sam no longer feared Trent. He reminded her of a puppy dog who hadn't grown into his body yet.

She held her skirt to the back of her thighs and sat down quickly. Her thong would offer little protection from the aged wood, and she didn't want to pick splinters out of her butt for the rest of the night. Furthermore, a strong breeze could give Trent another reason to rename the lake. Smirking at her private joke, she dipped her feet into the lake. The water felt cold but refreshing. Trent removed his socks and shoes before rolling up his pants. He sat down next to her, keeping some space between them.

He asked, "So do you have a new plan?"

"I'm still working on the details."

"Good, because I'm more of a big picture guy."

For a while, they sat in silence. Sam tried to let the tranquil location calm her nerves, but the idea of manipulating her family haunted her thoughts. Her mom and grandfather dealt with liars every day, so Sam would have to pull off an Oscar-winning performance for their scheme to work. Next to her, Trent smacked at the back of his neck. The blood-smeared remnants of a mosquito stuck to the palm of his hand, and he dipped it in the lake to clean it off.

"Anything yet?" Trent asked.

"Nope."

Trent said, "Couldn't we call your Grandpa and tell him that if Austin isn't released in the next twenty-four hours, he'll get pieces of you in the mail, like an ear."

"Are you sacrificing one of yours?"

He brought his hand to his head. "Umm . . . No."

"Well, don't look at me either."

But Trent was right; calling her Grandpa was their best chance of saving Austin. Sam was his only grandchild— his sole genetic legacy. Therefore, she knew he'd move heaven and earth to rescue her. Still, she was extremely nervous because there was a major problem with their plan. One problem, she couldn't find a way around.

"I don't think either of us has to surrender a body part— but there will have to be a sacrificial lamb if we want to free Austin."

"A what?"

"Umm . . . a scapegoat, a pawn, someone who sacrifices themselves for the greater good."

"Oh! Like when you're the quarterback running a triple option, and the linebacker reads inside."

"I guess, sure."

Trent nodded. "So I need to take the hit?"

"Will you?"

"I won't mind if Austin gets released. I assumed that's what would happen. A witness saw me take you, and they probably got my license plate, so the police will know it was me. There's no way around that."

She touched the side of his arm. "Are you sure?"

"Yes. I'd do anything for Austin."

"All right. That gives me something to work with. I think we'll use your idea but change it up a bit."

"How?"

She kicked her feet back and forth in the water, causing larger ripples. "How many people know about this place?"

"My family. A few friends. Not many people. Why?"

"Would the police know to look for us here?"

"I don't think so. Not unless my parents told them. It's still in my grandparent's name. Some kind of living trust thing. My Dad tried to explain it to me once, but it went over my head."

"Then we should be safe for a few days?"

"Yes," he said before casting a wary glance behind them.

"Good. I'll call my grandpa's cell phone and tell him that you're ransoming me for Austin's release. And that you want proof that it was done legally with a formal announcement from the DA."

"Shouldn't I make the call, let him know I mean business?" he asked.

Sam had doubts on Trent's acting abilities. He was not Zac Efron or Ryan Reynolds by any stretch of the imagination. He was more like a Golden Retriever; dependable, brave, and a little slow.

"No. If I really play it up with tears and tell him you'll hurt me or worse unless the charges against Austin are dropped, I bet he'll do it. As long as he gets to take his anger out on someone, he should be happy."

"And that someone will be me?"

Sucking in a breath, she said, "Yes. I'm afraid so."

"But you think it'll work?"

"I'd say the odds are better than fifty percent."

"I'll take those odds. Let's do it." He clapped his hands together.

The sound echoed across the lake as Trent stood up. Sam's empty stomach churned, threatening to eat itself from the inside. Their odds were probably less than fifty percent, and as low as twenty, but they were in too deep. If she backed out now, Trent wouldn't be in any less trouble, and Austin's life would still be ruined, so there was no sense procrastinating.

Keeping a hand on her skirt, Sam pushed herself up. The water puddled off her feet and onto the dock boards. It reflected in the moonlight like iridescent paint. She retrieved her phone from a shallow pocket and reattached the battery. The device powered up, a beacon in the night for every bug within a half-mile.

As she went through her contact list, the phone buzzed in her hand. She jumped, nearly dropping it in the lake. An image of her father came across the screen. Her thumb hovered over the red icon to decline the call when an idea struck her like a bolt of lightning.

Sam said, "I'm going to change things up. I'll trick my dad into helping us."

Trent shook his head. "I don't think that is a good idea."

"Trust me. I don't like it either, but this will improve our odds. My grandfather hates my dad."

She composed herself before accepting the call. Trent leaned in closer as she brought the phone to her ear. With a trembling voice, she said, "Daddy?"

"Oh my God, Sam. Are you all right?"

"I guess."

"Did Austin's brother take you?"

"Yes. Trent kidnapped me."

"Did he hurt you?"

"Not yet, but he will if Austin doesn't get released from jail."

"What?" Jake screamed.

Feeling unsteady on her feet, she whimpered, "Please! Talk to Grandpa. Trent says it has to look completely legal, like what Grandpa did with my fake prescription."

"I don't think he'll do that. He's pissed off and looking for blood."

"I know you, Dad. You'll think of a way to convince him."

"Ok, I'll try."

She sighed with relief. "Dad, I have to go."

"Wait, Sam! Why did you have your phone if you're being held hostage?"

Sweat broke out in Sam's armpits. Turning to Trent, she knew instantly that he'd be no help in fabricating an excuse. She stuttered, "B . . b . . because he gave it back to me to make the ransom demands when you called. He has a knife to my throat, but I answered it anyway."

Trent exhaled quietly next to her.

"Do you know your location?" Jake quickly asked.

"No."

"Are you at a lake?"

She froze. How could he possibly know where she was? Her mouth flapped up and down, but no words came out, luckily. He'd see through her lies. Trent hesitated and then grabbed the phone from her.

"This is Trent. We spoke earlier, but now I mean business. Austin gets released so that he never has to go back to prison. Make it legal and such, or you never see your daughter again, except in pieces."

"If you hurt her, I'll kill you."

"No. No, you won't. You're not calling the shots here. I am. Talk to me that way again, and Sam will suffer greatly. Do we understand each other?"

Jake made an audible groan. "Yes."

"Good. We'll call you in two hours. Austin better be free or else!"

"That's not enough time to– "

Trent disconnected.

Sam gave him a thumbs up. "That was awesome."

"Cool. Should we call your grandfather now?"

"No. Let's wait and see what my dad can do."

Chapter 37

The moon peeked out from behind the clouds as Jake pulled into the parking lot of Chestnut Towers, the luxurious new residence of his old friend. A person he prayed would help him despite their past. The drive hadn't given him enough time to calm down from Sam's phone call, so he took a moment to collect his thoughts before climbing out of the car.

Having only a vague location of the cabin, Jake was already in trouble. But now that he had two hours to convince Doyle to meet Trent's ransom demands, Jake was completely screwed.

A rational man would release Austin, the consequences be damned. But that response would draw attention to his judicial record and possibly expose his corruption. Doyle valued himself and his precious reputation too much to allow that. However, Jake had a plan to force Doyle's hand.

The exterior door to the building was locked, as Jake had expected. A gold-plated panel of call buttons was set into the wall. It was an outdated feature on an otherwise fancy high rise. Not wanting to tip her off to his arrival, Jake pressed all the little black switches in the first row. A voice came over the intercom, but Jake didn't respond. Several seconds later, the latch to the door clicked. He pounced on the handle and wrenched the door open.

Inside the lobby, a frumpy woman in a turquoise tracksuit stood by a row of mailboxes. A yappy little Shih Tzu circled her ankles. The dog's hair was so long it could pass for a member of ZZ Top. It strained against its sparkly leash, barking and gnashing its teeth.

'Sampson, heel," the woman said, eyeing Jake suspiciously.

Damn! Why did there have to be a busy body in the lobby? He gave Tracksuit a friendly smile and said, "Good evening, Ma'am."

"Good evening."

The scrutiny continued as he scanned the mailboxes. Thank god he'd decided to leave his weapon in the car. This woman would have noticed the bulge in the small of his back, for sure. Luckily, Jake found the appropriate name alongside number 1501 on the top floor, just as advertised. He stepped over to the elevator and pressed the button. It took longer than he liked, but eventually, the elevator binged with its arrival. Jake wasted no time getting inside.

"Stop right there." Sampson yanked his owner forward as she stretched out her free hand.

"Ma'am, don't worry about it. Your dog is fine."

She shook her head. "I wasn't talking to Sampson. I was talking to you."

"Me?"

"Yes." Wedging a foot in the door, Tracksuit kept the elevator from closing. "I saw you on the news."

Jake's pulse quickened. "I don't think so."

"Yes. There was an Amber alert for that cute little red-headed girl, Susan. You and another guy were listed as suspects. Your name is John Billings, right?"

"No. It's not," Jake said, trying to maintain a straight face. It was just his luck that she'd seen the Amber alert.

"I don't believe you." She pulled a phone from her pocket while Sampson attached himself to Jake's pant leg. "I'm going to call the police."

If Jake took the woman's phone and punted her yappy dog across the lobby, he could escape, but that would only make things worse. Doyle had to be to blame for adding Jake's name to the Amber Alert. Yet, Jake avoiding the detectives couldn't have helped his cause either. Thank God, the woman had his name wrong. He might be able to buy himself enough time to finish his task before the police caught up with him.

"My name is Jakob Bryant, not John Billings. I swear."

She shook her head. "But you look just like the man on the television."

Trying to appear unfazed, he shrugged nonchalantly. "I get mistaken for people all the time. I must have a very common-looking face."

"All right. Show me some ID," she demanded, returning her phone to her pocket.

"My, you're very brave," he said, extracting his wallet. "Because if you're right, I'm a dangerous fugitive."

"I'm not worried. I've taken several self-defense classes, so I'd crush you like a grape." She fell into a martial arts stance before snatching the ID from his hand. She studied his driver's license information and frowned.

"Satisfied?"

"I guess, but you look exactly like the guy on the television."

Jake took his wallet back. "Then I'll better be on the lookout for my evil twin."

Looking down at the floor, she said, "Sorry, but five years ago, my niece went missing, and they never found her. I take these things seriously."

"I understand. Where did it happen?"

"Right here in Chicago." Her eyes remained downcast, but she did remove her foot from the elevator door. "She was a sweet, sweet girl."

"I'm sorry for your loss."

"Thank you." She reeled in her dog and headed back to the mailboxes.

"Bye, Sampson."

The Shih Tzu growled his farewell while Jake hit the button for the top floor. The elevator ascended with a lurch, forcing his gut downwards. With the woman and her dog behind him, his thoughts turned to the real reason for this side trip. He prayed she had kept his bag, but it had been ten years and another apartment ago, so it was just as likely she'd thrown it out.

The elevator slowed, and his rolling belly moved up into his chest, next to his thumping heart. The polished metal doors slid apart, and Jake stepped into the beige-colored hallway. The floor held four apartments. The door to 1501 stood at the end of the hall, next to a tall window that provided a gorgeous view of Lake Michigan.

Sam's only hope rested inside this penthouse, so he pushed aside his nerves and knocked on the door. The sound echoed through the empty hallway. Light footsteps approached. The latch turned, and the door opened.

"Why are you knocking? Did you forget your key?"

Smiling, Jake said, "I think you have the wrong guy."

Maureen O'Malley jumped back like she'd seen a ghost. "Jake! Oh, Jesus. What are you doing here?"

Chapter 38

Jake said, "I need your help."

Maureen hung on the side of the door. "You do? After all this time?"

"Can I come in?"

Maureen considered his question like it was a story problem involving two trains traveling in opposite directions. She stuck out her bottom lip while she performed the calculation. He used the time to soak in her good looks. Maureen was still gorgeous. Her raven black hair cascaded in beautiful ringlets past her shoulders. She wore a silky green robe that contrasted nicely with her milky white skin. The long legs and full bosom brought back fond memories.

He gave her a boyish grin. "Please."

"I guess." She released the door and stepped aside.

Jake considered giving her a hug but didn't want to appear too forward. She escorted him into the apartment, gesturing towards a leather couch. He took a seat on the edge of the cushion, his elbows resting on his knees. She stood across the room from him, her arms crossed at her chest. If anything, she'd gotten more beautiful with age, adding weight in all the right places.

"You look great."

She smiled. "Thanks. You too."

"Nice place you have here."

"How did you find me?"

"Did you forget?" Jake shrugged. "I used to be a detective."

Maureen raised an eyebrow.

"And when I was at O'Malley's, Shane let it slip."

"Figures. He always talked too much."

Jake held up a hand. "Don't hold it against him."

"No worries. We have our own problems. Besides, you were one of his best customers, at least until you dumped me."

"I still feel terrible about what happened. I'm sorry. I was a jerk."

She tightened the tie on her robe. "It was for the best."

He gave her a tiny nod in agreement. "So I hear you're not waitressing anymore?"

"It got old. I buy and sell stuff online now," she said, pointing to brown cardboard boxes lining one wall. Packaging material lay under the window, along with computer printouts and shipping labels.

"Sounds interesting."

"Not really, but it passes the time. I lose money at it, but my boyfriend subsidizes my hobby along with paying for this place."

Moving to the chair across from Jake, she perched on the armrest. Her robe rode up, revealing a toned thigh and the bottom half of a butt cheek. His breath caught in his throat as he tried not to stare. Her butt had been one of the best things he'd ever laid a hand on. She noticed him looking and tugged her robe down.

Jake tried to act surprised. "Boyfriend?"

"Yes, boyfriend. I hope you didn't think I'd sit around pining for you."

"Not at all. A great woman like you, I figured you'd be married with a house full of kids."

"No." Her pale blue eyes glistened. "That wasn't in the cards. I guess I'm not wife material."

"Stop. You are— "

"Anyway!" Maureen stood up, glancing towards the door. "He should be here any minute, and I don't think he'll like finding you here."

She was right. There was no reason to bring up old history; Sam was his top priority. Jake stood up and rubbed his hands together. "Well, then let me get to the reason I dropped by. Did you keep my overnight bag?"

She raised an eyebrow. "And why would I do that?"

"Umm . . . I was hoping . . . the last night we were together at your old place, I left it behind. It had clothes and some papers. Do you have it?"

She snorted. "Me? Keep your old bag after all these years?"

"I wouldn't blame you if you threw it away. Did you?"

She looked down at the floor and back up at him sheepishly. "I might have kept it."

"Thank God. You don't know how important this is."

Grinning, she said, "I'm pretty sure it is in my bedroom closet."

He took a step towards her. "Then can I have it back?"

"Sure. It's yours. Follow me, but we should hurry."

"No problem. I'm already late for another engagement." He followed her to the back of the apartment.

She looked over her shoulder. "You are?"

"With my daughter."

"Oh."

The bedroom held a king-sized bed, a dresser, a chest, and two nightstands. She went to the closet and flung open the slatted doors. Getting down on all fours, she dug past an extensive collection of shoes. The silk robe rode up again, revealing matching green panties that covered a perfect peach of a butt. She cursed as clothes still on their hangers toppled onto her back. "Can you give me a hand over here?"

"Are you sure?"

She laughed nervously. "Sorry. I must be giving you quite a view, but we are in a hurry, or I would've put pants on."

"And it's nothing I haven't seen before," Jake added with an uneasy chuckle.

"True."

Jake removed the shirts and pants from her back and rehung them. She continued her digging in the closet while he averted his eyes when suddenly squeals came from the rear of the closet. So much for Jake dodging his perverted thoughts.

"I found it. I knew I still had it," she shrieked.

Maureen backed out, dragging his old duffel bag with her. She handed it to Jake and then adjusted her robe, ensuring she was properly covered. Working open the zipper, he heaved a huge sigh of relief. Everything was still there, a change of clothes, deodorant, a toothbrush, and a manila folder. His heart pounded in his chest as he opened the folder; inside was a thick stack of papers full of numbers. Whew! Doyle would have to release Austin, and Trent wouldn't have to harm Sam.

Holding the bag up, he said, "I can't thank you enough."

"No probl— " A key scraped in the apartment door, and the words died on Maureen's lips.

Jake said, "Is that the— "

"Shit! He's here."

"It'll be fine." He put a hand on her shoulder. "I'm just an old friend who stopped by to say hello."

She jerked free from his grasp. "No. You don't understand. He'll kill you if he finds you here."

"Seriously?"

"Yes. He has a terrible temper." She pushed him across the bedroom. "You need to get in the closet."

"No. I have to go," Jake pleaded.

"Please! Give me five minutes. I'll distract him, and you can sneak out."

Jake allowed himself to be pushed into the closet. The doors closed inches from his face. Maureen had saved the day, but there was no way he was waiting that long. Jake hissed, "Three minutes!"

Maureen didn't respond as she raced from the room. He did his best not to move around and rattle the clothes hangers behind him. Jake felt like a coward hiding in here. He tried to push aside this feeling because letting Maureen deceive her boyfriend was the quickest path to saving Sam. But Jake's ego was still dented.

At first, he couldn't hear anything, but eventually, he could hear voices though he couldn't make out the words. Jake waited, but nothing happened. Would Maureen give him a signal when it was safe to leave? The seconds ticked by. He wasn't claustrophobic, but the closet felt like it was closing in around him. He had to resort to counting apples to gauge the time since he'd make noise if he reached for his phone.

After what had been easily three minutes, he considered exiting the closet. This was taking too long— Sam needed him. Maybe he could pretend to be with Building Maintenance, and he'd answered a call to fix a leaky faucet. But where were his tools? In his duffle bag? No, that wouldn't work; any self-respecting handyman would use a toolbox.

The hell with it, Jake would just make a run for it. Though Shane had suggested the boyfriend was an athlete who might easily chase Jake down. Damn it!

As Jake was crafting a different escape plan, he heard the voices enter the bedroom. Quietly shifting forward, he brought his ear to the slats in the door.

Maureen asked, "How about you run a bath for us while I mix you a drink?"

A gruff voice answered. "A bath? I might get a call from work. I can't show up looking like a wet dog."

"Then can you run it for me?"

"Grrr . . . Can't we just make love? I could really use the release after the stunt that asshole pulled."

Jake thought the voice sounded familiar, but he couldn't place it. Was he a news anchor, perhaps?

Maureen said, "He's not an asshole."

"I hope you still don't have a soft spot for him," the mystery man growled. It was followed by a slap. Jake assumed it was a hand connecting with Maureen's curvy behind.

"No. I was a dumb kid."

"Well, you're not a dumb kid anymore."

"You're right. I'm not, which is why I'm with you. So draw me that bath while I pour you a double, and then you can wash my lady bits?"

"I told you I don't want to get wet."

Jake's back twitched from contorting around the clothes. He leaned slowly backward to relieve the pressure, but the hangers still made an audible metallic groan on their racks. The man didn't react, but he thought he heard Maureen suck in her breath.

"Silly, you don't have to get in. But I want you to get me all sudsy, and afterward . . . if it slips into the wrong spot . . . then, oh well!"

"Really?"

She said, "Really."

"You've never let me do that before."

"Then I guess tonight's your lucky night."

Jake ground his teeth together. Maureen was offering him the moon, literally, for Jake's escape. She said, "That should relieve some stress, right?"

Footsteps moved quickly across the room. "I'll start the water and add plenty of bubbles."

"And I'll get that drink."

In the bathroom, the faucet turned on with a loud rush of water. Jake waited a few seconds and then pushed on the center of the doors. They cracked apart with a squeak. Mo's face appeared in the opening, startling him. She pulled the doors apart, and he breathed in the fresh air.

Putting a finger to her lips, she whispered. "Come on. Hurry."

He followed her from the room, the duffle bag held protectively at his side. A bright light shone out of the bathroom, revealing a white countertop and toilet. But no man, the tub was hidden behind the partially open door. Pulling him by his shirtsleeve, Mo hastened their escape. They both broke into a hurried walk. It was all for naught; they only made it as far as the hallway.

A guttural scream stopped them in their tracks. "Jesus fucking Christ! You have another man in my apartment!"

Jake placed the voice. Slowly, he turned to face his old friend and future boss, Steve Hill.

Chapter 39

Steve Hill's jaw dropped when he recognized Jake. "What the hell are you doing here?"

"I could ask you the same thing," Jake said as vomit rose up in his throat. Maureen was sleeping with Hill's old wrinkly ass. Gross!

"Mo's with me now. And what does it matter, you guys were long over?"

"But she's half your age. She could be your daughter."

Hill glared at Jake. "Shouldn't you be searching for your own daughter and not trying to get back in Mo's pants?"

Taking a step towards the door, Jake said, "Trust me. That was the last thing on my mind. What's in this bag is part of Sam's ransom."

Hill took two steps of his own. "Did the kidnapper contact you?"

"Yes. On my cell."

"And what were the demands?" Hill asked.

"That's between me, Judge Doyle, and the kidnapper."

"Doyle? Fine. He'll tell m—"

"He'll tell you what?"

Hill shook his head. "And the bag was here with Mo?"

"Don't blame her. I asked Maureen to keep it for me," Jake lied.

"In my apartment!"

"I didn't know it was your place."

"Fine. Tell me, what's in the bag?" Hill asked.

The puzzle pieces fell into place. Why had Jake not seen it before now? Hill was not Jake's friend, not even close. Worse, he was in Doyle's pocket. How else could Hill afford this apartment along with his own house and two alimony payments? He couldn't. Not on a commander's salary.

"No. I need to go." Jake took another step.

"Stop right where you are, Jake. You're listed on the Amber Alert. I'm legally bound to detain you."

"Why am I on the Amber Alert? You know me. I would never take Sam."

Hill shook his head. "Do I, Jake? Sam was kidnapped right after you forfeited paternity. You pull a disappearing act and won't contact the detectives. It'll be best if you can come into the station until this gets sorted out."

"I can't do that, Steve."

"We'll see."

Hill's hand shot to his side, but he found only air, the shoulder holster already discarded for his tryst. A practiced mask covered Hill's true emotions, and he gave Jake a big smile. His hands held up in a display of surrender. With another tentative step, he closed the distance between them. "Come on, Jake. Work with me here. Just tell me what's in the bag?"

Jake retreated. "First, tell me how long?"

"I got with Mo long after you two split up."

Shaking his head, Jake said, "No, not that. How long have you been on Doyle's payroll?"

Hill's face scrunched up. "I don't work for Doyle."

"I know you're lying. How long?"

"Grrr . . . When we became partners."

"You son of a bitch!"

The total picture came into focus. Jake was so stupid. Doyle had been manipulating events from the start. Why else would Hill send Jake into a crazed gunman's house without backup? Why would Hill offer Jake his dream job, but in the worst part of town? Because Doyle was orchestrating everything, so eventually, Jake would wind up dead, but it would look like a horrible accident.

Mo stepped in front of Hill. "Steven, what is going on? You work for the Chicago PD."

Jake used her distraction to race down the hallway and into the living room. Instead of exiting the apartment, he went straight for Hill's jacket. He found it along with his sidearm resting on the back of a kitchen chair. Mo squealed like a train whistle as heavy footsteps pounded down the hall. Jake ripped the pistol from the holster and aimed it at Hill's chest, stopping him in his tracks. The adrenalin and the short run caused the older man's face to turn red.

Hill shouted, "Don't do anything stupid, Jake."

"Why shouldn't I kill you?" Jake said. "You've set me up with Leroy."

Hill grimaced. "I don't know what you're talking about."

"Yes, you do. And I bet you took the letter."

"What letter?"

"The letter that warned Leroy the police would murder him. That's why he pulled a gun on me. Now, sit down, or I swear I'll shoot you in the face."

Maureen gasped but kept her distance from them both.

Breathing loudly, Hill moved to the couch and sat on the armrest. "If there was a letter, I didn't take it. I wouldn't be surprised if Tasha made the whole thing up. I hear she is a crack head."

Everything that came out of his mouth was a lie, of course, he would claim a Tasha was a drug addict. Jake kept the weapon trained on Hill's head. "Shut up! I don't believe you. You ruined my life."

"God, you're vain, Jake. Destroying your career was only one of my assignments. And you made it so easy. I just needed to nudge you in the right direction. Provoke you, a little. You're such an impulsive asshole; it was only a matter of time before you hung yourself."

"Fuck you!"

Hill laughed. "Now what's in the bag?"

"I'll tell you," Jake said. "But I want your boss on the phone. He needs to hear it too, and I don't want to repeat myself."

"Which boss?"

"You're not funny. We both know I meant the Honorable Judge Doyle."

"My phone is in my jacket."

Jake leaned over and extracted the device from an inside pocket. Hill said, "Give it to me. I can find his number faster."

"Do you think I'm stupid? You'll call 911. Just tell me your code."

Hill did, and Jake unlocked the device. He scrolled through his contacts and found Doyle's number. Putting it on speaker, he set the phone on the coffee table between them. A loud ringing noise filled the room.

"Hello."

Hill said, "Hi, Patrick."

"Do you have any news about Sam?"

"Unfortunately, I don't. But I do have Jake here with me."

"You found him. Where was the son of a bitch hiding?"

"Umm . . . I found him under a rock. Jake says he's in contact with the kidnappers, and they'll swap Sam for the contents of a mysterious bag that is in his possession."

Doyle asked, "And Jake's with you right now?"

"Yes, you're on speaker."

"Jake?"

"Hi, Patrick. How's it going?"

Doyle's voice crackled loudly in the phone's speaker. "Don't play games with me, Jake. We all know you're behind this, and somehow you got that other Morrison boy involved."

Jake jabbed a finger at the disembodied voice. "I'm not playing games. And for the last time, I'm not involved in Sam's kidnapping. Trent is acting alone."

"Bullshit! Steve arrest this idiot. But not before you beat Sam's location out of him."

With the weapon still pointed at Hill's face, Jake said, "No, he won't. I have Hill's weapon. I'm in charge here."

"What the hell? How could you let this happen?"

Hill replied sheepishly, "It wasn't my fault. Jake surprised me at my girlfriend's apartment."

"You really fucked me, Steve," Doyle said.

"I know."

Jake yelled, "Don't blame him. You fucked yourself, Patrick because I have your undoctored tax documents."

"You what?"

Smiling, Jake said, "Yes. I still have the ones you thought were destroyed. The ones that prove you were getting kickbacks to fill the juvenile detention centers."

"It's not possible. You're lying."

"Sorry. It's true."

"Let Hill look at them."

Jake unzipped the bag and pulled out the files. Jake stayed out of arm's reach and awkwardly flipped through the document with one hand while aiming the weapon with the other.

"It looks like a tax return," Hill said. "And it has your personal information on it."

"Jesus Christ, Hill! You really fucked up," Doyle shouted.

"Me? You're the one who let Jake get them, asshole!"

Jake returned the file to the bag and moved back across the room. "All right. Good. Now that we can agree, I hold all the cards here. You're going to listen to me and do exactly what I say, right, Patrick?"

No answer.

"Right!"

"Yes," Doyle hissed.

"Great. I want you to tell the authorities I had nothing to do with Sam's kidnapping and have me taken off the Amber alert."

"Fine."

"After that, you'll have the charges against Austin Morrison dropped."

"What?"

"You heard me," Jake said. "That is Trent's one demand if we want Sam released unharmed."

There was a long delay before Doyle responded, "You know I can't do that."

Chapter 40

Jake said, "You can. And you will."

"Even if I could," Doyle replied. "It's logistically impossible."

"Nothing is impossible. Don't you want to save your granddaughter's life?"

"I do. But the boy was selling drugs to children!"

"It was a few pills. It shouldn't cost him the next ten years of his life."

"That's the law."

"You've broken all kinds of laws, Patrick. You should be locked up twice as long, and yet you're still free."

"I've done n— "

"Shut up!" Jake shouted, "You're going to call the prosecutor and get Austin released, or I'll drop these documents off at the Attorney General's office. I'm sure he'd love to take you down."

Doyle unleashed a string of obscenities. After he ran through every cuss word, Doyle said, "You wouldn't dare. I'll ruin you."

"Go ahead. I only care about Sam. Once she's safe, I'll give you the files. Then you can destroy them and me."

Maureen gasped but remained on the opposite side of the room, shifting her attention between the two men and the phone as Hill said, "Wait! Maybe we don't have to go to such extremes. Did the kidnapper give you any clues on where he was keeping your daughter?"

"He didn't," Jake lied, suspecting Hill would ask that question. Hill would call in the SWAT team, and the night would end in a bloodbath, the exact thing Jake had fought to prevent. "So we have only one option. Give Trent what he wants."

"Fine." Leaning forward, Hill cleared his throat. "But I have a lot to lose here too. How do we know that you'll do what you say, Jake?"

"You'll have to trust me."

"Do you swear on your daughter's life?" Hill asked.

Jake shook his head. "Haven't I already?"

"True."

"Bullshit," Doyle snarled. "I'm not doing anything until I personally talk with Sam."

"That's not going to happen." Jake looked down at the clock on the wall. "We have an hour to meet Trent's demands, and you're wasting time posturing like a peacock."

"Me? You're the one posturing."

Hill moved to a couch cushion and crossed his legs. "Patrick, stop. I agree with Jake. You need to get the boy released. It's the smart move for you and your granddaughter."

"You can't be serious. You're taking Jake's side?"

"No. I'm taking MY side. I have no intention of going to jail. Do you really want the Attorney General looking into your bank accounts? I'm sure he'll find my payouts for the last twenty years. Or your case history? How many kids have you had locked up that didn't deserve a harsh sentence? Fifty? A hundred? Let's get through tonight, and then we can worry about Jake."

Jake's hand tightened around the gun. He'd shoot Hill right here if it wasn't for Maureen. The bastards would double-cross Jake the first chance they got. Jake knew that, without a doubt, but he'd be ready for them.

Snarling, Doyle said, "Fine! Maybe I can get Austin out."

"Maybe?"

"I will get him out."

"You better, or it's your ass," Jake said.

Doyle said, "Don't threaten me. I will."

"Good." Hill nodded. "That's the smart move, Patrick. You won't regret this."

"If my business associate hears that I've been compromised, we'll all regret this deal. By the way, Steven, did your girlfriend hear any of this conversation?"

"No. She's in the other room." Hill said as he frowned at Maureen.

"Are you sure?"

Jake snorted. "Don't worry about her? You need to focus on Austin's release. Because if you don't call me in the next hour, then I'll be paying a visit to the Attorney General's office. Are we clear?"

"Yes," Doyle mumbled.

"What?" Jake asked to emphasize his point.

"Austin will be released tonight."

Jake ended the call and headed for the door, high on emotions of anger, fear, and hope. Maureen remained in her spot on the far wall, but Hill jumped up from the couch. "Stop! You can't take my gun."

Removing the magazine and ejecting the round from the chamber, Jake tossed the empty weapon across the room at Hill. "Here, but I want you to remember that if I lose Sam, I'll have nothing left. I'll burn everything to the ground, and I won't care who I bring down with me."

Hill glared back at Jake. "I understand."

"Good, and if you're smart, you'll stay here tonight and have Maureen make you another drink." Jake slammed the door behind him and ran down the hallway. He dropped Hill's clip in the potted plant before he jumped on the elevator.

Chapter 41

Trent rocked in his chair while he watched Sam prepare their modest meal. "I'm so hungry I could eat a dead rhino's ass."

"I hope my cooking tastes better than that." Sam poured the powdered cheese onto the macaroni noodles. Without any milk in the cabin, she'd used bottled water instead. An old stick of butter that she'd deemed unspoiled had also found its way into the pot. It wouldn't be great, but it should be better than a deceased animal.

Trent asked, "But how will we know?"

"I'll pass. But if you can find a rhinoceros, you can have your own taste-test."

"No, silly. I mean, how will we know when Austin is released?"

She stirred the concoction with a large wooden spoon. "I assume my dad will call and leave a message with an update for the next time we power up my phone."

"And you think your dad can pull it off?"

"I do," she said with a tiny smile. "Where are the bowls?"

Trent pointed to a cupboard to her left. She pulled out two and scooped half of the macaroni into each one. Not asking, she found the silverware drawer by trial and error and got them each a fork. He licked his lips as the bowl was set down in front of him.

"Thank you."

"You're welcome."

Sam pulled out the chair opposite him and sat down. She had been hungrier than she thought and finished before Trent. Too bad the lone pack of hotdogs was freezer burned. They shared a sleeve of stale crackers and a jar of peanut butter for dessert, but Sam was still hungry afterward. Trent rummaged in the cupboards but came up empty.

From the fridge, Trent held up a beer. "Do you want one?"

"I don't like beer."

"No?"

"I think it tastes like piss."

Closing the fridge door, Trent said, "You know what piss tastes like?"

She rolled her eyes. "Shut up. You're the one who wanted to eat a dead rhino's ass."

He laughed and set a water bottle down on the table for her. Falling into his chair, he took a long pull on the beer while rubbing his knee. "Where did you learn how to cook?"

"Robert, my step-father, does a lot of the cooking now, but before that, I had a nanny. I was a picky kid, and I didn't eat much, but I'd eat mac and cheese. Rosalie taught me how to make it with real cheese."

"Why didn't your mom make dinner for the family?" Trent asked.

She snorted loudly. "Duh, you know she's a big-time prosecutor. She would always get home late, stressed out, and grumpy. No time for anything else. That's why I don't want to be a lawyer."

"Right, you want to be an artist." Trent finished his beer and stifled a belch. "What type of art do you do?"

"Painting. Mostly still life and landscapes." She practically bounced in her seat as she responded. It pained her that she didn't have her supplies with her. The scenery here would have provided some wonderful landscapes to paint while they waited for their answer on Austin.

"I'd like to see them sometime."

She smiled. "Really?"

"Yeah." Trent nodded as he peeled the label off his empty bottle with his thumbnail. "Is there much money in being an artist?"

"Not really, but I don't care. Give me a paintbrush and a blank canvas, and I'm happy. Even meals like tonight don't scare me. Five years from now, I picture myself living in a drafty loft with a mattress on the floor, wearing second-hand clothes but with my work in a show at a fancy gallery."

"You're definitely not the type of girl that Austin usually dates."

"We turned a lot of heads in the beginning."

"How did you two end up together?"

"I don't know. It just kind of happened. He sat behind me in math class, and we would talk. He was nice, not like those other jock jerks. Then one day, he asked me on a date. We went to the movies and out for ice cream. The rest is history."

"I'm glad. He deserves someone like you. For however long."

A pang of guilt stabbed Sam in her side. "No, he deserves better. I got him into this mess."

He leaned back in his chair and stretched out his bad leg. "Hey! I'm responsible too, but we're doing everything we can to fix it, right?"

"Yes, you're right."

Sam never would have thought she'd be with Trent on the lam with a crazy plan to spring Austin from prison. It was like something out of a movie. Hopefully, this story would have a happy ending. Pushing her bowl in Trent's direction, she said, "And since we are in this together, how about you clean up?"

A quizzical look crossed Trent's face like she had asked him to perform brain surgery. From Austin, she knew their mother never let the men in her life lift a finger in the kitchen, but Trent should be capable of washing their flatware and placing it in a drying rack.

Hesitantly, he stood up. "I guess that's fair."

Sam watched as Trent found dish soap and a dried-out sponge under the sink. He hummed while he scrubbed at the orange cheese residue. Looking back at her over his shoulder, he asked, "So what's next?"

She was afraid he'd ask that. She didn't like being the leader of this operation. "I don't know."

Trent took the pot from the stovetop. The cleaning brush banged around inside the pot, clearing away the last of the cheese. Trent ran water inside it and checked for any residual food. He said, "Maybe we should turn back on your phone. It's almost ten o'clock."

"Probably," Sam agreed.

Reaching across the table, she grabbed her phone and replaced the battery. The phone powered up with a series of beeps, and the provider's icon danced across the tiny screen. After a minute, the phone finished its initialization, and she checked her voice mail, but there were no messages. She said, "Damn. Nothing."

"Should you try calling him quick?" Trent set the bowls and forks along with the pot in the drying rack and returned to the table.

"I guess." Sam dialed his number, putting it on speaker.

Her dad answered on the second ring. "Honey. Oh, my God. Are you Ok?"

"Yes. I'm fine."

From the background noise, she could tell Jake was in the car.

"He hasn't hurt you, has he?"

Trent leaned over the receiver and shouted, "Not yet, but I'll hurt her bad if Austin isn't out? Is he out?"

"Austin will be out by morning. So you better not harm a hair on Sam's head, or you'll regret it. That's a promise."

Trent let out a growl. "And you better not be lying, or we'll all have regrets."

Sam grimaced but knew Trent's theatrics were necessary if their ploy was to be taken seriously.

Jake said, "I'm not lying. Sam's grandfather is working on Austin's release as we speak."

"Good."

"How do you want to handle the transfer?" Jake asked.

"Transfer?"

"Yes. The trade. Austin for Sam."

Trent's face went blank as Sam's mouth fell open. She should have thought of that eventuality, but they'd been too focused on Austin's release. Shoot. The seconds ticked by. Without paper and pencil, she had no way to give Trent a silent recommendation.

Stammering, he said, "T... They'll be no transfer. Put Austin in a cab. Make sure he gets his phone back, and that it's charged up. Don't follow him. When he's safe, he's to call me, and I'll set Sam free."

"No way. We don't release Austin until I have Sam with me unharmed."

Sounding like he was the Joker, Trent laughed with manic glee. "I told you. You're not calling the shots here. I am."

"I'm warning you if— "

"Good night, Mr. Bryant."

"Don't hang up!" Jake cried out.

Sam ended the call, impressed with Trent's act.

Quickly, she removed the battery and set the phone aside. They'd talked for less than a minute, but she felt exhausted, mentally and physically. "God, I hate this. But it's the only way, right?"

Trent nodded. "Right."

She exhaled loudly, rubbing her temples. Her head hurt again, and acid bubbled in her stomach. "I hope he doesn't kill me when this is all over."

Trent shook his head. "If he's going to kill anyone, it'll be me."

"No. I won't let him. I promise." She smiled nervously at Trent as she pretended to hold it together on the inside.

Chapter 42

"Damn it!"

Even though it had been an hour since the call, Trent's laugh still echoed in Jake's head, scaring him. Animals and people were always dangerous when they were cornered. Adding to Jake's frustration, he'd been driving in circles looking for the stupid cabin.

GPS was no use in this neck of the woods, and Barbara's directions had been sketchy at best. Why had Jake thought he could find it on his own? There were a hundred little lakes in this corner of Illinois. Had he expected to see a neon sign at the end of their driveway announcing the location?

"Fuck!" Jake came to what he thought were the same crossroads he'd passed twenty minutes ago. Yet, a convenience store with two gas pumps magically appeared in the distance. Maybe he hadn't been down this section of road before, but Jake swore he had. Hopefully, the clerk could give him directions to the Morrison's cabin if he played his cards right. Jake signaled and turned into the station.

A truck that had been following him at a distance drove on, never slowing. Good. Earlier, it hadn't gone around him even when Jake had slowed down, which was worrisome. Though in the other driver's defense, the roads were narrow and twisting. Still Jake waited until the taillights faded into the night before he got out. It was better to be safe than sorry. Doyle could have more crooked cops on his payroll.

Pulling open the glass door, a buzzer announced Jake's presence. An elderly woman looked up from a newspaper. She sat on a wide wooden stool. A red and black flannel shirt covered her generous frame. Gray frizzy hair sat askew on top of a plump face. She reminded Jake of a mad witch complete with bulging eyes and a hairy wart on her cheek.

Jake gave her his best smile. "Good evening."

"Evening." She replied, turning back to the paper.

The store was empty except for the two of them. On top of a small refrigerator advertising bait, an old-style boom box played a sad country song. She didn't give Jake a second look as he went to the back cooler to retrieve a bottle of Coke Zero. After grabbing a giant-sized candy bar and a bag of corn chips, he headed to the counter. Avoiding her reading material, he set his items off to the side.

He asked, "Interesting story?"

"Not really." She eased off the stool and folded up her paper with much ceremony.

The scanner beeped with each item as she rang him up. The woman reminded Jake of an actor in a movie, but the exact character slipped away through his fingers like an eel. Worse, the clerk caught Jake studying her and frowned.

"That'll be eight dollars and fifty-seven cents."

The price seemed exuberant for road snacks, but he bit his tongue and handed over a ten-dollar bill. "Slow night?"

She let out a tiny snort as she handed him back his change. "Yeah. We don't get busy until summer. That's when all the city slickers trash the lakes in their fancy boats and buy up all my beer. Nightcrawlers too. The idiots could find them in their yard for free."

She laughed at her own joke as she put his candy bar and chips in a small paper bag and slid it across the counter. Jake laughed along with her. She smiled and returned to her stool, grabbing a fresh section of newspaper.

Jake turned to leave but stopped halfway to the exit. "I hear that Bo Morrison has a place around here."

"Who?" she asked with a voice gravelly from years of smoking.

"Bo Morrison. You know, the NFL star who played for the Dolphins. I'm a big fan. If you can believe it, I played against him in high school."

"Never heard of him." She answered curtly and quickly looked down at her paper.

The lie was evident.

With his hand resting on the door, he shrugged. "I understand that you don't want to tell me for privacy reasons. I'd do the same thing in your position."

She ran a hand through her wavy gray hair. "Listen, Mister, I don't know who you're talking about. But if you had an address of a house you couldn't find, then I might be able to help ya."

"You would?"

Looking at him suspiciously, she said, "Yes."

He let go of the handle and returned to the counter. "I don't have Bo's address, but I really am his friend."

She shook her head. "I don't believe you. A lot of fellers come in here claiming that."

"So you do know Bo?"

She frowned.

"I swear, I just talked to Mr. Morrison earlier tonight. Along with his demure wife, Barbara, and his older boy, Trent."

The frown deepened. "If you're his friend, then why don't you know the address?"

Sticking out his hand, he said, "I should have introduced myself. Hi, I'm Jakob Bryant."

Annoyed, she shook his hand like it was a rotten piece of fruit.

"Anyway, my daughter Sam is dating Bo's youngest boy, Austin. They're normally good kids, but the two of them ran off for the weekend to do what kids do. Now, Bo is trying to protect his son, and I'm trying to do the same thing because girls have a lot more to lose. Am I right?"

Her head nodded slowly.

Jake continued, "You know teenagers. They can make some pretty stupid decisions when they're in love. Heck, we did the same thing at their age. Barbara and I are pretty sure they ran up here for the weekend, but she didn't do a real good job with her directions. I've been up and down this road at least three times. But that is so Barbara, am I right?"

The old woman smiled.

Jake leaned an elbow on the counter, making sure to not wrinkle her paper. "Do you have kids?"

"Three. Two girls and a boy. They are all grown and have kids of their own."

"Then you know what I am talking about, and I'm sure you did everything possible to protect them."

She sat up straighter. "I still am. Why do you think I'm working here at this late hour? Because one of them needs my help with diapers and formula. I tell you, a mother's job is never done."

Slapping the counter, Jake said, "Exactly! From the moment I walked through that door, I told myself that you were a good person. And I just knew that you would help me. So, for my daughter's sake, do you think that you could give me directions to their cabin?"

"I don't know."

"Please, from one parent to another!"

Her eyes bored into him. "Your daughter is really dating Bo's son?"

"If you had a bible, I'd swear on it. You got one?"

"Not here."

"Well, I swear."

She looked to the door, but they were still alone. "You're close, but you never would have found it."

"I was afraid of that."

"You need to make a right out of here, go down a half-mile, and turn left. After about two miles, drive really slow and look for a turnoff on your right. Are you with me so far?"

"I think so," Jake said. "Right, Left, drive two miles, then another right."

"You got it. The last right is tricky. Without a sign, it's easy to miss, plus the driveway is hidden between a pair of trees. One of them was nearly split in two by lightning. I think Bo lets the drive be overgrown on purpose."

"I would if I were him."

Nodding her head, she said, "His place is at the end of that lane. You can't miss it. A log cabin right on the lake."

"I can't thank you enough." He pulled out his wallet and rifled through the bills, laying two twenties on the counter.

She pushed the cash back towards him. "I can't take your money."

"It's not for you. It's for your kid, the one that needs it. Us parents have to stick together." He walked to the door with his drink and snacks.

"My daughter thanks you," she called after him.

Half out the door, he said, "I never caught your name?"

"Marge. People call me Large Marge."

"It was nice meeting you, Marge."

Holding up the bills, she said, "You won't rat me out, will you? Bo spends a lot of money in here."

"I wouldn't dream of it," he yelled as the door shut behind him.

Climbing into his car, he tore open the Snickers bar and ate it in three giant bites. The chocolate gave his system a jolt adding to his good fortune. After a sip of the pop, he started the car and made a right out of the station.

Before Jake made the left turn, he looked over his shoulder and found the store's lights had been turned off. Marge must have decided to close for the night. Who could blame her? It was the slow season, and she'd just made a quick forty bucks.

The only thing behind Jake was a pair of headlights off in the distance.

Chapter 43

The trunk of the large oak was split almost in two. It was a wonder it was still standing, but the driveway was just past it like Marge had foretold. Jake never would have found it without her help. The witchy clerk was a lifesaver.

Jake doused the headlights and parked the car behind a trio of scrub pines. He retrieved his weapon from the glove box. The weight of the pistol felt good in his hand. He didn't want to use it tonight, but it would be better to have it and not need it than the alternative. Slipping out the door, he closed it as silently and quickly as he could to extinguish the interior lights. The trees should have concealed his arrival, but he inched his way to the end of the driveway and watched for a response.

None came. Not that he could see or hear.

The night had an eerie quality that he couldn't put his finger on. On the surface, everything appeared normal. A gentle breeze ruffled the leaves overhead while crickets hummed at his feet, bullfrogs croaked down at the lake, and bats flapped overhead on their nocturnal hunt for insects. All regular noises for the setting, but it still felt like an ice cube had been dropped down his shirt. Jake shivered as he tried to brush away his jitters.

When his eyes adjusted to the darkness, Jake examined the property. The driveway was long, at least fifty yards ending at a sprawling cabin. Behind it, he could just make out the small lake. Its surface reflected the moonlit sky above. The place was as isolated as Barbara had described, not another residence for miles.

From his vantage point, only two windows in the cabin were illuminated. A window shade concealed most of the light from the one on the right, most likely a bedroom. The other was a high window with red-checkered curtains, which had to be the kitchen.

Luckily, the exterior porch light was off, so even if Trent was watching, he shouldn't see Jake's approach.

Walking slowly and silently, Jake made it to the next set of trees. He paused to see if there would be a reaction from the cottage but was met with silence. Out of the corner of his eye, he thought he saw movement by the road. Shit! Was Trent sneaking up behind him? Maybe the boy wasn't as stupid as Jake had hoped. He scanned the shadows intently but didn't see anything. It must have been a trick of the moonlight. Or he was still a bundle of nerves— probably that.

Making it safely to the corner of the house, Jake took a second to catch his breath with the gun resting against his thigh. Behind him, the only motion was the leaves in the trees as they rustled and swayed. When he had his nerves back under control, he methodically crept along the side of the house. He reached the shaded window and peeked in at the seam. A sliver of the room was visible. Part of the bed and a dresser were in view. A red-haired girl passed in front of him and sat down on the bed.

Sam!

Jake's heart soared into his throat. His daughter was here, mere feet away, and she appeared unharmed. He blinked away the tears of joy. Things were going to work out. He'd save her. He knew it. It took extreme willpower not to tap on the glass to get her attention, but Jake couldn't afford to do anything rash. Trent might be in the room with Sam but out of sight. Jake needed to get eyes on the boy before he acted, so he tiptoed to the other window. Hastily, he stuck his head up, gave it a quick look, and ducked back down.

No exclamation or sound came from inside the cabin. Jake tried to process what he saw in his brief glimpse. Through the window, he'd seen a typical rustic kitchen. A man with his back to Jake sat at a long pine table. It had to be Trent. Past him was a living space with couches, a rocking chair, a fireplace, and a large-screen television. Obviously, the cabin has some modern amenities, but not many.

With less trepidation, Jake popped his head back up. Trent remained seated with a game of solitaire spread out in front of him. The boy flipped over three cards from the deck as he listened to an oldies station on the radio. Through the thin glass panes, Bob Seger sang about life on the road. And next to Trent, a shotgun leaned against the table.

Fuck!

Of course, Trent would have a gun. Jake had hoped for the contrary but wasn't every cabin required to have at least one shotgun. Nevertheless, this limited Jake's options.

Sure, he'd told Trent that Austin would be released in the morning, but that had been to buy Sam time. The truth was Jake didn't know when Austin would be released. Maybe, he already had. Jake prayed that was true. However, he didn't know anything for sure; Doyle had not updated Jake on his progress.

Backing slowly away from the cabin, Jake retreated into the trees. He tucked his pistol in his waistband and pulled out his phone, covering the screen to hide the glow. He found Doyle's name in his contacts and dialed the number, but the phone beeped in an odd tone. Jake checked the screen to find he had no signal. Damn it! Why did he have to go with the cheapest service provider?

He crept back to the road, but it didn't improve the reception. So Jake walked down to the lake, thinking an open space would get a better signal. One bar appeared on the display, which was an improvement. Another bar would allow him to make a call, so he cautiously stepped onto the beach as the leaves rustled loudly behind him.

Jake froze.

Whatever it was, it sounded big, possibly a man or a bear, but Jake reminded himself that in the woods at night, everything sounded large. He ducked back into the tree line and looked in the direction of the noise but saw nothing. He waited but still couldn't put eyes on the noisemaker. Yet, when Jake left his hiding spot, someone or something stepped on a stick. It snapped like a shotgun blast.

Quickly, Jake moved his hand to his pistol, but before he could draw the weapon, a fat raccoon waddled into the clearing. Ignoring Jake, the nocturnal thief ambled to the lake, got a drink, and then returned to the forest. Jake exhaled and then verified that nothing had changed at the cabin. All was quiet, so he walked down to the water, but the signal didn't improve. The weathered dock stretched out in front of him. Should he dare? He'd be completely exposed. However, if he didn't know the latest news on Austin, Jake might as well walk up to the door naked to confront Trent.

Tentatively, he took a step out on the dock. The boards groaned. On his phone screen, a second bar joined the first but then disappeared. He looked over his shoulder for any sign of Trent. Nothing. The only sound was a mild breeze rippling across the surface of the lake. Cautiously, he continued his dangerous trek to the end of the dock, and the second bar returned and stayed as a dragonfly landed on the lake. Its narrow feet did not break the surface tension of the water. A loud smack echoed through the darkness as a bass swallowed the unsuspecting insect.

Jake couldn't help but feel like the bug as he redialed Doyle. It rang through this time, but after seven beeps, it went to his voice mail. Unbelievable. What was the man doing? Doyle only had one job, to get Austin released and report back. Damn him.

It would kill Jake to wait; he was so close to saving Sam, but he had no choice. He couldn't storm the cabin with Trent wielding a street howitzer. Jake dropped the phone to his side when it rang. Thank god. Doyle must be calling him back.

Though when Jake checked the screen, he saw Bo's number. Weird, but it still could be good news about Austin's release from the opposite front. "Hello?"

"Jake, it's Bo." His voice carried across the night.

Cringing, Jake looked back at the cottage but saw no sign of Trent. "Hi. I assume you're calling me about Austin's release."

"You're God damn right, I am."

Jake's shoulders sagged with relief. "So Austin is out?"

"No," Bo growled.

The answer jabbed at Jake like a needle through the eye. "What?"

"Austin's still locked up. I got a call earlier from the prosecutor's office saying that they would drop the charges and release him. I run down there, and then they tell me there was a mistake. That he is still being prosecuted and to show up Monday. They wouldn't even let me see him."

"That can't be true."

"Yes, it is. Welcome to my fucked-up life. Are you involved in this cruel joke? You are, aren't you?"

Shit! Doyle had screwed them. And Sam. What the hell was he thinking? "No! I got word he was supposed to be released too. I'm as confused as you are, I swear."

"I don't believe you. I bet this is payback for my son knocking up your daughter."

"What?" The night fell silent. The only sound was Jake's heart hammering in his chest.

Bo said, "You heard me. It takes two to tango, so your girl was just as much at fault. She's the one who let her bloomers down, but that said, we still paid for the abortion, so why are you ruining my son's life."

"Abortion?"

"Quit your dumb act. I'm on to you. If I ever see you again, I'll knock your teeth in. That's a promise."

"Bo. Wait."

The line disconnected.

Jake's arm fell to his side, but he somehow hung onto the phone. The sound of his pulse rushed in his ears like a freight train. Completely lost in his own thoughts, he turned to stare into the darkness.

Sam had been pregnant.

There'd been an abortion.

And they'd kept it a secret from him.

No. It wasn't possible. Jake would have known. Sam couldn't hide something like that from him. Unless it happened when he was back in Michigan. Still, she'd have said something to him. They were close, or so he thought. Bo was angry and lashing out. Or he was confused. It had to be one of Austin's other girlfriends. Not his Sam.

One of the scariest sounds in the world brought him back into the moment.

A shotgun ratcheted behind him. His bowels wanted to loosen, but he steeled his nerves. He turned around slowly. Trent pointed the shotgun at Jake's face. He was trapped at the end of the dock. Even if he jumped in the water, he'd be a sitting duck, literally.

"Trent, I just got word that Austin will be released soon."

"Liar. I heard everything."

Jake tried to swallow, but his throat was too dry. "Listen. It's not as bad as you think."

"Yes, it is. Now we're both fucked."

"Trent— "

"Shut up! Drop your phone in the water."

Jake extended his hand to the side and let the phone fall into the lake.

"Your gun too," Trent commanded. "And don't try anything cute, or Sam will die a slow and agonizing death."

Jake used his thumb and forefinger to retrieve the weapon from his waistband. He dropped that in the water next to the phone. It sank into the abyss along with Jake's hopes of saving Sam.

Chapter 44

Sam locked the bathroom door behind her. She tested the knob; it held firm. She trusted Trent— but still, Sam was about to get butt-ass naked, and she had an uneasy feeling that she just couldn't shake. It had started in the bedroom where she swore she was being watched, which was ridiculous. The cabin was in the middle of nowhere. There wasn't another living soul for miles.

Besides, if the police had found them, they would've knocked down the front door— not stared through a crack in the shade like a pervert. And it hadn't been Trent. Sam had checked. He'd been at the kitchen table playing solitaire after finding her a set of his mom's pajamas.

So since they had time to kill before Austin should call, Sam had decided to take a shower. She felt itchy, dirty, and tired. Hopefully, a hot shower would make her feel better and allow her to catch some sleep before things got crazy again. Pulling open the shower curtain, she turned on the water and tested the temperature. It quickly grew blistering, just how she liked it. Her pale skin would be pink and squeaky clean when she was done. Perfect.

Before undressing, she visually checked the lock one more time. It was still locked, so she pulled her sundress over her head and removed her bra and underwear. Stepping into the shower stall, she pulled the curtain closed behind her. After getting her hair wet, she turned around and let the water beat on the spot between her shoulder blades. Ahhh, heaven. Was there a better feeling in the world? She was hard-pressed to think of one at the moment as the water washed away her stress.

Sam's thoughts drifted as they usually did in the shower. It was where she did some of her best thinking. Wistfully, she ran a hand over her flat belly, blaming herself for the pregnancy. Kate had put Sam on the pill when she turned fifteen. Kate didn't want Sam making the same mistakes she had, but then Sam had made them anyway.

She and Austin had done it several times. Had sex, that was. The last time Sam had suggested they skip the condom. She wanted to know what it felt like without one. Selfishly, she wanted the extra intimacy, and they already had protection, right? Wrong! She didn't know what happened since she'd never missed a pill, but it happened. She'd gotten pregnant at seventeen, two years younger than her mother.

When she broke the news to Austin, he didn't run away. A lot of guys would have, but he stood by her. Nor did he pressure her in any way. He said he'd stand by her no matter what her decision was, even though they both knew it would affect his football prospects. She'd been overwhelmed. The decision too big. In the end, she'd let Kate push her to the answer that wouldn't affect Sam's future either— though the decision would probably haunt Sam forever. Yet, it was the best choice for everyone involved, or so she kept on telling herself.

Sam didn't hate Kate. She was her mother, after all. Mothers and daughters had complicated relationships, and Sam and Kate's were no different. Sam knew her mother had good intentions when she pressured Sam to excel, but the ends didn't justify the means. And for as smart as Kate was, she should accept that Sam didn't want to follow in her footsteps. She wanted to blaze her own trail, make her own mistakes, and have a little fun along the way. What was wrong with that? Nothing.

Her life didn't have to follow a straight path. Her dads hadn't. She'd only wished he'd been home when she'd gotten pregnant. It would have been awkward, but she would've liked to have his opinion beforehand. But he'd been in Michigan, and it would be too weird a conversation to have over the phone. Plus Sam didn't want to add to Jake's troubles right after his best friend had died.

God! Why was she such a screw-up? The pregnancy. The Adderall pills. And now getting involved with Trent in this crazy scheme to free Austin.

Sam was brought back to reality by the water shifting from hot to warm. She brushed the wet hair from her face. Her skin was blotchy red, and mist filled the air. How much time had passed? She wasn't sure. At home, it took twenty minutes before the hot water tank ran dry. She would know; it was a daily occurrence. Hurriedly, she washed her hair and body before the water turned ice cold. When she was finished, she grabbed a towel from the rack and dried off.

The mirror was steamed over, hiding her reflection. With a hand towel, she cleared a spot off and checked her forehead. The bump was nearly gone, and her headache had all but disappeared too. Through the closed door, she heard muffled voices. Odd? It didn't sound like Trent, and why would he be talking to himself?

Was he listening to the radio? That was the only answer that made any sense. She pressed her ear to the door. It sounded like a radio tuned to an oldies station. No cause for concern, so she finished drying off and put on the borrowed pajamas minus her underwear. Hopefully, they had a washer she could run them through for tomorrow. Or she could just hand wash them in the sink. That would work too. The pajamas were a little big, but she rolled up the pant legs, so she wouldn't trip over them.

Exiting the bathroom, she peeked in the kitchen. Trent was gone while the DJ continued with his inane chatter. Maybe, Trent had stepped outside to relieve himself; Sam had definitely occupied the lone bathroom for a long time.

Going into the bedroom Trent had given her, she laid on the bed and closed her eyes for a minute. Boy, was she tired. It had been such a long day, and who knew when she'd get to rest again. Sam quickly drifted off to sleep.

Chapter 45

Jake stepped off the dock and purposely stumbled on the loose dirt by the shore. He fell towards Trent, but the boy backed up quickly, keeping the shotgun out of Jake's reach.

Trent growled, "I said, don't try anything cute."

"Sorry. I tripped."

"Bullshit. Don't let it happen again, or I'll blow a hole in your chest." Trent frowned while motioning for Jake to walk ahead of him.

The long blades of grass swished around their shoes as they cut a path to the cabin. Jake had lost control of this situation, but he thought he could get it back if he could get Trent to listen.

Looking over his shoulder, he said, "We can still get Austin out."

"How?"

"Why don't you put the gun down, and we can discuss it?"

The barrels jabbed into Jake's spine. "Not a chance."

"Be reasonable. I'm your only hope of getting out of this alive."

"So you think I'm going to die?"

Jake shook his head. "I didn't say that."

"Then what did you say?"

"Trent, you kidnapped a district court judge's granddaughter. Do you think the Feds will think twice about putting a bullet in your head to get her back?"

"They'll have to find me."

"I found you."

"You did. How?"

Jake considered whether he should tell the truth. He decided if he could play on Trent's emotions, it might work to his advantage. Jake said, "Your mother told me where to find you."

"She did?"

"Yes. She's concerned about you. I promised that I would bring both you and Sam home safely."

"Why?"

"Because I care." Jake stopped, turning to face Trent.

His eyes narrowed on Jake. "You don't give a shit about me. You only care about your daughter. Now move!"

"Where are we going?"

Trent thrust the shotgun at Jake again. "The garage. There's a door along the back corner of the cabin."

Jake begrudgingly did as he was instructed while weighing the odds of spinning around and wrestling the weapon away from the boy. But what if something went wrong, and he got shot? Jake wasn't as fast as he used to be. Would Trent tie up the loose ends and kill Sam too, before he made a run for it. Maybe. Probably. No, Jake needed to wait for a better opportunity. One with a higher chance of success.

"Fine. You're the boss."

In the moonlight, Jake saw the glint of a brass knob. It turned freely in his hand, and he pushed the door open. Fumbling around, he found the switch. Yellow light blinded him. He brought his arm up to shield his eyes.

Trent stood a couple feet away. With the gun, he motioned Jake inside. "There's some clothesline on the tool bench. Grab it. And remember, don't try anything cute, or you'll regret it."

"I heard you the first time," Jake sighed.

Dropping his arm, Jake let his eyes grow accustomed to the light. In the center of the garage, an aluminum boat with an outboard motor sat on a trailer. Gas cans, yard tools, and a beat-up lawnmower littered the back wall next to a workbench. He found the white rope hanging from a hook and met Trent back outside.

"Whatever you're planning, you don't have to do it. No one's been hurt yet. We can come up with a story where it was all a big misunderstanding, and I'll back you up," Jake said.

"And how will that save Austin?"

"Umm . . . I'm sure we can think of a way to get Austin out too."

"Sure." Trent shook his head. "Once you're tied up."

"If that's what will make you comfortable?" Jake swallowed hard, knowing he couldn't allow himself to be bound.

"It will. Now, get moving."

Jake entered the cabin. The kitchen was empty. Good. With Sam still locked in the bedroom, she was out of the way. And safe. Jake wanted to keep it that way until after he made his move.

Trent's eye twitched towards the kitchen table. He whispered, but it came out as a hiss. "Sit down and put your arms through the spindles of the chair. Cross your hands over one another."

Tossing the rope on the table, Jake pulled out a chair and sat down. He did as he was directed. "Son, you don't have to do this. There's —"

The barrel of the gun snapped to attention. The sights aimed square at Jake's skull. "I'm not your son, and remember no— "

"Yes. I remember— no funny business. I've got it. You have the gun. You're in charge. Whatever you do, just please don't hurt Sam. She's innocent."

"No one here is innocent. No one!"

Jake's heart hammered in his chest. The boy was losing it; Jake would have to tread carefully. Trent snatched the rope off the table and paused behind Jake. He must have realized his dilemma. With the shotgun in one hand and the rope in the other, Trent would need two hands to secure Jake to the chair properly. A low groan escaped his lips. Jake waited.

Eventually, Trent made his decision. He leaned the shotgun against a kitchen counter. Just out of arm's reach for both of them. It was now or never. Relaxing all the muscles in his body, Jake got ready to make his move. Trent unfurled the rope; the coils hit the hardwood floor with a hollow thud. Trent grasped Jake's wrists, pressing them tight together. He wound a length of rope around them once.

When Trent went to wrap a second loop around Jake's wrists, he lunged forward. Trent let out of surprised scream. The rope scraped across Jake's hands, removing layers of skin, but more importantly, slowing him down. One hand broke free, but Trent latched on to the other one, trapping Jake's left hand in the chair. Jake pushed off with his legs, fighting to get free, but Trent was strong. They crashed to the floor.

With the full weight of the chair, Trent landed on top of Jake.

Snap.

Pain erupted up Jake's arm. White stars flashed in his eyes. From the sound, his left wrist had to be broken. Trent twisted Jake's arm to maintain control. Jake's vision darkened, and he cried out in agony.

"Dad!" Sam ran into the kitchen wearing pajamas that were too big.

"Sam?" Jake continued to struggle with Trent while he pointed to the door with his good hand. "Get out of here. Run!"

Instead of running, she ran to Jake. "Trent! Stop it!"

"I can't."

"Of course, you can," Sam shouted.

"No. They lied to us. Austin wasn't released."

She pushed Trent away from Jake. "Get off of him. Can't you see my dad is hurt?"

Trent rolled off Jake and lunged for the shotgun.

Jake gingerly extracted his throbbing hand from the chair. "Sam, I said, get out of here. He has a gun."

Sam's mouth fell open in surprise. She jumped in front of Trent, shaking a finger at him like a disappointed schoolteacher. "Why do you have that? That was never part of our plan. Put it down before someone gets killed."

The strain on Trent's face was evident to everyone in the room. "That's what I'm worried about. He's here to kill me and save you. I can see it in his eyes."

"Sam?" Jake frowned. "You said 'our' plan. What the hell is going on here?"

"Umm . . . Trent and I are working together to get Austin out," she answered meekly.

Jake stood up with his broken wrist clutched to his chest. Stockholm syndrome couldn't have kicked in that fast. "I don't believe you. Why are you lying for him?"

"Sorry, I'm not," Sam said before turning on Trent. "And why were you wrestling with my dad? He's on our side."

"He might be on yours, but he's not on mine!" Trent said with the weapon aimed at the ground. "Besides, it's his fault. He started fighting me. I was just going to tie him up after I found him sneaking around the lake."

"Why were you tying him up?"

"I told you. Austin's not getting out."

Jake pulled his daughter by the shoulder to face him. "Sam! I need you to tell me what is happening here?"

Guiltily, she studied his red swelling wrist. "I know it was stupid, but Trent and I hatched this dumb kidnapping plot to get Austin out. It's not fair that he's in trouble, and I'm not. We never intended for anyone to get hurt. We were just trying to make things right."

Jake didn't release his grip. "So you weren't kidnapped?"

Her eyes fell to the floor. "No. No, I wasn't."

The lie was obvious, but it didn't change their current predicament. Jake could only assume that Trent had nabbed Sam outside of his apartment in a desperate attempt to save Austin.

Sam's guilt and love for the boy had made her a willing participant at some point in the evening. Then, she'd attempted to use Jake to leverage Patrick. He didn't blame her. He considered it an honor that he was the one man she knew she could count on.

Jake exhaled slowly. "Well, your plan almost worked, Sam. But your grandfather double-crossed us. Austin is still in jail."

Trent raised the gun slightly. "See. I told you."

"Are you sure?" Sam asked.

"Yes. As Trent heard, I just talked to Bo. Austin's release was arranged and then canceled. He'll be arraigned on Monday."

"No. It can't be." She pulled free of Jake's grip.

"I'm sorry, honey. I tried my hardest. I blackmailed your grandfather with some files I had hidden. It should have worked. He'd face some serious trouble if the truth got out, so I don't know what happened."

Trent leveled the shotgun at Jake's head. "I know what happened. You're lying to us, Mr. Bryant— you're part of it too. Austin was never getting out. Now get back in the chair and don't try anything stupid this time, or I'll break your other arm."

Jake stepped back. "I'm not lying to you. Trust me. You need me now more than ever. Things are about to get bad. Really bad. It's only a matter of time before the police find this place. Let me help you. Please!"

The strain on Trent was apparent as his face contorted with emotion.

Sam jumped in front of Trent again, holding up both palms. "How about we all just remain calm? We can sit down and come up with a new plan."

Trent closed his eyes and took two deep breaths. His eyes popped open like a jack in the box. "No, I'm not sitting down, and I'm not remaining calm. Look where that has got us."

"Trent!" Sam begged.

"No! I've got a new plan. You're going to call your grandfather and tell him I've got two hostages. And somebody is going to die unless Austin gets out. Tonight! How about that for a plan?"

The back door opened slowly, and an all-too-familiar voice said, "There is no need to call me. I'm right here."

Chapter 46

Doyle shut the door behind him and locked it. The deadbolt slid home with a solid clunk. Smiling, he said, "Don't worry, I'm up to speed. I've been listening at the door."

With a shiny pistol at his side, Doyle walked to the center of the room like a gunslinger at high noon. He stopped just far enough away that Jake couldn't make a move without getting shot. Jake's heart fell into his stomach. Damn him to Hell. But before he went to that fiery place, Jake had questions. Like, how did Doyle find the cabin? Or why hadn't he released Austin? Were the police and Hill on the way? And why was he such a bastard?

Firstly, Jake asked, "How did you find us?"

"It wasn't that hard, and it's a good thing too because it looks like you really fucked things up here, Jake." Doyle inclined his head in Trent's direction. "Put the gun down, son."

The shotgun pivoted in the judge's direction. Trent said, "Everyone better stop calling me son, and who the hell are you, old man?"

"My grandpa," Sam grumbled.

"Your grandpa?" Trent exclaimed.

Doyle nodded. "Samantha, sweetheart, you need to get out of here. Is there a backroom you can go to? Or better yet, go out to my car and wait for the men to settle things here."

Like a child, she stamped her foot. "No!"

Jake said, "Sam, please. There are too many idiots here with guns. Somebody is going to get hurt, and I don't want it to be you."

"For once, your father's right, honey," Doyle agreed.

Jake snorted. "About there being a lot of idiots in the room?"

Doyle glowered at Jake and then turned to his granddaughter. "Samantha Marie, I said leave!"

She shook her head. "I'm not some baby to be put in the corner."

Doyle threw up his free hand. "You're just like your father—you're too smart for your own good."

Sam's nostrils flared. "I'll take that as a compliment. And the joke is on you. I was never going along with your plan. I'm going to go to art school, and you can't stop me."

"Over my dead body. You're better than that."

"You don't get to decide what is best for me." Sam shouted, "I do!"

Doyle laughed and pointed at Jake. "So I'm just supposed to let you become a loser like him."

Jake put his good arm around Sam's shoulder. "Fuck you, Patrick."

"Enough!" The shotgun tapped loudly on the counter. They all turned in Trent's direction as he brandished the weapon wildly. A vein throbbed in his forehead. Trent snarled, "You can argue about Sam's future later. Right now, I only care about my brother. Now tell me why Austin isn't out of prison?"

"Now settle down, son. I'll— "

Trent leveled the shotgun at Doyle. "I said, don't call me, son!"

"I'm sorry. It's Trent, right?"

"Right."

Doyle put the safety on his handgun and tucked it in the back of his pants. Slowly, he extracted a phone from his pocket and held it up. "I'll have Austin released tonight. The prosecutor is waiting for my call. That's what you want, right?"

The barrel dropped slightly. "That's the only thing I want!"

"Then I'll make that call. I promise, but the thing is Trent, a SWAT team is twenty minutes away. There is no way I can stop that. You'll have to surrender, or they will kill you, but with the mitigating circumstances and time off for good behavior, I can make sure you're out in two to three years. That sounds like a fair trade for Austin's freedom, right?"

The gun fell to Trent's side. "You promise?"

"Cross my heart," Doyle said.

Sam shook her head. "You lied before, Grandpa. How do we know you're not lying now?"

Jake stepped forward to look into Trent's eyes. "Don't listen to him. He can't be trusted."

"Me?" Doyle looked incredulous. "Did you know Jake murdered a suspect back when he was a cop? That's why he was fired from Chicago PD."

"You did?" Trent asked.

"Yes . . . No . . . It's not that simple. He was armed and dangerous."

"Like me?" Trent scoffed.

Doyle smiled. "See. I'm your only chance. I can let you talk to Austin on the phone before the police get here, but we have to hurry."

"I can?"

"Yes. Definitely."

"Then what are you waiting for? Make the call," Trent pleaded.

"I will, but first, we need to stage the scene."

Jake laughed. "Here's the catch, Trent."

Doyle ignored him. "It does have to look like a real hostage situation. I see you already have some rope. Good. Cut it in half. Take Sam into a back bedroom and tie her to a bed. Tight knots. Make it look real. I'll do the same with Jake in the kitchen."

Jake held up his good hand. "No way. I won't allow it."

Trent looked at Jake. A muscle twitched above his eye, and his breathing was ragged. "Shut up. You're not in charge here. I am."

Doyle nodded. "Yes, Jake. Shut up. I'm only trying to protect Sam, and you too. If Trent's willing to take the fall, then the rest of us can walk away scot-free tonight."

Trent moved to get the rope. "Let's do this."

Sam looked at Jake. "Dad, what do we do?"

Jake's mind raced. Time was of the essence. If the SWAT team got here before Trent knew that Austin was released, then things could get ugly. The boy was on the edge. No. He was over the edge. There was no telling how he would react if the doors were kicked in, but it would be bad. Very bad. Sam needed to be out of the line of fire.

"Yes. Sam, go with Trent. It will be Ok."

"Are you sure?"

"Yes."

"All right. If you're sure."

Doyle slipped the phone back into his pocket. "Go on, sweetheart, you have nothing to worry about. I promise."

Trent set the shotgun against the kitchen counter with the barrel pointed up. He dug in a utensil drawer until he found a large butcher's knife. Using it, he cut the long length of rope into two pieces and tossed one to Doyle. Sam gave Jake a kiss on the cheek. She looked so incredibly small and fragile as she left the room. Trent followed her with the rope and the knife.

The shotgun remained on the counter behind Doyle. He grinned devilishly from ear to ear as he rubbed his hand together. Jake got a bad feeling in his gut. The final puzzle pieces fell into place. He'd been wrong, but it didn't change the fact that he wanted Sam safely tucked away in the back of the cabin. Jake righted the chair, but it was too heavy to wield with one hand. He added his bad hand, but the broken bones rubbed on nerves. He fought back a scream. Damn! Jake needed to incapacitate Doyle before Trent got back and could manipulate him further with his silver tongue.

Doyle snarled, "What are you waiting for? Sit down."

Jake shook his head. "The SWAT team is not twenty minutes away, right?"

Doyle removed the pistol from his waistband. "Like I said, you're too smart for your own good."

Chapter 47

Doyle clicked off the safety and aimed the weapon at Jake's chest. "It's a shame too. After I tied you to the chair, I was going to break your nose."

"Never did get over that, did you?"

"No. I didn't. I guess I'll have to settle for killing you."

Jake's stomach clenched. "So that's your plan?"

"Not exactly." Doyle smiled. "I'll have the boy do it for me."

"And how will you pull that off?"

"Because you were right— SWAT isn't coming. So I'll have plenty of time to convince him it's the only way out of this mess."

"Don't you know about villains and their monologues? You're so confident that it will work that you told me your plan first?"

"Yes. You're smart, but not smarter than me," Doyle said.

Maybe. Maybe not. Jake stared down the dark eye of the pistol while the shotgun stood proudly behind Doyle. If Jake could distract Doyle long enough to get the shotgun, then he'd have the upper hand. "Can you at least tell me how you found me?"

Doyle nodded. "When Detective Hill called me, I was in my car and not that far away from that whore's apartment. I raced over there, so that I could tail you because I knew you were lying. You knew where Sam was."

Jake took a couple steps to his left. He continued to ask questions, playing into Doyle's ego. "Smart, but then why did you arrange for Austin's release?"

"I couldn't be sure you would lead me to her. You might handle things remotely. And then you nearly lost me on that deserted road, but you reappeared and came straight to this cabin. With you, Sam, and Austin's brother here, I could cancel Austin's release and still salvage my career."

Jake groaned. "You're such an asshole."

"Shut up."

"Fuck you." Jake took another step. "You're playing with Sam's life."

"No. You are. I know you won't let the detention centers go. And if my associate finds out that you have those documents, I'm a dead man along with everyone that I love. So it's either you or us."

Beads of sweat broke out on Jake's forehead. "I can let it go for Sam."

Doyle frowned. "I don't believe you, so I'd stop trying to make your way to that shotgun."

Jake's foot hung in midair. "I swear. I'll hand over your tax documents right now."

"Right. The files you left in your backseat? The ones I dropped in the lake?"

Jake opened his mouth, but Doyle held up a finger. "Don't bother. I know it's the only copy. There were no stops to an all-night copy center, the Attorney General's office, or the newspaper."

Jake's shoulders slumped in defeat. So much for outmaneuvering Doyle. The room felt suffocating. But that didn't stop Jake from shivering.

Chuckling, Doyle asked, "What's the matter, Jake? Did someone walk across your grave?"

Trent walked into the room and studied the two men. He pointed at Jake. "Why isn't he tied up too?"

Doyle lowered his gun. "Good thing you're back. Jake has ruined things with your brother, and I'm not sure I can get him out of jail now."

"What!" Trent's nostrils flared.

Leaning forward, Doyle whispered, "Can I trust you with the truth, Trent?"

"Yes."

"Well, to get reelected and make our streets safer, I accepted money from a donor. But at the time, I didn't know he was an unscrupulous man, but Jake is threatening to use that relationship against me."

Trent's brows pinched. "Ok?"

"This man is very powerful. More powerful than you or I. If his crimes are revealed, he could make us disappear without a trace and have your brother killed in prison. Do you understand?"

Trent's complexion turned grey. "I guess."

"So Jake needs to be taken care of."

"Taken care of?"

"Yes. I can't risk releasing your brother until Jake is removed from the equation."

Trent shook his head. "You have to kill him?"

Doyle nodded. "But I'll need your help."

"Me?"

"You want Austin released, don't you?"

Jake took a step forward. "Trent, listen to what he's saying. It doesn't even make sense. He's trying to manipulate you."

Smirking, Doyle said, "Stop it, Jake. You can't deny it. You tried to blackmail me."

"I tried to blackmail you TO get Austin out."

Doyle shook his head and frowned. "No, you did it to keep Austin in. You hated him. You wanted him to rot in jail for getting your daughter pregnant."

Trent's mouth dropped open. "You lied to me!"

"No." Waves of shock and sadness washed over Jake. He couldn't believe it. Did everyone know about Sam's pregnancy but him? Why hadn't she trusted him? He wouldn't have been angry. He could have helped her. Damn. Like he was helping her now— maybe that's why she hadn't trusted him?

"You're right. He's lying," Doyle proclaimed.

Keeping an eye on Jake, Doyle walked slowly towards Trent. He put a hand on the boy's shoulder. "But I understand. They were stupid kids. We've all been there. How do you think my daughter ended up married to Jake? Katey couldn't keep her knees together, and she got pregnant with Sam. It happens. I understand. But Jake couldn't let it go. He hates Austin. That's why he's putting us all in jeopardy."

"Don't listen to him," Jake shouted.

Trent looked from one man to the other. "I don't know who to believe."

Doyle said, "Trust me. Eliminating Jake is the only way to get Austin out. I wish there was another way, but there's not."

"I just don't know," Trent cried.

Jake considered his options as Trent wrestled with his own decision. If Jake ran for the door, it would take too long to unlock it before Doyle shot him. If he went for Doyle, the old man would shoot him and then Trent. And Jake couldn't go in the other direction and risk a stray bullet hitting Sam. He couldn't win, but at least he could save two souls tonight.

Jake met the boy's eyes. "You're a good guy, Trent. Don't do it. You'll regret killing me. It'll haunt you. Make him do it if he wants me dead so bad."

Trent turned to Doyle. "He's right. I don't think I can do it."

"Sure you can. Just pick up the shotgun and pull the trigger. It will all be over in a second."

"Think of your poor mother when you're convicted," Jake pleaded.

The look on Trent's face was one of utter despair. "Yes. I'll be a murderer."

"No. It's self-defense. I'll vouch that Jake tried to kill you. We both know that's the real reason he came here tonight. And who wouldn't believe a district court judge?"

Leaning over, Trent picked up the shotgun. "Isn't there another way?"

"I wish there was, but there's not. Do you want Austin's life to be over before it started?"

Jake raised his hands. "Please! You don't have to do this."

Trent slowly brought the gun to his shoulder and sighted the barrel on Jake's chest. Fuck! Doyle had won, but Jake didn't plan on dying just yet. He had one chance to get out of this, but it would require split-second timing and lots of luck. He'd drop before the first shot, diving under the kitchen table. He could turn it over and use it to absorb the second shot. After that, Jake would have to improvise, but he knew he wouldn't stop until both men were beaten unconscious, and Sam was safe.

"Come on!" Adrenalin coursed through Jake's veins. "If you're going to do it, then get it over with."

Doyle turned to Trent and nodded. "Go ahead. You heard him."

Jake tensed. Hesitantly, Trent raised the gun. Sweat dripped into his eye. Trent shook his head and removed a hand from the stock to wipe his brow. Jake met his stare with calm intensity while every muscle in his body was ready to react. However, the barrel dropped to the floor, and Trent handed the weapon to Doyle. "I can't do it."

Doyle set his pistol on the counter. "Fine. I'll do it myself."

He raised the shotgun without hesitation and leveled it at Jake's chest. His finger hovered above the trigger. Jake prepared to make his leap when Trent knocked the weapon from Doyle's hand. "No!"

"You stupid son of a bitch," Doyle shouted.

The shotgun clattered to the floor. Doyle jumped on top of it, and Trent pounced on Doyle. They fought for control of the gun. They rolled back and forth as limbs flailed like windmill blades. It appeared the younger man would win the struggle, so Jake took the opportunity to run for Sam. Both men were far from sane, and Jake couldn't trust either one not to do something stupid. If he was quick, they could be in the tree line before Trent or Doyle were the wiser. He sprinted to the bedroom. Using the knife that Trent had left behind on the nightstand, Jake cut his daughter loose.

"Hurry!" He grabbed Sam by the hand. "We have to get out of here."

She followed him without a word. From the kitchen, the shotgun discharged. Someone cried out in gut-wrenching pain. With Sam behind him, Jake ran into the hall, where they were met by Doyle and the shotgun. Smiling, Doyle raised the weapon at Jake.

"No. Don't," Jake pleaded.

Doyle pulled the trigger as Jake was pushed hard from behind. He hit the floor face first. The shotgun blasted over his head. The sound was deafening.

Something or someone fell heavily to the floor.

No. No! NO!

Chapter 48

There were no screams. No cries of pain from behind Jake, but his ears rang so loudly he could be temporarily deafened. Jake prayed Sam had fallen down with the push, and the shot had missed her too.

In front of him, Doyle stood on wobbly feet, mumbling to himself. The shotgun had dropped from his hand. The old man clutched the wall for support, his face ashen.

Stumbling to his feet, Jake turned around. Sam lay curled on her side in the narrow hallway. She looked like she'd decided to take a nap right there. Yes, she's only asleep, he told himself. He crouched beside her limp form. Rolling her over gently, he cradled her neck in his arm.

"Sam?"

"Dad," she said weakly.

That's when he saw it. Fuck! It was bad. Real bad. The gun had been loaded with cartridges, not buckshot. There was a gaping hole in Sam's chest. He pressed a hand to the wound, but blood oozed around his fingers. It would be impossible to staunch the flow.

Jake screamed at Doyle, "Call an ambulance. Now!"

Doyle didn't move, only continued to mumble to himself. From the other room, Trent yelled, agreeing to make the call for what good it would do. Jake turned back to his daughter. "Honey. Why did you do that?"

She coughed. A thin film of blood coated her lips. "I had to save you."

"No. I'm the parent. I was here to save you," he said as tears spilled down his cheeks.

"Sorry. I guess I screwed up again."

"Don't talk like that." His face twisted up with emotion. "You're perfect. You're the one good thing in my life."

She smiled. Closing her eyes, she rested her head on Jake's lap. "It really hurts."

"Help is on the way. Everything will be all right. I promise," he lied, his heart breaking in two.

Her eyelids opened a crack. "I have something to tell you."

He caressed her cheek like he'd done when she was a little baby. It still felt so soft and smooth. "Whatever it is, it doesn't matter."

"It does. You need to know."

"Sam, the only thing I need to know is that you're my daughter, and I love you no matter what. I don't care what you've done or not done. Do you got that?"

"All right." Her eyes fluttered shut.

He whispered in her ear. "Stay with me, Sam. The ambulance will be here soon."

"Dad?"

"Yes, honey?"

"I . . . I . . . love . . . you"

She sagged in his arms.

"Sam!" He squeezed her shoulder.

She didn't respond. He put two fingers to her neck and felt for a pulse. Nothing. He shook her. No response. He shook her harder. Nothing.

She was gone.

The tears poured down his face. He held her tight, rocking her back and forth. He never wanted to let her go. It was noticeably different. He could feel it. The world felt empty without her.

From some far-off place, he heard someone clear their throat. He looked up to see Trent in the doorway to the kitchen, a bullet wound in his bad leg. His belt cinched tight across his thigh.

Trent said, "The ambulance is on its way. Is it . . . Is it too late?"

"Yes." Jake's lip quivered.

"Fuck!" Trent stumbled backward and leaned against the wall for support.

Jake kissed Sam on her rapidly cooling cheek. Brushing a stray piece of hair from her face, he tucked it behind her ear and laid her gently down on a threadbare rug. Standing up slowly, he took deliberate steps toward Doyle, who had sunk to the floor. Patrick scrambled for the shotgun at his feet. Jake kicked it away and smacked him hard across the face.

Doyle said, "It was an accident."

Jake kicked him in the ribs. "It doesn't matter. You killed her."

Flinching, Doyle asked, "Is she . . . Is she really dead?"

"Yes."

"But you made me do it."

"I made you do it?" Jake growled. "You pulled the trigger."

"I had no choice. It was either you or me."

"And it wasn't going to be you, was it? You, selfish prick!"

"Me?" Doyle looked up. A look of hatred in his eye. "If you'd just left her alone, none of this would have happened."

A veil of red descended across Jake's vision. He didn't say a word as his fists rained down on the judge. A fist connected with Doyle's chin, and he curled into a ball. Jake continued to punch him in the side and back, working out his anger. However, footsteps tottered towards him, and Jake was yanked back by the shoulders.

Trent held Jake tight as he shouted, "You should be dead too!"

Doyle nodded. "Do it. Please."

Shaking his head, Jake said, "No, that would be too easy on you. You'll rot in jail for what you've done."

Sirens bleated faintly in the distance. They'd gotten here quicker than Jake had thought possible. Suddenly, Doyle pulled the pistol from his pocket and pointed it at Jake.

Glancing back at Sam, Jake thought it wouldn't be so bad if Doyle shot him. He'd give anything to be dead and not her. He was the screw-up, not Sam. Why did it have to be her? Death followed him. Tom. And now, Sam. Yes, if Doyle killed him, Jake wouldn't have to live with the fact that Sam died because of him. He could join them; that was if heaven would let him in.

"This is all your fault!" The sirens grew closer, and Doyle jammed the gun in his mouth.

"Don't!" Jake screamed.

Doyle smiled and pulled the trigger. Bits of brain and skull splattered the pine wall. Doyle collapsed to the floor in a heap, mere feet from his lifeless granddaughter.

Chapter 49

On the wall, a clock with a sweeping red hand counted the seconds. Each one felt like an eternity. Jake knew a life of pain stretched out in front of him. One without Sam. It was true that some eternities could be longer than others, and each second without his daughter felt a little longer than the last.

His baby girl was growing cold in the morgue while he sweated in this stupid interrogation room with a one-way mirror on the opposite wall— though he couldn't bear to look at himself. Not after he'd failed Sam. Instead, he studied the wooden table and focused on his throbbing wrist.

The officers claimed it was the only room available, but he'd used that lie himself back when he was on the force. They'd also offered him medical attention, but he'd refused it. He deserved the pain for screwing up so badly. There were a hundred things Jake could have done differently to keep Sam alive. Doyle was right; she would have been better off without him.

Dropping his chin to his chest, Jake took a deep breath through his nose and smelled himself. He stunk of sweat, dirt, and regret. So many regrets. His gaze dropped lower to his bloodstained hands. They were covered in Sam's blood. They'd already taken his clothes into evidence. Maybe with some spit and the shirt they'd given him, he could wipe them off. Though he'd look pretty silly sitting in the interrogation room shirtless. They'd think he'd gone insane. Fine. Let them.

Jake started to undo the buttons, but before he reached the second one, a light rap on the door stopped him. It swung open, and an older detective walked into the room, followed by a younger man. The detective took the chair across from Jake and gave him a small nod. Jake returned the gesture, and the man smiled wider.

The twinkle in the detective's eye foretold Jake his fate. It should have been no surprise. If Doyle's associate was as powerful as he claimed, Jake didn't stand a chance. Evidence would be planted. A false confession would be wrung out of him. The case against him would be iron-clad. That was all right. Being locked up for the rest of his life would be a fitting punishment for failing Sam.

The younger man propped himself in the corner. He took off his wide-brimmed hat and held it in both hands. He rotated it nervously like a steering wheel. He reminded Jake of Deputy Dewey from the *Scream* movies but more bumbling and pathetic if that was possible.

Deputy Dewey asked, "Can I get you anything? Something to eat or drink?"

Obviously, he was the good cop in this farce of a questioning. Jake shook his head. "I'm fine."

Putting his hat back on, the younger man pushed himself off the wall. "But you've been locked in here for hours. I'm going to get you a candy bar and a coffee. Ok?"

"I guess."

"Great idea," the detective said.

The deputy pointed at the detective. "Do you need something, Boss?"

The detective shook his head. "No. I'm good. But why don't you make a fresh pot for our friend here? He doesn't deserve that stale stuff. Take your time."

"Got it." The deputy left the room.

The door locked behind him with a loud click. Checking the camera on the wall, Jake noticed the red light was off, indicating that it wasn't recording. Figures. They planned on beating a confession out of him. Fine. Someone had to go down for an influential judge's death.

Jake sagged down deeper in his chair, his hands folded in his lap. The clock ticked behind them. The detective got up and paced around the small room. The tension was thicker than taffy swimming in molasses. Stopping in front of Jake, the detective cracked his knuckles. He looked like a tough old bird. In a fair fight, Jake might have trouble with him, but this wouldn't be a fair fight. Jake took a deep breath, closed his eyes, and waited for the predictable punch to his chin.

However, the detective cleared his throat and dropped his hands to his side. He said, "Jake. Can I call you, Jake?"

"You can."

"We're going to let you go, Jake."

Jake raised an eyebrow. "You are?"

"Yes." Glancing at the mirror, the detective said, "The most you did tonight was obstruct justice. The DA doesn't want to take that to court. No way."

"Really?"

"Really. Especially considering the crimes your Ex-Father-in-law committed. The scumbag locked up all those kids to line his pockets. The press will have a field day with this for weeks, not to mention the time to go through every case he tried. I bet they just open the doors in Juvenile Hall and let the bad out with the good."

"So you found his tax records in my car?"

"Tax records?" The detective frowned. "No. A crooked cop on Doyle's payroll is singing like a canary for immunity."

Hmm. Jake should have guessed. It was the smart play for Steve Hill if he didn't want to end up dead. Better to be in witness protection than be assassinated in jail. Still not wanting to believe they would let him walk out of here, Jake said, "But I tried to blackmail Doyle into getting Austin Morrison released. I'm at least guilty of that."

The detective shook his head. "You did that under duress."

"No. I knew what I was doing."

"It doesn't matter. No jury would convict you. You're the victim here. I would have done the same thing if it was my daughter."

"I'm not a victim."

"You are, Jake. Your daughter is dead."

Chapter 50

A tear spilled down Jake's cheek. Somehow hearing a stranger saying she was dead made it more real. Worse, Jake realized he'd never get to talk to his daughter again as the detective continued, "Trust me. Everyone wants to close this case quickly and move on. Everyone!"

With that major question answered, Jake had two more. "So . . . what's going to happen to Trent Morrison? You should know that Sam was a willing partner in their fake kidnapping plot, and he saved my life tonight."

"Good to know. That's his story too, so we'll be taking that under consideration. Trent should get off considering what a farce the deceased Judge Doyle has turned the Cook County legal system into. His brother, Austin too."

Jake nodded. "And Leroy Jones, Jr.?"

"Who?"

"Another boy that Judge Doyle probably locked up unfairly. Could you make sure his name is added to the file so that someone can review his case?"

"Sure. If he's innocent, I'm sure any competent lawyer can get the conviction overturned."

Jake frowned. "It never should have happened in the first place. Not if I hadn't been so stupid."

"Stupid? How?"

"Never mind."

The detective crossed his arms over his chest. "You shouldn't beat yourself up over this. No one is perfect."

Jake laughed. Little did this man know that Jake was a world-class self-flagellator and the complete opposite of perfect. Jake was a horrible person, detective, and father, and he deserved more than a beatdown.

Deputy Dewey knocked on the door. He entered, carrying a coffee, a donut, and two candy bars. Saving a snickers bar for himself, he set Jake's food on the table. Deputy Dewey returned to the corner and tore the wrapper on his bar open with his teeth. Hot steam poured from the Styrofoam cup. The room suddenly felt very cold, and the coffee would help even if he wasn't thirsty. Jake picked up the cup, but his hand shook, and the beverage sloshed onto the scarred wood table. He wiped up the liquid with his sleeve.

Sitting back down, the detective said, "Jake, we have a really good psychologist on staff. You'll like her. She's helped a lot of guys through some very bad stuff. How about I send her in when we are done."

"No. I'll pass."

The detective reached out to touch his hand. "Jake— you need help."

Jake jerked his arm away. "I'll be fine."

Biting his lip, the detective said, "Guys who talk like that are not fine. Your daughter died in your arms, for Christ's sake."

Jake hated him for saying it. Through clenched teeth, he said, "I'll. Be. Fine."

The detective opened his mouth and then closed it. Jake cast his eyes down to study the table. He thought he could see a picture in the grain like one of those 3-D pictures that held an image of Marilyn Monroe if you could trick your eyes to look past the geometric pattern. But instead of the famous blonde, Jake saw his daughter's limp body. Deputy Dewey finished his candy bar and shoved the wrapper in his pocket. The noise brought Jake back to reality.

"So, am I free to go?" Jake asked without looking up.

The detective turned to the mirror. Someone knocked twice. It must have been a positive sign because he turned back to Jake and smiled. "You're free to go anytime; you're not under arrest."

Jake stood up and wiped at his face. "Yeah, I think I need to crash in my own bed. I feel like I could sleep for days."

"I bet."

"Why don't you give me the number of that psychologist too? Maybe, I'll sit down with her and talk things through next week," Jake said with no intention of following through with it.

"Great. I'll get you her number."

The deputy opened the door, and Jake got to his feet.

"Hold on." The detective held up his hand. "Your car is still in evidence. I can have a deputy drive you wherever you want, but you have family here at the station that I know wants to see you first."

The only family Jake had left was his mother, and he couldn't imagine she'd made the trip from Michigan already. "Family?"

"Your ex-wife."

"Kate's here?"

"Yes. She's being questioned as well, though she lawyered up pretty quickly. However, she did request a private meeting with you."

"More like demanded." Deputy Dewey chuckled.

The last person Jake wanted to talk to was Kate. There would be no reconciliation. The two of them would not come together over their common loss. All her blame would be reserved for Jake and not the monster that had raised her. He said, "I'd prefer not to."

The detective nodded his head. "Don't worry, I can run interference for you. That lady is a piece of work— a chip off the old block. Also, you have a friend that's called the desk three times. Misty? Mallory? She's very persistent."

Jake's brow pinched. "Mary?"

"Yeah, that's it."

Oh, God. Jake didn't want to talk with her either. He would crumble into a thousand pieces from her unconditional love, and she would try to put him back together. Jake didn't deserve her sympathy today. Maybe not ever. Jake flopped back down in his chair. "Can I have a minute before we go?"

"No problem," the detective said.

Dewey smiled. "I can drive you home. Let me know when you're ready."

"Thanks."

The detective straightened his tie. "FYI. Your ex-wife is in a conference room down the hall on the right."

"And I'll be at my desk straight out the door making a few calls," Deputy Dewey said.

The two officers walked out the door, leaving it open behind them. Jake waited while the clock ticked on the wall behind him. After two minutes, he stood up and exited the room, turning left. The deputy had his back to Jake with his phone pressed to his ear as he scribbled notes on a pad of paper. The detective was nowhere in sight.

In a back hallway, Jake found a fire door. He pushed it open. A loud buzzing alerted the building of his escape, so he broke into a jog. Once he was across the parking lot, he turned around, but no one was there to stop him. Perfect. Not looking back again, Jake walked away from everything and everyone to wallow in his misery.

REGRET

ABOUT THE AUTHOR

Henry Scott is the author of numerous short stories and novels since he began writing in 2015, though he's been an avid reader since the age of five. He lives in metro-Detroit with his family, two lovable golden retrievers, two cats, and a turtle. Fans can see plenty of pictures of them on his Instagram, @henry_scott_. He enjoys coffee, deep-dish pizza, true-crime TV shows, bonfires on cool nights, and his Triumph motorcycle.

Please visit his website and join his newsletter to learn about upcoming releases and the latest news.

www.henryscottauthor.com

Made in the USA
Middletown, DE
16 March 2022

62769655R00126